THE BUZZARD TABLE

This Large Print Book carries the
Seal of Approval of N.A.V.H.

THE BUZZARD TABLE

MARGARET MARON

THORNDIKE PRESS
A part of Gale, Cengage Learning

3 2210 00368 0813

GALE
CENGAGE Learning®

Detroit • New York • San Francisco • New Haven, Conn • Waterville, Maine • London

NORTH BABYLON PUBLIC LIBRARY

Copyright © 2012 by Margaret Maron.
A Deborah Knott Mystery.
Thorndike Press, a part of Gale, Cengage Learning.

ALL RIGHTS RESERVED
This book is a work of fiction. Names, characters, places, and incidents are the product of the author's imagination or are used fictitiously. Any resemblance to actual events, locales, or persons, living or dead, business establishments, is coincidental.

All chapter captions are taken from the official website of The Turkey Vulture Society, a nonprofit scientific corporation (http://vulturesociety.homestead.com/), and used by its permission. Its purpose is to promote scientific studies of the life habits and needs of the turkey vulture, to protect the vulture and its habitat, and to inform the public of the valuable and essential services this bird provides to mankind and to the environment.
The publisher is not responsible for websites (or their content) that are not owned by the publisher.
Thorndike Press® Large Print Mystery.
The text of this Large Print edition is unabridged.
Other aspects of the book may vary from the original edition.
Set in 16 pt. Plantin.

LIBRARY OF CONGRESS CATALOGING-IN-PUBLICATION DATA

Maron, Margaret.
    The buzzard table / by Margaret Maron. — Large print ed.
        p. cm. — (Thorndike Press large print mystery)
    ISBN-13: 978-1-4104-5145-3 (hardcover)
    ISBN-10: 1-4104-5145-3 (hardcover)
    1. Knott, Deborah (Fictitious character)—Fiction. 2. Women judges—Fiction. 3. North Carolina—Fiction. 4. Large type books. I. Title.
    PS3563.A679B89 2012
    813'.54—dc23   2012032027

Published in 2012 by arrangement with Grand Central Publishing, a division of Hachette Book Group, Inc.

Printed in the United States of America
1 2 3 4 5 6 7 16 15 14 13 12

NORTH BABYLON PUBLIC LIBRARY

For Barbara Mertz, who extended a
generous hand
to a ragtag bunch of unknowns

DEBORAH KNOTT'S FAMILY TREE

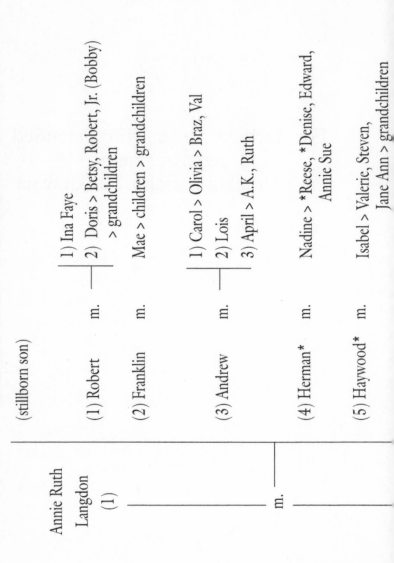

Annie Ruth
Langdon
(1)

m.

(stillborn son)

(1) Robert   m.
- 1) Ina Faye
- 2) Doris > Betsy, Robert, Jr. (Bobby) > grandchildren

(2) Franklin   m.   Mae > children > grandchildren

(3) Andrew   m.
- 1) Carol > Olivia > Braz, Val
- 2) Lois
- 3) April > A.K., Ruth

(4) Herman*   m.   Nadine > *Reese, *Denise, Edward, Annie Sue

(5) Haywood*   m.   Isabel > Valerie, Steven, Jane Ann > grandchildren

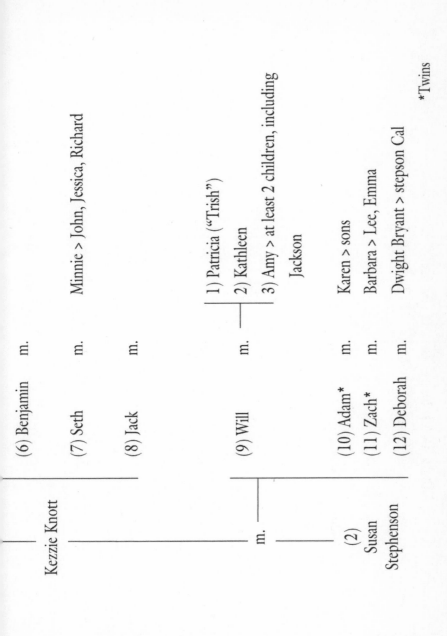

Kezzie Knott

(6) Benjamin — m. — Minnie > John, Jessica, Richard

(7) Seth — m.

(8) Jack — m.

(9) Will — m. —
1) Patricia ("Trish")
2) Kathleen
3) Amy > at least 2 children, including Jackson

m.

(2) Susan Stephenson

(10) Adam* — m. — Karen > sons

(11) Zach* — m. — Barbara > Lee, Emma

(12) Deborah — m. — Dwight Bryant > stepson Cal

*Twins

Somalia — Late 1993

She sits huddled on the dirt floor in near darkness, her knees drawn up to her chin, her arms clasped around her legs to keep them from trembling. A dim battery-operated lantern gives barely enough light for the guard to keep a watchful eye on her and another journalist. So far as she knows, they are the only two westerners still alive from the UN group who came to this village to deliver food, water, and medical supplies. Humanitarian aid. It was supposed to have been a safe day trip out from Mogadishu. Instead, their trucks were ambushed and strafed with bullets, their drivers' mangled, bloody bodies thrown into the nearest ditches. Beyond the walls of this hut, bursts of gunfire and shrieks of terror still mingle with the screams of villagers and their children dying in agony.

Unless they have been separated to hold for ransom — a not unrealistic hope, the other journalist whispered before their guard ordered them to keep silent with a wave of his rifle — it will soon be their turn to die.

She knows she is not brave. Given the chance, she will probably cower and beg for her life, but she has passed from paralyzing fear to calm regret for her daughter and her onetime lover. Her daughter is grown, well launched on a satisfying career; but the life she could have built with her old love, even supposing he still cares for her, had been a glimmer of light through the dark tunnel of the guilt that drove them apart. Now she will never know if the breach could have been healed or if —

Her thoughts are cut off by a rustle in the doorway. The guard's rifle swings toward the two Arab men in native robes who duck through the opening, kicking a bundle of some sort before them.

"Assalamu alaikum," says the first man, while the second steps forward and points toward the two prisoners. He seems to be questioning the guard about them with assured authority.

Distracted, the guard turns his back on the first man to answer, when that one suddenly slips his arms under the guard's, locks his hands behind the man's head, and forces his neck to bend so sharply that she hears his spine pop and sees his body go limp before she fully understands what has just happened. The second man grabs the fallen rifle.

He points it at the woman and her colleague and in heavily accented English, says, "We go now."

The first man lets the guard's body slide to the ground, then pushes the bundle toward them and says something in Arabic. The second man nods. "You put on."

She pulls at the cloth. Two burkas, complete with head scarves. Her colleague does not hesitate, but instantly slides one over his head and helps her with the other. He adjusts their scarves till only their eyes are visible.

"Keep your hands hidden and your head down," he tells her, "and don't look anyone in the eye even if they speak to us."

The assassin gives a murmur of approval and motions for them to follow.

Outside, they keep to the shadows, and the woman has almost begun to allow herself hope when a tall Ethiopian soldier with an automatic rifle blocks their way. His teeth glisten in the light from a nearby burning hut and she does not need to know the language to understand that he is claiming her as his own booty. He grabs her by the breast, but before he can rip off her burka, he is felled by a blow to the nape of his neck with the butt of the rifle the second Arab carries.

Minutes later, they are bundled into the backseat of a battered and bullet-pocked car and are speeding back to Mogadishu through the darkness over rutted, bomb-shelled roads. She unclenches her hands from the folds of her burka and realizes that they are coated in something sticky. She holds them up to her nose and smells.

"Oh my God!" she says. "This burka. It's soaked in blood!"

The assassin, who is driving, gives a short bark that could be a laugh, and the other man says, "She not be needing it. You, yes."

"Who are you?" the other journalist asks. "How did you find us?"

"No talk," he says.

When they finally reach a relief camp on the outskirts of the city, they are ordered out of the car. Before their rescuers drive away, the assassin calls to her and holds something out in his hand. A camera.

"He say sorry," the other man tells her. "Only this one he can save."

Although smaller than the Leica she has lost, this is her favorite and the camera she uses most frequently.

"Tell him thank you," the woman says. She grasps the man's hand before he can pull away. "Thank you both for saving us."

His eyes gleam oddly in the lights of the camp as he jerks his hand back, throws the car into gear, and speeds away.

"Sweet friggin' Jesus! What a story!" her companion says as they stumble toward the fire and safety. "I've heard you can break a man's neck with one good yank, but that's the first time I ever saw it done."

DECEMBER

Subject: Arrived
  From: 983.MC4762@me.com
Date: Dec 27, 2010 12:23:14 PM EST
  To: 68RRipley0108@me.com

The situation is better than I hoped. I have the use of an abandoned house out in the country. Weather at the moment is much like London: cold, but not freezing. Sending this from a computer in a nearby library. Should be safe.
Tell Michael I found the guitar picks he wanted and will mail them next week.

JANUARY

Subject: ???
  From: 68RRipley0108@me.com
Date: January 18, 2011 03:16:12 PM EST
  To: 983.MC4762@me.com

What's happening? Nothing from you in two weeks. R.

Subject: Re: ???
  From: 983.MC4762@me.com
Date: January 19, 2011 01:26:21 PM EST
  To: 68RRipley0108@me.com

Intel was good, but I got it too late. He came in after dark and left before noon next day. Not to worry, Rihana. Sooner or later, etc. We've waited this long, we can be patient. Otherwise, things are going as planned. The vultures are beginning to trust me. One has let me band his leg without spewing all over me.

16

FEBRUARY

Subject: It Works
  From: 983.MC4762@me.com
Date: February 2, 2011 04:26:02 PM EST
  To: 68RRipley0108@me.com

The first pictures are crisp and clear. Still waiting though. Turns out that security may not be a problem. Have learned there's a better option.
If it won't embarrass him, give my godson a birthday hug for me and tell him I've deposited £50 to his iPod account for his birthday. 16! If only Gerry could see how much he's matured this last year.

CHAPTER 1

In America, the term "buzzard" is often employed incorrectly to describe vultures. This probably dates back to the arrival of the first English colonists. There are no vultures of any type in England, so these pioneers probably gave the common term "buzzard" to all the soaring figures above the New World.

— The Turkey Vulture Society

Midafternoon and the thin February rain was making a total nuisance of itself — too light to turn the windshield wipers on steady, yet too heavy to let them clear the glass between intermittent sweeps. At least it wasn't cold enough to turn the rain to ice. Frustrated, my nephew Reese fiddled with the adjustable settings while I tried to find where he'd hidden the NPR station on his radio.

Up ahead, I caught a glimpse of movement on the wet pavement.

"Look out!" I cried, automatically stomping on brakes that weren't there because I was buckled into the passenger side of the pickup.

Too late.

With a sickening *thunk,* the front right tire hit flesh.

Reese glanced in his rearview mirror, braked, and immediately threw the truck in reverse.

"What are you doing?" I asked.

Looking into my own mirror, I saw no motion, only a splash of bright red blood that the rain had washed from the crushed head. No way could that small body still have a spark of life in it, but Reese kept backing up till we were even with it. Luckily, this was a deserted country road with nothing but scrub pines and bare-twigged underbrush on either side and no other vehicles behind or ahead.

"Won't take a minute," Reese said, hopping out of the cab. I twisted around in my seat to watch him push aside the tarp that covered the neon sign we'd just picked up from the auction house so that he could get at a plastic tub that was secured to the side of the truck bed with a couple of bungee cords. He picked the dead squirrel up by its fluffy tail, dropped it in the box, and snapped the lid back in place. Through the translucent plastic, I could make out another small shape.

All of my brothers and their children grew up cooking and eating whatever they shot when out hunting — deer, rabbits, game birds — but roadkill? Besides, I've heard Reese on the subject of tree rats too often to think he was going to take that squirrel back to his trailer and dress it out. Even Haywood's quit eating squirrel except when Daddy gets Maidie to stir up a washpot of Brunswick stew big enough to share with the whole family.

(According to Daddy, "It ain't a real Brunswick stew if it ain't got a squirrel in it.")

Like some of my equally squeamish sisters-in-law, I sort of pick around any dubious chunks of meat and fill up on the vegetables.

I hadn't paid any attention to that box when he and my brother Will slid the sign into the bed of the truck. I was too excited that Will had come through on his promise to find me the perfect piece of retro neon for the back wall of the pond house we planned to build this summer. The battered pink metal sign was pig-shaped, measured about five feet long by three feet tall, and spelled out BAR-B-CUE & SPARE RIBS in bright orange neon tubing on the side. Normally it would have been out of my price range, but one side was so damaged that it could no longer swing freely and be viewed from both sides. It was going to need some electrical work, too, but hey, when one of your eleven brothers and two of his kids are electricians, you get the family discount. I figured a case of beer and all the barbecue Reese could eat for the next month at our cousin's barbecue house would just about cover the cost of getting that pig up and oinking.

For the record, Will is three brothers up from me and runs an auction house on the west side of Dobbs, our county seat.

Reese's dad, Herman, is four more up from Will, one of the "big twins," which is how we differentiate Herman and Haywood from Adam and Zach, the "little twins" who were supposed to be the end of the line. I was an unexpected bonus — a "change baby" and the only girl. Herman's in a motorized wheelchair now, so Reese and his sister Annie Sue do most of the electrical work these days, but Herman still keeps his hand in with whatever jobs he can do sitting down. Between the three of them, that pig was going to look just fine.

But first I had to get it stashed in one of the outbuildings on the farm before Dwight got wind of it.

My husband thinks neon is tacky, and so far I haven't found the right place to hang the blue guitar sign I stole when I was sixteen (and spent the summer working off), the bright multicolored OPEN TILL MID-NIGHT sign that came home with me one New Year's Eve, or the pink-and-white WED-DING CHAPEL sign that Will and Amy gave us when we got married. I'm hoping that when the pond shelter is built and Dwight sees that back wall filled with vibrant tubes of colorful lights that he'll change his mind about neon and agree that this is exactly what's been missing at our family get-togethers.

"What's with the squirrel?" I asked Reese when he came around the side and opened the door.

He shook the rain from his cap, then climbed back behind the wheel and wiped his face dry on his sleeve.

"Guy I met a couple of days ago," he said, finally getting the wipers set the way he wanted them before he put the truck in gear. "I told him I'd bring him any roadkill

I found as long as it hadn't been dead too long. Hey! Don't change the station. I like that song. Beside, it's appropriate."

Diverted, I cocked my head, trying to get a fix on the music. The song was something I'd heard before, but the band?

Reese grinned. "Squirrel Nut Zippers."

My answering smile became a frown when he turned off the paved road onto one that was dirt and gravel. We were still a couple of miles from the farm and I was in no mood for one of his side trips, not when Dwight was due home in less than an hour. As Sheriff Bo Poole's second in command, his normal hours are eight to four, and it was already a minute or two past four.

Reese is about as reliable as a three-dollar watch. I couldn't trust him to stow the sign where Dwight wouldn't see it the minute he dropped in on Daddy.

"This is no time for a detour," I said. "Where're we going?"

"I told you. Guy I just met. I need to drop off those squirrels before they start smelling."

"He wants roadkill? Why?"

"You'll see."

This road was a deserted dead end with no houses for the last half mile and I hadn't been on it since I was in high school. A lane meanders off to the left to wind up at the creek, and it used to be a popular makeout spot. Might still be for all I knew. Back then, it was way too close to the farm for anything except a few chaste kisses in the moonlight before my date drove me home. A bootlegger —

(*"Former bootlegger,"* said the preacher who lives in the back of my head.)

(An amused snort came from the more cynical pragmatist who dwells there, too.)

Former or not — and as a district court judge, I live in fear that he's going to turn up in a colleague's courtroom one of these days — a bootlegger keeps tabs on anything happening around him, and Daddy seemed to have a pair of eyes everywhere when I was growing up. If I'd tried to park here with someone on the basketball team, word would have gotten back to him and Mother before the car windows fogged up good, so I'd kept the foggy window thing at least ten miles away.

The road ended, but another, nearly invisible lane continued on through the dripping trees, then leveled out into a sloped clearing next to a meadow that ran down to a creek. Beyond the creek was a stand of mixed hardwoods and I realized that those bare trees marked the western boundary of our family's land.

A weathered clapboard tenant house with a rusty tin roof sat at the top edge of the meadow. Smoke drifted from the chimney and was pushed down by the heavy wet air to cloud around the rooftop.

I searched my memory and asked, "Isn't this the old Ferrabee place? I thought it got bought up as part of Talbert's housing development."

Reese shrugged. The last Ferrabee died long before either of us was born, and Reese had been brought up in Dobbs, so the name meant even less to him than it did to me. I tried to think who might own this forgotten slice of woods and meadow, but nothing popped to the surface. I'd have to ask Daddy. He would certainly know. In fact, he'd probably put in an offer if the land had changed hands anytime recently. Daddy's like one of those old Iron Curtain countries: land-poor, yet always trying to extend the buffer between our homeplace and the outside world.

Reese pulled up to the porch and blew his horn.

No response. Not even a telltale twitch of the sun-faded shades that were tightly drawn over the windows.

"Must not be home," I said. "I don't see a

26

car. Let's go."

He tapped the horn again.

Rain dripped from the porch overhang onto the single homemade wooden step. When I made a pointed show of looking at my watch, Reese eased off the brakes and the truck moved forward to circle past a corner of the house that had, till now, blocked our view of a rusty old black Ford pickup down near the creek. A muddy track was all the invitation Reese needed, and even though I yelled at him, we went bouncing across the rough meadow.

The black truck was parked beside a broad slab of cracked concrete. The slab was half enclosed by the stubby remains of a wall that was now only three or four bricks high and had probably served as the foundation for a barn or storage shelter years ago. This time of year, night comes early and the gathering dusk blurred the landscape. As we neared the ruins, what had looked like a clump of dark wet rocks suddenly morphed into three big black birds that pushed off from the slab and flew away.

Buzzards.

Reese drew even with the driver's side of the other truck and powered down his window. After a moment or two, the man inside lowered his and I looked into an unfamiliar face.

Late fifties or early sixties if the graying hair at his temples and a grizzled unkempt beard meant anything, the stranger wore a ratty black derby that had seen better days, a heavy black work jacket zipped up over what looked like black twill coveralls, and an unfriendly scowl. He could have been any dirt farmer in the county, annoyed by unexpected guests.

Except for his eyes. There was no curiosity in those cool gray eyes, yet I felt that we were being scanned and catalogued and that everything about us was being filed for future reference.

"Yes?" he said.

"Reese Knott," my nephew said. "I was over a couple of days ago. Remember?"

"You remember hearing I don't like company?"

"Just buzzards. I know," Reese said cheerfully, ignoring the man's frosty tone. "I brought them some squirrels."

He hopped out of the cab and headed around to the back of his truck.

The man continued to stare at me through the open window.

"I'm Reese's aunt," I said, annoyed by the awkward situation. If he'd warned Reese off before, then clearly we were trespassing and his rudeness was somewhat justified.

Before he could respond, Reese called from over near the slab. "Do I just throw them on top or off to the side?"

I glanced in his direction and saw the remains of a deer carcass on the concrete slab where the buzzards had been before. The rib cage poked up from a mound of fur.

"No!" the man shouted back, exasperation written all over him. He stepped out into the misting rain and pulled a plastic garbage bag from under the toolbox bolted beneath the truck's rear window. The box looked new and its unchipped white enamel was a marked contrast to the rusty dents in the truck. "I told you before that I don't want anyone bringing them food out here but me. Put them in this and I'll feed them after you've gone."

Reese was clearly disappointed, but finally got the message. He dropped the squirrels into the plastic bag and headed back to the truck. The stranger remained where he was, looking up into the gray sky.

"Man," Reese said, sounding like a little kid again as he turned the ignition key. "I was hoping he'd let us watch them land."

As we drove back through the pasture, I leaned close to the window so that I could follow the man's gaze. High above us, those three buzzards circled without flapping their wings. They seemed to bank and wheel almost absentmindedly whenever the thermals started to carry them away. A slight dip or rise in those big white-tipped wings brought them drifting back until they were overhead again, floating gracefully on the wind.

Waiting.

CHAPTER 2

Vultures prefer to eat fairly fresh meat.
They will turn their nose up at rotten meat
if there is a fresher alternative available.
They also prefer the meat of herbivorous
animals.

— The Turkey Vulture Society

"What was all that about?" I asked Reese
when we were back on the road home.
"Who *is* that guy and what's his problem?"

He shrugged.

"So how did you meet him?"

Reese turned into a lane that would cut
across the farm and bring us out near one
of Daddy's barns. "I've been noticing buzzards hanging around over there off and on
since right after Christmas and I couldn't
figure out why. I mean, deer aren't like
elephants, are they?"

"Not that I've noticed," I said dryly. "For
one thing, elephant antlers are a lot bigger."

He grinned. "You know what I mean. Elephants have graveyards, right? But who ever heard of a deer graveyard? I figured that it had to be a pretty sizable animal, though, and more than one of 'em to keep those buzzards circling in the same place for so long. Anyhow, a couple of days ago I drove over in that direction as far as I could and hiked the rest of the way. When I got across the creek, I saw that guy trying to get a deer carcass out of the back of his truck. He looked to be having trouble — I think there's something wrong with his arms — so I went and helped him."

"He doesn't strike me as somebody who'd welcome help," I said.

"You got that right. But as long as I was there, he let me hoist it out and onto the table."

"Table?"

"That's what he calls that old foundation. His buzzard table. Anytime he finds some fairly fresh roadkill, he picks it up and puts it there."

"Why?"

Reese shrugged. "All I know is that his truck box is stuffed with tripods and camera equipment. He says he's doing a photographic study of American vultures."

I had noticed the stranger's slight accent.

"He's British? An ornithologist?"

"Oh, hell, Deb'rah. I don't know. It's not like he's somebody who'll tell you the story of their life the first minute you meet 'em. I didn't even get his name."

"But you must have talked about something when you were helping him move that deer."

"Just buzzard stuff. Hey, did you know that they don't like the taste of dogs or cats?"

"Really? I thought buzzards eat anything dead."

"Not meat eaters if they can avoid it. They will if there's absolutely nothing else, but he says they'd rather have animals that eat plants. Like squirrels and deer."

That made me smile. "Who knew buzzards were that picky?"

"Or that stuff could be too rotten even for them?"

He coasted to a stop under one of the shelters that jutted off from the barn and we soon had my neon pig safely stowed in a stall that hadn't been used since Daddy quit keeping a milk cow.

There was no sign of Daddy's truck up at the house, so Reese dropped me at my own back door, then headed on down the lane to see if he could scrounge some supper from one of my sisters-in-law. Most of them have a soft spot for him.

I let the dog out, started a load of laundry, and set a spinach lasagna that I'd made the weekend before out on the counter to thaw for our own supper. Children aren't supposed to like spinach, but it was one of my young stepson's favorites.

When I married Dwight December before last, the courthouse women — judges, clerks, and attorneys — gave me a recipe shower. The consensus seemed to be that Dwight would otherwise starve to death. Never mind that he'd been cooking for himself since his divorce a few years earlier. This lasagna was from Portland Avery, an attorney in Dobbs, and my oldest and closest friend. Weird to think of getting healthy recipes from her after all the Butterfingers, bacon cheeseburgers, and double-buttered popcorn we consumed together growing up.

The rain had begun again, heavy now, and gave signs of setting in for the night, so Bandit, Cal's terrier, was ready to come back in almost immediately. I gave him a rawhide chew and sat down at the computer to check my email. The last message, sent only minutes ago, was from Dwight's sister-in-law Kate and was headed "TURN ON YOUR PHONE!!" in all caps. The message itself read, "Did you forget about tonight?"

Tonight?

I quickly switched on my phone and saw that I'd missed two messages from her and one from Dwight. It seldom occurred to either of them to try the landline first.

I immediately called Dwight, and after he got through fuming because I won't keep my phone on 24/7, he got around to telling me what he had forgotten to tell me several days ago. "We're supposed to go to Mrs. Lattimore's for dinner tonight."

"What?"

At least he had the grace to sound abashed. "Sorry, shug. Kate passed on the invitation last week, but things were sorta hectic that day. That arson case, then Cal's molar. Remember all the blood?"

I did remember. Dwight and I contribute to the nanny that Kate and Rob hired to watch their own three. The oldest, Mary Pat, is in the same class as Cal, so he rides the school bus home with her every afternoon and Dwight usually picks him up because he gets off work earlier than I do. That molar hadn't quite been ready to turn loose and Cal had grabbed an apple from the bowl of fresh fruit the nanny keeps for them. Two bites into it on the drive home and the molar tore free. In his determination not to swallow the thing, Cal had wound up with chunks of apple and bloody saliva down the front of his jacket, on his face and hands, and on the seat and armrest of Dwight's truck before that tooth was found and securely wrapped in a tissue. At nine and a half, Cal's not entirely sure there really is a tooth fairy, but he wasn't going to take any chances of losing a potential moneymaker.

So yes, it was understandable that Dwight might have forgotten an invitation to dinner, especially to one that promised to be somewhat stiff and formal.

"Sigrid Harald's down and her mother, too," he told me. "I can understand why Mrs. Lattimore would want Kate and Rob to come, but why us?"

Why indeed?

Until age and cancer overtook her, Mrs. Lattimore had been a force in Cotton Grove, our nearest town, using her money and her family connections to get things done the way she wanted them done.

My mother and Mrs. Lattimore had been distant cousins, so distant that they were not in the same social circle, especially after Mother went and married "down," choosing a disreputable bootlegging tobacco farmer with eight motherless little boys instead of a white-collar professional from further up the social scale.

Our homeplace is a much-added-onto structure that began as an old-fashioned four-over-four wooden farmhouse out in the country, surrounded by several hundred acres of rolling fields and scrub woodlands.

The Lattimore house is a three-story Victorian clapboard and shingled "cottage" with steeply pitched roofs, a turret or two, and extensive verandas. It sits on a large corner lot one block away from the town square. A life-size bronze deer stands amid head-high hydrangea bushes and stares moodily through the tall iron railings at the passing cars. Given the current price of scrap copper and brass, the Cotton Grove police chief keeps predicting that someone's going to try and steal that deer one of these nights even though his office backs up to Mrs. Lattimore's yard.

"I don't want to be left looking like a fool," he says gloomily.

"It'll take a crane and flatbed to move that thing," Dwight tells him. "I'm sure some-body would notice a crane."

"You think?"

I'd never been inside the scrolled iron gates, but Mrs. Lattimore was related to Kate's older son through Kate's first husband, so her daughter and granddaughter had known Kate for years.

We had met that granddaughter a few weeks earlier when we finally took a honeymoon trip to New York and stayed in the apartment that Kate still owned. Upon hearing our plans, Mrs. Lattimore asked us to take along a small bronze sculpture that she wanted to be rid of, which was how we came to know Lieutenant Harald, a homicide detective with the New York City Police Department.

A careless word on my part had led to my having to tell Sigrid that her grandmother's cancer had returned and that she was not expected to make it past spring.

Through Kate, I knew that Sigrid's mother, Anne, had made a quick trip down the day after we got back ourselves. She'd been in New Zealand when we were in New York and Kate said she'd gotten off one plane and right onto another without even going home to change. Now she was evidently back in Cotton Grove again, and this time with Sigrid, whom we'd met after a killer used that bronze to smash in someone's head.

Sigrid and Dwight had gotten along okay professionally during the subsequent investigation, but she and I hadn't exactly bonded and I didn't expect to see her again before the inevitable funeral.

"Sorry, shug," Dwight said again, but his tone turned hopeful. "I don't suppose you could just call and get us out of it?"

"Not at this late date."

I heard him sigh. "I guess that means a dress shirt and silk tie."

For work, he usually wears a soft shirt and a comfortable knit tie that comes off as soon as he gets to the office. Dinner at Mrs. Lattimore's would surely be more formal. No footmen or finger bowls, but definitely Sunday best.

I called Kate, who confirmed the dress code. She also offered to let Cal stay with her brood till we got home. "Aunt Jane's not up to late nights, but just to be on the safe side, why don't you bring over his pajamas and you and Dwight ride with us?"

Until his last growth spurt, Cal and Mary Pat could wear each other's PJs in an emergency. No more. He's a good two inches taller than she now and almost up to my shoulder.

Dwight was later than usual getting home, which didn't give him much time to shower and change. Just as well, because his first question was, "Where's your car?"

"I left it at Will's," I said, opening his closet as he started to undress.

"Why? It's not acting up, is it?"

"No, I finished up early today and stopped by to see him. Reese was there and offered me a lift. I thought I'd save a little gas and ride in with you tomorrow." I held out two ties that would go with the brown wool sports jacket he would be wearing. "Which one?" I asked.

As I'd hoped, it was enough to distract him from asking more questions about why I'd left my car in town, and our talk turned to the Dobbs woman who had disappeared last week.

Rebecca Jowett had presumably gone jogging Saturday evening, taking nothing with her but her cell phone and a house key that she could tuck into the pocket of her sweatpants. She had not been seen again. Her car was still parked in the drive, her purse and iPad were on the dining table, and her husband swore that none of her clothes were missing.

A licensed Realtor who worked for a local agency, she habitually ran at least four evenings a week. Unfortunately, there was no fixed routine to her runs. Sometimes she circled the neighborhood where a new listing had lately come on the market, sometimes she took one of the trails that led from the town commons along the river to a historic house near the old cemetery. More times than not, she would loop around the cemetery and jog home through the quiet, tree-lined streets. The Jowett neighborhood boasted half-acre lots with mature trees and head-high azalea bushes; and although there were streetlights on every corner, she often ran past the houses unnoticed.

"It's not like you could set your watch by her," a concerned friend said.

As with every town, Dobbs has its troubled pockets of poverty and crime, yet no one could remember any incidents of violence along the routes Becca Jowett might have taken that night. Yes, someone had exposed himself to two teenage girls on the river path two summers ago, but after closely questioning all three parties, the Dobbs police officer, a sensible woman with no tolerance for sexual harassment of young girls, had concluded that the exposure was unintentional. The guilty and highly embarrassed old man had simply not stepped far enough into the bushes to relieve himself.

"Which is not to say someone didn't lie in wait for her along the river that night," Dwight said. Both the town police and several sheriff's deputies had gone over all the missing woman's usual routes and had found nothing of significance.

"Cold as it was?" I scoffed. "It must have been someone driving by. Someone she knew, because nobody gets in a car with a stranger. Unless it was her husband or a boyfriend?"

He shot me a questioning look as he jangled his keys. "You hear something I need to know about? I thought you didn't know the Jowetts."

"I don't. One of our clerks — Robin Winnick? Her sister does the Jowett woman's hair. She said her sister said that she thought the marriage was dying on the vine, and besides, aren't husbands and boyfriends automatically at the top of the list?"

"On the top of what list?" Cal asked, coming down the hall with his pajamas stuffed in his backpack.

"Of men important to a woman," I said. "Like husbands and stepsons."

"You can't tag Dave Jowett for this," Dwight's brother Rob said firmly on the short drive to Cotton Grove. "We were in school together and I never saw him fly off the handle or lose his temper to the point of violence, not even when that Dobbs pitcher

42

tried to beanball him. He just isn't the type, Dwight."

"Even if his wife was slipping around on him?"

"Do you know for a fact she was?" Rob asked, glancing back at Dwight in his rearview mirror.

"Don't know much of anything yet," Dwight admitted.

Sometimes it's hard to realize that these two are brothers. Dwight looks like his father: tall and rangy, with brown eyes and brown hair. Rob is built like their mother: small-boned, wiry, with green eyes and russet hair. Dwight's face is broad and open, while Rob's is more pointed, with a foxy slyness that tends to make opposing lawyers decide to settle out of court.

Rob is maybe half an inch under six feet so he was never tall enough nor muscular enough to follow Dwight onto the West Colleton varsity basketball team, but he had been an excellent shortstop on the same baseball team as Dave Jowett. Not that either of them was on my radar screen back then. Portland and I'd had our sights trained on the captain and quarterback of her school's football team, so I had nothing to add to the discussion. Except for that one clerk's comment, there wasn't even any good gossip going around the courthouse.

"You still tight with Jowett?" Dwight asked.

"Not really," Rob said. "His office is down the block from mine in Cameron Village so we run into each other at lunchtime now and then, and I've met his wife. He thinks it's funny that I've wound up with three kids when he was the one who wanted to coach some sons through Little League."

I saw Kate lean toward him with a contented smile. All the children were related to each other through Kate, but only R.W. was his by blood. Late last summer, though, Rob had adopted Kate's son Jake and together he and Kate had adopted Mary Pat, her orphaned cousin.

Cal had been fascinated and asked a million questions about how adoption worked and did this mean that Mary Pat and Jake were his real cousins now that Uncle Rob was their real dad?

Before Dwight and Rob could pick up again on Dave Jowett's missing wife, I asked Kate what tonight's dinner was in aid of.

"If I know Aunt Jane, it's to take the spotlight off her health for one evening. Sigrid doesn't hover and Anne tries not to, but it's hard on all three of them. Anne wants to tell her sisters and Aunt Jane absolutely refuses. I can't say I blame her. Mary and Elizabeth both are such take-charge types that they would hound her to go for chemo or radiation or else spend the next two months berating everybody in Cotton Grove for not telling them sooner, back when it might have helped."

"But it wouldn't have helped, would it?" I asked as we entered town and Rob slowed the car to a sedate 35 miles an hour. "Not once it's in the liver and pancreas?"

"And so far, she's not in too much pain. Or so she says. She's told Anne that she doesn't want the others to know until it's time for hospice. I just hope they won't take it out on Anne." Kate turned to face me around the headrest of her front seat. "Be prepared for Aunt Jane to give you a bit of a hard time, though."

"Me? What did I do?"

"You were the one who told Sigrid, remember?"

Rob turned at one of Cotton Grove's three traffic lights, and a moment later we glided through the open iron gates to follow the circular drive to the imposing front door.

"Nobody swore me to secrecy," I said. "And besides, Sigrid had already figured out that something was wrong."

With rain pounding on the car roof,

Dwight reached for the umbrellas on the rear ledge and passed one up to Rob.

Chivalry is not yet dead in the South.

CHAPTER 3

These peaceful animals pose no risk.
— The Turkey Vulture Society

I was not surprised when Chloe Adams opened the door. A licensed practical nurse, she has an easy, reassuring manner that makes her a good companion for someone ill or dying. Early fifties now, with a trim build that belies her physical strength, her children are grown and her husband is a long-haul trucker who is on the road for such long stretches that she can move right into a spare bedroom if that's what's wanted and be on call 24/7.

Elderly whites who were tended by black nursemaids in their long-vanished youth are doubly comforted by her calm professionalism in the evening of their lives. Sent to bed early by a stern parent, they could remember a soothing pat and a low voice crooning in the darkened room. "There, there, baby.

Stop your crying and go to sleep now. Things'll be better in the morning."

Mrs. Lattimore has never struck me as someone who would cry herself to sleep, not even with death staring her in the face. All the same and despite her wealth, she had hired Mrs. Adams rather than a fully accredited RN. I doubt if her choice had anything to do with money.

Chloe Adams took our umbrellas and coats and told us to go on into the living room, then discreetly vanished.

"Come in, come in," said Mrs. Lattimore. Seated in a high-back wing chair, she gave a welcoming gesture with her thin hands. "How nice to see you all."

She wore a stylish cranberry wool dress with a high neck and long sleeves, and a quilted velvet throw was tucked around her legs although the room was quite warm. She seemed even more fragile than when I had last seen her at Kate and Rob's Christmas dinner, yet she was still beautiful. Good bones always last.

In any conflicts with school boards, town officials, or county commissioners, I'm told that Mrs. Lattimore had always begun with honey. "Although you knew the vinegar was coming if they didn't fall in line," my own mother had said with a grin. Over the years,

I had heard so many stories about the vinegar that I admit I was slightly intimidated by her when we met at Christmas. Now I was seeing the honey as she welcomed us.

She did not rise from her chair by the fireplace where realistic-looking gas logs burned, but Sigrid stood and so did the woman I assumed was her mother. Anne Harald resembled her mother more than her daughter, the same bones, the same beauty, the same easy poise when meeting new people. She was shorter than Sigrid, and her dark curls were heavily threaded with silver. Like her mother, now that I was noticing, her eyes were the same indeterminate bluish gray while her daughter's were more silvery. A green silk scarf, loosely looped around her neck, brightened her dark blue sweater and slacks, and sapphire earrings caught the light as she greeted Kate and Rob with warm hugs, before turning to Dwight and me with outstretched hands.

Charm and beauty seemed to be this family's birthright and Anne Lattimore Harald had apparently inherited both her share and Sigrid's, too.

She's a prizewinning photojournalist, semiretired now, and Kate reminded her that I'd gone to the opening reception when she exhibited some of her photographs at the art museum in Raleigh a few years back. "But of course you won't remember me," I said. "You must meet so many people."

"I'll remember you after this, though," she said. "Especially since Sigrid's told me so much about you both."

Although Sigrid murmured politely that it was good to see us again, Anne's bubbling warmth was in sharp contrast to her daughter's cool reserve as she drew us over to the couch. "I'm so sorry you wound up cutting your honeymoon short. Maybe if I'd been there to take that odious bronze thing off your hands the first day, things would have turned out differently."

Dwight shrugged. "Not necessarily."

Once we were seated, I was emboldened to ask Mrs. Lattimore, "If it's not too personal, how did you come by such a piece?"

With a graceful air of frankness, the older woman said, "At my age, I have very few secrets left, but I probably ought not to confess with so many law people in the room."

Sigrid smiled. "I'm sure the statute of limitations has run out by now, Grandmother."

"Thank you, dear. Very well, Deborah. I

stole it. Took it from my history professor's private office when no one else was around and stuck it in my bookbag. But where are my manners? What can Anne give you to drink?" She waved her hand toward a well-stocked wet bar in the corner of the room and held out her empty cocktail glass to Rob. "Would you, dear? Another martini? Light on the vermouth, please."

As Anne and Rob moved over to the bar to mix our drinks, I said, "But why on earth would you steal such a thing?"

Amusement lit her thin patrician face. "So you saw it, did you?"

I had. And although I am not easily shocked, I have to admit that it was quite a surprise to open the package she had asked me to take to New York for Anne. Cylindrical in shape and roughly the size of a tall can of beer, the small bronze sculpture was obscenely offensive, hardly the sort of thing I'd ever suspect Mrs. Lattimore of owning.

"My parents had sent me north to a little New England school with good academic qualifications and a reputation for respectability. Carolina did not accept female undergraduates back then and my father had heard disturbing rumors about lesbians at Woman's College, although of course he couldn't tell me that. Too, there was a young

51

man here that he felt was an unsuitable match, so I was packed off north to a school where the morals were very much the same, just better hidden. I'm afraid I wasn't quite as innocent and unknowing as my father hoped, although I was just as priggish in my own way. Ah, thank you, Rob," she said and took a sip of the fresh martini he had brought her.

"I thought my professor was a hypocrite because he flirted with my favorite teacher even though I knew that he preferred men. She clearly didn't realize it and I hated him for leading her on. It never occurred to me that the poor man had no real alternatives. Back in the forties, it was stay in the closet or lose your job. The times forced him into hypocrisy. I didn't think the piece was very valuable, but even if it was, I knew it was so vulgar that he could never describe it to the police once he missed it. I was going to be the avenging hand of God and punish him for hurting Miss Barclay."

Remembering her youthful indignation, she shared an indulgent smile with us. "As a judge, Deborah, I'm sure you're well aware how foolishly self-righteous the young can be."

I nodded in wry agreement as I smeared some soft brie on a cracker, then slid the cheese tray down the long low table toward Sigrid and Dwight to make room for the drinks Anne handed us. "So you kept it and brought it back home with you without realizing that it was by a famous sculptor?"

"Ah, but he wasn't famous then," Mrs. Lattimore said. She took another sip of her martini and let her head rest against the back of the chair. "I had planned to leave it in some conspicuous spot on campus at the start of our Christmas break, but the war was getting worse and I came back from class one day to find my mother waiting for me. She and Father wanted me to transfer to Woman's College immediately. WC might have been a den of iniquity, but its academic standards were just as high as Stillwater's and it was much closer to home in case the Germans landed on our shores or started bombing us. It was all I could do to roll that thing up in one of my nightgowns and lock it in my dressing case before Mother caught sight of it. She found the case in the attic a few years later and brought it over to me to see if I still had the key."

She cradled the cocktail glass in her thin hands and smiled at us. "As I told Anne, I took it straight up to the attic storeroom here and promptly forgot all about it. It would have been something for her and her sisters to puzzle over someday had I not read that article in the Smithsonian's journal and realized how valuable it probably was now. I'm just sorry it was used to kill someone."

Her mention of the murder prompted Dwight to ask Sigrid where that case stood now.

"You heard the confession," she told him. "In return for an immediate guilty plea, the DA's decided to save the state the cost of a jury trial and just go with three counts of manslaughter."

"I guess two of them weren't premeditated," he agreed.

"What about attempted murder?" I asked, indignant that the killer hadn't been charged with nearly suffocating me.

"That really was unpremeditated," Sigrid reminded me dryly, and the conversation turned to other topics.

Although I no longer felt intimidated by Mrs. Lattimore's reputation for bluntness, I was glad that she seemed to have forgotten to scold me for letting Sigrid know about her cancer.

Our drinks were nearly finished when Anne turned to Mrs. Lattimore and said, "Mother, don't you think — ?"

"Yes, of course," the older woman replied.

"We won't wait any longer. Tell Martha that we're ready to begin."

She pushed aside the lap robe and reached for her cane and Rob immediately offered his arm to help her rise.

As the rest of us stood, the doorbell rang.

Mrs. Lattimore looked over to Sigrid. "Would you get that, dear?"

We waited awkwardly while Sigrid went out into the vestibule. We heard the door open and a male voice.

A moment later, the man entered the living room and went straight to our hostess. Of medium height and average build, his hair and neatly trimmed short beard were steel gray, and there were deep lines around his eyes. He wore rimless square glasses, a black turtleneck sweater, and a gold chain. His black wool suit had good lines but something about the way it hung made me think he might have lost weight since he first bought it. He took Mrs. Lattimore's hand in both of his own and in that light British accent said, "So sorry to hold everyone up, Aunt Jane. My truck didn't want to start."

It was the buzzard man.

CHAPTER 4

In many parts of the world, vultures have become very brave and comfortable in the presence of humans.
                              — The Turkey Vulture Society

"Do you remember Anne?" Mrs. Lattimore asked him.

The man shook his head. "I'm sorry. I don't. I was what? Five? Six?" He smiled at Anne. "Sorry I missed you when you were here a couple of weeks ago, but I'm glad to see you now."

There was a puzzled look on Anne's face as she peered into his eyes. "Have we met before? I mean since that time in Washington when we were children? Your face seems familiar."

"Family resemblance perhaps?"

Anne frowned and shook her head, staring at him more intently. "Did you always have the beard?"

"It comes and goes, depending on the weather. Without it, I pretty much look like everyone else, although there *is* a man in London that I run into once or twice a year and he's convinced we were on the same rugby team in Colchester. I've never been to Colchester in my life and I've never played rugby."

"Me either," Anne said with a laugh. "Shall I still tell Martha to begin, Mother?"

"Please," said Mrs. Lattimore. "Unless you'd like a drink first, Martin?"

He waved away the offer and looked expectantly at the rest of us.

"Martin is my late sister's son," Mrs. Lattimore told us as she completed the introductions. "Martin Crawford."

"We met this afternoon," I said.

His smile broadened. "So we did. I hope your nephew wasn't offended by my abruptness. It's been a difficult week for me. Did my aunt say you are a judge?"

He was all genial politeness now as Anne led the way into the dining room — more of the family charm? The long formal table could accommodate twelve, so there was plenty of room for the eight of us. Mrs. Lattimore took the chair at the head of the table with her nephew on her right and Dwight on her left. Kate was next to Martin and Sigrid next to Dwight, then Anne and I across from each other and Rob at the end.

Salads were already at our places, and as the silver boat of creamy dressing went around the table, conversation was general at first, despite the curiosity I was sure the others must share about this unfamiliar nephew.

I hadn't known that Mrs. Lattimore had a sister and I gathered that Kate hadn't known either. As a quasi-relative, though, Kate was free to ask all the questions I couldn't.

"We were never particularly close as children," Mrs. Lattimore explained. "As much my fault as hers, probably. And it didn't help that she was engaged to my husband first."

Again that graceful shrug, followed by the same wry smile we'd seen when she announced earlier that she had no secrets left. By the time the entrée was served, we had learned that after Mr. Lattimore broke off his engagement to Ferrabee Gilbert and proposed to her sister Jane, Ferrabee had gone to live with a college roommate in Washington. A month before the Lattimores married, she eloped with a young attaché assigned to the British embassy there. Soon afterwards, he was posted to North Africa, and she never came back to America.

"Father never forgave her and Ferrabee never forgave me."

"Ferrabee?" I asked Martin Crawford. "Does that mean the old Ferrabee place belongs to you?"

"Not to me," he replied. "To my aunt. She's letting me camp out there."

"My mother was a Ferrabee," said Mrs. Lattimore, "and I inherited it."

Turning back to Martin Crawford, she said, "I'll be forever sorry that your mother and I never got a chance to mend fences."

"And I'm sorry I waited so long to come looking for her people," he said, lifting a forkful of warm poached salmon. "But in all honesty, I barely remember her myself. I had a good stepmother, though. She's still living in London. In fact, I hope to be there for her eightieth birthday next month."

"You'll be finished with your research on turkey buzzards by then?" I asked.

"With a little luck," he answered cheerfully.

"Research?" asked Sigrid.

"I'm not the photographer your mother is," he said, raising his glass to Anne diagonally across from him, "but I've managed to cobble together a living as an ornithologist.

I lead tours to exotic-sounding places for serious birders who want to add to their life lists, and I do a little teaching. I've also had a bit of luck getting a couple of books published. We lived all over when I was a boy, and my stepmother always bought me a guide to that country's birds. What would you like to know about *Neophron percnopterus,* the Egyptian vulture also famously called Pharaoh's Chicken?"

Diverted, Kate asked, "Chicken? How does a vulture get mistaken for a chicken?"

"It's supposed to be a humorous comment on how often the vulture is depicted in ancient hieroglyphics," he told her. "An archaeological joke. Archaeological humor can be as dry as the Sahara, I'm afraid."

He smoothed his short beard and turned back to Sigrid. "But to answer your question, raptors are my specialty and I'm writing an illustrated piece for a North African nature magazine. My agent interested them in a comparison of African vultures with the vultures here in your American South."

Mrs. Lattimore touched his hand. "Whatever your reason for coming, I'm glad you didn't leave it until too late. I do wish you would stay here with us, though. We have plenty of bedrooms and that house out there is nothing but a shack. No electricity. No plumbing."

"I've stayed in much worse," he assured her. "Besides, I rather doubt your neighbors would like it if I fed dead animals to vultures in your back garden. Especially if they began roosting on the surrounding rooftops."

Kate grimaced. "Aren't they the ugliest, most disgusting birds around?"

"Not a bit of it," he said and launched into an enthusiastic defense of what he called "nature's dustmen," reeling off facts and figures to bolster their importance in the circle of life. "In fact, their very name — *Cathartes* — means 'purifier.' The acid in their stomachs can kill cholera germs."

"You've certainly made a believer out of my nephew," I said and amused the others by telling how Reese had stopped to pick up a dead squirrel to drop off for Crawford's buzzards.

"Not mine, actually." He held out his glass for Dwight to top off his wine from the bottle between them. "It's against the law for private individuals to keep vultures in captivity. I merely feed them so that I can get close enough for some good pictures. They can be quite friendly once they trust you. And of course, it doesn't hurt to provide them with a steady diet of fresh kill."

He turned to me with a rueful smile.

"That's why I asked your nephew not to feed them there himself. I quite selfishly want to encourage them to think of me as their one dependable food source in this area."

"You keep calling them vultures," Rob said. "Aren't buzzards the same birds?"

"Technically no, idiomatically yes," he said. "Here in the States, what you call buzzards actually *are* vultures. There weren't any vultures in the British Isles, so the early English settlers lumped them under the common name for buteos, and the name gradually transferred over to your vultures to differentiate them from hawks, the way your American thrush got called a robin simply because it has a red breast similar to the English bird's."

"But why turkey vultures?" asked Kate, whose city roots sometimes betray her. "They don't eat turkeys, do they?"

Dwight, Rob, and I smiled at that.

"Red head, no feathers on it," Rob told her. "Just like a wild turkey."

"I'm not sure why the turkey's bald," said Crawford, "but for vultures, it's a cleanliness thing. Not to get gross here while we dine, but when you consider how and what vultures eat, fluffy head feathers would be a serious handicap."

Anne's fork clattered onto her plate. "Changing the subject," she said firmly, "what magazine is the article for?"

His reply was unintelligible, and at our blank looks he said, "Sorry. In English, I suppose you could call it *Modern Nature* or *Wildlife Today*."

"Was that Arabic?" Anne asked.

He nodded.

As the import of his nod sank in, I was impressed. "You're writing it in Arabic?"

He looked embarrassed. "It's actually easier than trying to translate it back from English."

"How many languages do you speak?" Sigrid asked.

He shrugged, but Sigrid persisted.

"Fluently? Only five or six."

With an amused lift of her eyebrow, Anne said, "But you can read — ?"

"Eight," Martin admitted. "No credit to me, I'm afraid. A child's brain is like a sponge. It can soak up anything, and we didn't stay behind the embassy walls. My stepmother always did her own shopping in the marketplaces wherever my father was posted, and they sent me to the local schools. And, of course, she was Pakistani, so I had a leg up there."

"He was being modest before," Anne told

us. "That book you brought Mother? There are some wonderful pictures of birds flying over the pyramids and seen from above. How on earth did you get that angle? And what sort of camera did you use?"

Mrs. Lattimore sent Sigrid up to her bedroom for the book in question, and while it went around the table, Crawford and Anne went back and forth on the merits of different cameras and lenses. The book was coffee-table quality, beautifully printed on heavy glossy paper, and the plates were in full color. Unfortunately, except for the Latin names of the birds beneath each picture, the text was in Arabic.

By the time dessert was served — warm peach cobbler swimming in heavy cream — Mrs. Lattimore was clearly starting to fade. She left her spoon on the plate and shook her head at the offer of coffee. I could see that it was an effort for her to maintain her ramrod posture, and when her shoulders slumped of their own volition, she pushed back from the table.

Chloe Adams appeared as if by magic until I realized there was probably an old-fashioned foot bell within reach of Mrs. Lattimore's shoe under the table. They had likely worked out a signal. One ring for

Martha, two for Chloe.

"Please don't get up," she said to the men, who had begun to rise. "So tiresome of me, but you'll hurt Martha's feelings if you don't stay and finish her wonderful cobbler. No, Anne, you really don't need to come with us. Chloe will take care of me."

Anne ignored her mother's protests. "I'll say good night, too," she told us, "but I'm sure I'll see you all again. Martin, I'll drive out one day if I might. I'd love to see those birds up close and I still think our paths might have crossed somewhere. You weren't in Peru five or six years ago, were you?"

Martin Crawford's face brightened. "Actually, I was!" he said. "I led a tour group to the Andes to watch the condors. What a coincidence if we wound up in the same hotel or airport lounge. We'll have to compare notes."

After Anne left, we finished our dessert, and when there was a lull in the conversation, Sigrid invited us back to the living room for more coffee and brandies, but Kate reminded us that tomorrow was a school day. I remembered that I had an early appointment with an attorney from Wilmington, while Dwight pleaded the need to check up on the search for that missing woman.

"If you have some free time and want to see how a county sheriff's department works, I'd be glad to show you around," he told Sigrid and gave her his card.

Rain was still sluicing down heavily when we reached the porch, so Martin Crawford did not linger on the steps. "Quite glad to have met you," he said and splashed off to that dilapidated truck.

"Nice man," I said as Dwight slid into the backseat of Rob's car with me. "Interesting, too. How long you think it'll take your mother to rope him into talking to one of the science classes?"

Miss Emily was the principal at West Colleton High and never missed a chance to provide enrichment for her students.

"About buzzards?" Kate asked, shaking her head. "Yuck!"

"Teenage boys usually like yuck," Rob said. "Right, Dwight?"

All the same, when we saw a dead rabbit lying by the roadside, Rob did not stop and pick it up.

CHAPTER 5

Vultures have excellent eyesight, but, like most other birds, they have poor vision in the dark.

— The Turkey Vulture Society

Sigrid Harald — Tuesday night
Anne Harald came back downstairs to find Sigrid tidying up the wet bar in the corner of the living room. While they were at dinner, Martha had washed and dried their drink glasses and they now sat on a tray waiting to be put away.

Sigrid took one look at her mother's face then filled two of the glasses with ice cubes from the silver bucket that had been in the Lattimore family for at least four generations and poured them each a stiff bourbon, no water.

"Thanks, honey," Anne said. She sat down in the wing chair by the fireplace and took a deep swallow.

Sigrid sat in the chair across from her and said, "How's Grandmother?"

"Chloe gave her a shot and it put her out pretty fast." Anne drank again, a smaller sip this time. "She was really hurting by the time we got her into bed, though. We shouldn't have let her sit so long at the table."

"Try telling her," Sigrid said dryly. "You know she doesn't want us to baby her." She lifted her own drink and let the sweet smoky scent fill her nose.

Her grandmother did not economize when it came to providing drinks for her guests, and the bourbon was almost half as old as she was. "Sippin' whiskey," Oscar Nauman had called it when he contributed this particular brand to her liquor cabinet shortly before his death, "so don't you-all go addin' any mixers to it."

Her lover's attempted drawl was nothing like the soft Southern accents that had flowed around her since she and Anne had arrived a few days earlier. It wasn't that Southerners talked slower, she had long ago decided; it was that they added extra syllables and stressed those syllables so differently that she had to keep mentally processing what she was hearing in order to understand and keep up. It was like wading in honey. Back in New York, Anne's accent was only slightly noticeable. After three days here, she had almost totally reverted.

"Why have I never known you had an aunt and a cousin?" Sigrid asked.

"Frankly, I had almost forgotten myself," Anne said. "It's not as if Mother ever talked much about her sister. You heard her. Ferrabee took herself out of the family when Dad dumped her and proposed to Mother. She died young and Dad died when I was still a child, so who else would keep her memory green?"

"Quite a coincidence that you two should both become professional photographers."

"And wind up in Peru at the same time . . . if that's where it was." Anne drained her glass and went over to the bar to pour herself another.

"Does it really matter?"

Anne stared into the flames that flickered from the gas log. "I suppose not," she said, but Sigrid could see that it was clearly going to bother her till she remembered.

The ancient gas range was fueled by a tank of propane gas that sat outside the kitchen window. When the kettle began to whistle, Martin Crawford poured part of the boiling water into the teapot on the counter and wrapped a towel around the pot to keep it hot while the tea leaves steeped. The rest of the water went into a basin in the sink and he tempered it with a dipperful of cool water from the nearby bucket. The sink itself was a homemade tin tray and fresh water came from a hand pump. A kerosene lantern gave enough light to see himself in the cloudy mirror over the sink.

While rain hammered on the tin roof overhead, he made a mental note to pick up a can of shaving cream the next time he passed a store. Wetting his beard, he made a lather with a bar of hand soap. Fortunately, he still had a razor in his toiletries kit. He had not intended to shave off his beard until he got back to London, but he could not risk having Anne remember where she'd seen his bearded face before.

Stupid of me not to realize she'd looked at us with a photographer's eye, he thought as his strong chin emerged from the under-brush.

With a little luck, maybe this beardless face would soon blur her memory of the old one. He just hoped that the vultures would accept his new look.

When they first married, real estate prices were so insane that Ginger and Wesley Todd could not touch any house on this side of town, much less a house in this neighborhood; but by the time the floundering economy had sent this 2,200-square-foot dream house into foreclosure, their pest control business was doing well enough to let them put in a serious offer. Four bedrooms, two and a half baths, a master suite with a huge walk-in closet, finished basement, and a two-car garage on a large lot thick with trees and bushes, and not too far from her parents' more modest neighborhood.

The only hitch was that the agent who first showed them the property had gone missing. Fortunately the agency owner had stepped in and was proving just as helpful.

"So if your daughter's bed doesn't fit in that dormer room, it's going to be a dealbreaker?" Paula Coyne asked as she unlocked the front door for them shortly before 10:30 that evening.

They left their wet umbrellas dripping outside the door and wiped their shoes on the welcome mat.

Ginger Todd knew that she was being silly, but Ms. Coyne's tone was teasing so she smiled back. "It's really nice of you to come out this late, in the rain and all, so we can take one last look, but this is such a huge step for us, and when we remembered the ceiling . . ."

"It's a lot of money," the Realtor agreed, flipping on the light switches. "I don't blame you a bit for wanting to be sure. That's what we're here for."

The house had been minimally staged: a couch and some chairs in the living room on the right, a table and four side chairs in the dining room on the left. "They'll get the furniture out of your way as soon as you close on Thursday," Ms. Coyne said, moving briskly to the staircase.

The younger woman started to follow, but her husband fumbled for the light switches on the interior living room wall.

"You know, hon, I really do like that couch. It's long enough to stretch out on when I watch TV." He looked up at Ms. Coyne, who was already halfway up the stairs. "Is there any chance you could get them to leave it?"

"We can certainly ask," she said.

"But that color," his wife said. "Will it go with the rest of our things?" She moved past him to consider the couch's potential. She rather liked the pattern — large dramatic bunches of red roses and green leaves on a white background. "I don't think our red chair will match this red, though."

"Sure it will," Wes Todd said confidently. In contrast to his wife's habit of dithering and second-guessing herself, he usually knew his own mind and made snap decisions. "Besides, it's really more green-and-white than red." He whipped off the bright red afghan that had been draped over one end of the couch. "See?"

His wife started to agree, then made a face. "Forget it, Wes. Look at that yucky stain."

"Stain?" Ms. Coyne frowned and came back down to join them. Selling houses in this economy was hard enough with fresh paint and pristine décor. Stained furniture was unacceptable in the listings she handled. She remembered admiring the couch when she did her walk-through yesterday, so the afghan must have hidden the stain because no way would she not have noticed this ugly —

"Oh, dear Lord!" she said. "Is that blood?"

CHAPTER 6

Turkey vultures usually hiss when they feel
threatened.
— The Turkey Vulture Society

Wednesday morning

I had been half joking when I said that my
mother-in-law would probably cajole Martin Crawford into talking to a class at West
Colleton High. It never occurred to me that
she would rope Anne Harald in for something as well. Yet when I came back to my
courtroom after the midmorning break,
there sat Miss Emily on the front bench
with Anne Harald on one side and Richard
Williams on the other. Miss Emily wouldn't
meet my eyes, but Anne gave me a rueful
smile and Richard beamed with his usual
friendly optimism.

As the youth minister at the Methodist
church here in Dobbs and an advocate for
troubled kids, Richard was in and out of

the courthouse several times a week pleading that his charges be given another chance to straighten out their lives before they were sentenced to serious jail time. He could be here for the shoplifter, one of the D&Ds, the malicious vandalism, or for anyone else under the age of twenty-five.

But Miss Emily?

I ran my finger down the calendar until I came to Jeremy Patrick Harper, charged back in December with trespassing, and I remembered that she'd asked me where a charge of trespassing on state property would be tried. In district court or superior?

There had been another flurry of peace demonstrations at the small county airport that forms the bottom of a triangle between our house and Cotton Grove, and it had made the national news because the protestors were claiming that the field was again being used for rendition flights. Sheriff Bo Poole's picture even landed on the front page of the *Washington Post* because he had sent deputies out to keep order and they wound up arresting a photographer who had breached the chain-link fence and tried to get a look inside one of the privately leased hangars.

"I don't have a problem with people exercising their constitutional right to protest," Bo was quoted as saying, "long as they don't go trespassing on other people's constitutional rights."

Like most Americans who like to think that global events don't really touch their small safe lives, I had been appalled to learn that our country's war on terror had included torturing suspected terrorists and even more appalled to think that some of the planes that ferried prisoners from Guantanamo to be tortured in foreign countries might have used the little airstrip here in Colleton County as a refueling or transfer stop. Yet this was what the news media claimed six or seven years ago. Call me naïve, but till then I'd been under the impression that it was just a convenience for eastern North Carolina business executives who wanted to park their Lears and Gulfstreams at less congested and somewhat cheaper hangars than Raleigh. Since I don't own a plane and don't know anyone who does, I hadn't paid much attention to that airport except to vaguely wonder why there were no commercial commuter flights in and out. Dwight says its true purpose was the worst-kept secret in the county, but I must have been the last law-connected person in Dobbs to hear that while the field was officially owned by the state, it had been built with CIA money and that the planes that did fly in and out weren't all corporate jets by any means. Or rather, they *were* corporate jets, but the corporations were shells set up by the CIA and Blackwater to hide their true ownership.

Blackwater, the guns-for-hire company that originated in the swampy northeast corner of the state within commuting distance of the Norfolk SEAL base, has been renamed Xe. The last I heard, its ex-SEAL founder now lives in Abu Dhabi and claims he's out of the government contracting business. I don't know about our own government, but if you Google "Abu Dhabi" and dig down a couple of layers, you'll find allegations that their government has hired mercenaries to protect the oil fields and prevent another Arab Spring within the emirate. Oh, and the Pentagon is still shelling out millions to buy airplane fuel from them through noncompetitive contracts.

So what else is new?

When Jeremy Harper's name was called shortly before noon, the teenager who had been seated behind Miss Emily came forward and stood at the defendant's table beside his attorney, Reid Stephenson, who happens to be my first cousin, once removed, and a former law partner from when I was in private practice with Stephenson and Lee.

Small-town courtrooms can sometimes seem incestuous to strangers, but if judges recuse themselves every time a friend or relative stands up to argue a case for or against another friend or relative, court calendars would become an exercise in futility. No one's ever accused me of favoring Reid. If anything, John Claude Lee, the other partner in my former firm (and yes, another cousin), complains that I always lean too far backwards in my determination to be fair. He himself won't come into my court unless his case is totally ironclad.

Today's ADA was Claudia O'Hale (no kin to any of us), and after she'd read the charges, I said, "How do you plead, Mr. Harper?"

"Not guilty, ma'am." For one so tall and skinny, Jeremy Harper had an unexpectedly deep voice. He had a prominent Adam's apple on a slightly longer than usual neck, and it didn't help that he had very curly, very thick, and very light blond hair that poufed up all over his head. When the light hit it, his fair hair was closer to silver than gold. As he and Reid sat down, those frizzy white curls and the long neck gave him a vague resemblance to a dandelion gone to seed. If I wanted to get fanciful, I could almost imagine that his dark green sweater formed the dandelion's basal leaves.

Resisting the temptation to look for further parallels, I gave my attention to Claudia O'Hale, who had called the arresting officer to the witness stand. Deputy Tub Greene wasn't much older than young Harper, but he was the complete professional in his crisply pressed shirt and creased wool slacks, despite a utility belt that strained against his disappearing waistline as my clerk swore him in. Hard to stay in shape when you sit in a patrol car too long and snack on Moon Pies and RCs.

Upon being asked about that December day, Greene described how the protestors had been issued a permit that clearly stated they had to stay outside the fence, but that the defendant had later been caught trying to get inside one of the locked hangars with his camera. When given the chance to leave the premises without penalty, Mr. Harper had become foulmouthed and verbally abusive, whereupon he was placed under arrest.

Reid stood to cross-examine. He's tall and good-looking, with such a boyish face that women jurors have a hard time voting against him. Unfortunately for him, this was not a jury trial.

"When you say my client 'tried to get inside,' Deputy Greene, what do you mean?"

"When apprehended, he was carrying a crowbar."

"Did you see him actually use it?"

"No, sir."

"Did he threaten you with it?"

"No, sir."

"So you arrested him merely because he was carrying a perfectly legal carpenter's tool."

"No, sir. I arrested him because he was trespassing and refused to leave."

"Were you aware that my client is a freelance reporter and has had some of his pictures published in the *Dobbs Ledger* and the *Cotton Grove Courier?*"

"No, sir, not at that time. Besides, he wasn't wearing a press badge."

"No further questions," Reid said and sat down.

I looked over at the ADA. "Ms. O'Hale?"

"Redirect, Your Honor. Deputy Greene, were there any members of the press at this demonstration?"

"Yes, ma'am. There was a reporter from the *News and Observer* and two television stations. There were also stringers for the *Washington Post,* the *New York Times,* and the Associated Press."

"And did any of these real reporters —"

"Objection," said Reid.

"Sustained," I said. "Less pejorative, please, Ms. O'Hale."

"Sorry, Your Honor." She turned back to the deputy. "Were those reporters wearing press badges?"

"Yes, ma'am."

"And did any of the reporters with credentials push their way onto the field?"

"No, ma'am. They poked their long-lens cameras through the chain-link fence, but they respected our instructions and didn't try to get in. Just Mr. Harper."

"Any of them get foulmouthed because you kept them from entering?"

"No, ma'am."

"No further questions, Your Honor."

I looked at my cousin. "Redirect, Mr. Stephenson?"

Without rising, Reid said, "What about you, Deputy Greene? Weren't you the one who got foulmouthed first?"

The young officer flushed a deep brick red. His mother goes to the same church as one of my born-again sisters-in-law, a church that does not hold with cussing. "I don't remember," he said, avoiding my eyes.

"No further questions," Reid said.

"Ms. O'Hale?" I asked.

"The State rests," she told me.

"Call your first witness, Mr. Stephenson."

Reid touched the young man's shoulder and told him to take the stand. Once Harper had sworn to tell the truth, the whole truth, and nothing but the truth, he told us his name and that he had turned eighteen a week after the incident.

"In your own words, Jeremy, why did you go out to that airstrip and what did you hope to accomplish?"

Despite his resemblance to a dandelion, there was nothing fuzzy about the boy's response. He sizzled with self-righteousness. "We heard that they'd started up the rendition flights again and we called for a demonstration against it."

"Who is 'we'?" Reid asked.

"P-A-T. Patriots Against Torture. We're a loosely organized Internet group of concerned citizens from wherever these flights touch down — Nevada, Maine, North Carolina. We're people who don't believe America should sanction torture no matter what the excuse or provocation."

"Where are your headquarters?"

Young Harper gave an impatient jerk of

his head. "We don't have a headquarters. I told you. We're an Internet group on Yahoo! and I'm one of the group's administrators. It's like Facebook except that it's not as visible. You can't just Google PAT and enter our website. You have to join and get the password before you can read or post. We have links to some other activist groups, so when we heard that one of the suspect planes had been seen using the Colleton County Airport, the people over in Kinston called for that demonstration. We hoped to get fifteen or twenty people, instead we got nearly forty. And it was really cold that day, too."

Reid glanced down at his notes. "You've told me that the demonstration was supposed to be peaceful and nonconfrontational. Why were you arrested?"

"Because I tried to get inside one of the hangars to get a look at the identifying numbers on the fuselage of that Gulfstream jet. I was really hoping to take a picture of them changing the numbers."

"Changing the numbers?"

"Rendition planes routinely get new numbers painted on the fuselage to keep people like me from keeping track of where they are. I thought if I could get inside that hangar I could find the paint sprayers and maybe some of the stencils they use for the new numbers, and that would be visual proof that the CIA was using our airport for these illegal activities."

"Illegal? What's illegal about the CIA flying in and out of the county?"

"Because they're flying prisoners suspected of terrorism to foreign soil. *Suspected.* Not *proved,* because they won't put those prisoners on trial."

"Again, what's illegal about that?" Reid persisted.

Harper's hands tightened on the armrest of the witness chair and his curls bounced like springs as he grew more impassioned. "It may not be illegal in the technical sense, although the Constitution mandates speedy trials, but it's hypocritical and immoral. Our soldiers aren't fighting and dying so that America can turn into one of those fundamentalist countries where laws don't protect its citizens. We're supposed to be Christians. We say we don't torture people, and it's illegal for Americans to do it, so we fly them to a different country that's not so hypocritical and let them be tortured there. We —"

Reid held up his hand to cut off the boy's rant.

Jeremy Harper sank back into his chair, but instead of waiting for Reid to frame another question, he looked up to me beseechingly. "If they didn't think it was wrong and that we would care, why do they mess with the planes' registration numbers?"

"Do you know for a fact that they do?" I asked.

"Yes, ma'am. One of our members called the FAA in Oklahoma from the Kinston airport. You're supposed to be able to give them a fuselage number and they have to tell you who it's registered to. He gave them the number and they told him there was no such plane with that number. He said, 'Ma'am, I'm standing here looking at the plane and those are the numbers,' and the woman said, 'Sir, you don't understand. There *is* no such plane,' and then she hung up."

"Hearsay, Your Honor," Claudia O'Hale murmured.

"Sustained," I said.

"Let's go back to the day in question," Reid said. "You knew you were not supposed to go inside the fence?"

As if the tenor of that question had abruptly reduced his actions from high-minded nobility to juvenile misbehavior, Harper gave a sulky, "Yes, sir."

"Deputy Greene gave you an opportunity

to move back behind the fence without any charges, why didn't you take it?"

"Because he was acting like citizens and taxpayers have no right to question anything the government does, and when he called me a Muslim-loving motherfucker — sorry, Your Honor — I called him something right back and told him he was like a Nazi soldier. Just following orders without asking if those orders were legal or ethical."

Seated behind the prosecution's table, Deputy Greene stared straight ahead, stony-faced except for a dull red flush creeping up from his tight collar.

To my mind, *Nazi* is an epithet too freely tossed around by people who have no true sense of what it means, but again, as when I'd sustained the hearsay, I held my tongue.

"Thank you, Mr. Harper," Reid said. "If it pleases the court, Your Honor, my client will change his plea from not guilty to guilty with extenuating circumstances."

I looked at Claudia, who said, "One question, if I may, Your Honor?"

"Proceed," I told her.

"Mr. Harper, you talk about citizenship and taxpayers. May I ask how much tax you paid to the IRS last year?"

Now it was Harper's turn for a red face, but he jutted out his chin and his Adam's apple bobbed up and down. "Nothing," he said pugnaciously. "I'm a high school student. The only job I can find doesn't pay enough to let me help pay your salary."

"No further questions," Claudia said.

"You may step down," I told Harper.

When Reid said he had no further witnesses, I looked at Claudia. "What's the State asking, Ms. O'Hale?"

Several of her male relatives are in the National Guard and she doesn't have much tolerance for civil disobedience where the military is concerned. She suggested some jail time and an injunction against the young man ever stepping onto the airfield again.

"Mr. Stephenson?"

"Your Honor, as you know, Mrs. Bryant is the principal at West Colleton High School. Before you pass sentence, she'd like to speak on his behalf."

Dwight's mother stood up and placed her hands on the rail between her and the defense table. Mid-sixties now, her once fiery red hair has softened into a rusty white, but her commitment to her students still blazes brightly. She described how young Jeremy Harper had entered her school as a freshman with a chip on both shoulders. His parents were in the middle of a bitter divorce, their house was in foreclosure, and as if this weren't enough, the older brother he idolized was killed in Iraq before midterm exams. He came very close to flunking out.

"When his brother's effects were sent home, though, they included a good digital camera, and that camera saved him."

She said the yearbook's faculty advisor saw some of the pictures he took over the following summer and invited him to join the staff if he could get his grades up. "Last year, we won an honorable mention from the American Scholastic Press Association and they cited the photographs for their excellence."

I glanced at the clock on the wall above the jury box. It was somewhat past my usual time to recess for lunch. Miss Emily followed my eyes. "I'll get to the point, Debor— I mean, Your Honor. As you know, Anne Harald is a Pulitzer Prize winner. She's seen Jeremy's photographs and she thinks he has a genuine talent. She's willing to give him pointers about getting good pictures that tell the story without violating legal and journalistic protocols."

She paused and looked up at the man on her left. "Richard?"

Reid cleared his throat. "Mr. Williams would like to add to that, Your Honor."

As Miss Emily sat down and Richard Williams stood, I said, "Mr. Williams?" and tried very hard not to beam back at him, but he has one of the most infectious smiles of anyone I've ever met. His hazel eyes twinkled behind his glasses, and when he beetled his thick white eyebrows at me, I almost lost it. I knew that if I asked him how he was, he'd say, "Awesome! Absolutely awesome!" and we'd be off and running.

A large tall man of late middle age, his soft white hair was retreating toward the crown of his head. He wore pleated gray slacks and a navy windbreaker that carried the logo of a Methodist youth camp.

Unlike most denominations, Methodists are required to bring in a new head minister every three or four years. I suppose it's an attempt to keep their churches from forming cliques and splitting up every six or seven years the way the Baptists seem to do every time half the congregation starts to feel that the minister is listening only to the other half. But Richard has been youth minister at the Methodist church here in Dobbs for as long as I could remember. Not that I was ever anything other than a visitor there when invited to attend an event by some of my friends. I was brought up Southern Baptist and have never seen a reason to convert to something else.

I wasn't quite sure what Richard Williams, who lives and works in Dobbs, would have to do with Jeremy Harper, who attends the high school out near Cotton Grove, twenty-odd miles away.

"Jeremy's grandparents are members of our congregation, so I've known him since he was born," Richard said. "And now that he and his mother are living with them —"

He didn't have to explain further. The Cotton Grove house must have gone down the same drain as the parents' marriage.

"Jeremy's keeping up his grades and he works weekends at Burger King. I've been trying to counsel him about the best way to channel his peace efforts, but I don't know anything about photojournalism, so when Mrs. Bryant called and told me about Mrs. Harald's generous offer, it occurred to me that between us we could come up with something meaningful for him to do to fulfill the community service hours you're going to give him."

I did have to smile at that. "And just how do you know I'd planned to give him community service instead of jail time?"

He beamed back at me. "Because you're a kind person," he said. "Besides, you've had nephews who've had trouble with the law and you've seen the difference between meaningful service and jail time that doesn't teach them anything."

"And you think you and Mrs. Harald can design a program that will let him accomplish something more significant than spending a hundred hours picking up trash from our roadsides?"

"Absolutely!"

"Very well," I said. "Mr. Harper, I sentence you to three days in the county jail, the sentence to be suspended on condition that you not trespass on the Colleton County Airport property and that you complete seventy-two hours of community service as designed by Mr. Williams and Mrs. Harald, subject to the approval of this court."

Before I could bring down my gavel, Richard said, "What about court costs, Your Honor?"

I sighed. A recent statute requires us to make a special finding before we waive the court costs, but a student with a limited income certainly qualifies.

"Court costs waived," I said, making the appropriate notation on the form in front of me. "This court will be in adjournment until two o'clock."

CHAPTER 7

Turkey vultures do not have a voice box and thus have limited vocalization capabilities.

— *The Turkey Vulture Society*

Major Dwight Bryant — Wednesday morning, February 9

The skies had finally cleared and bright winter sunlight flooded through the tall windows of the family room, making the bloodstain on the end of the floral patterned couch look like a misplaced bunch of darker roses that had trailed down onto the sand-colored carpet. Dwight Bryant stood in the archway with the owner of Coyne Realty and watched while Percy Denning, who headed the department's crime scene team, finished going over the area inch by inch. They could hear voices echoing through the empty rooms as other officers dusted for fingerprints on doorknobs and handles.

"I know you went over everything with the officers last night," Dwight said, "but I'd appreciate it if you would take us through it again this morning."

"It's Becca Jowett's blood, isn't it?" Ms. Coyne asked. She had stressed the *Miz* in a businesslike tone when they met, then smiled. "Or you can just call me Paula."

Late fifties, with a tipped-up Irish nose and a body kept taut by daily horseback rides, the real estate agent normally had an easy laugh. She was not laughing now.

"It's too soon to tell," Dwight said. "All we can say for sure is that it's human."

"O-positive?"

"Is that her blood type?"

Paula Coyne nodded. "We give to the Red Cross every two months. I'm A-positive and she's O. It *is* Becca's blood, isn't it?"

"Now, Ms. Coyne —"

"And she's still missing. As soon as I saw that stain, I was afraid we were going to find her stuffed in one of the closets."

"How long has Mrs. Jowett worked for you?"

"Six years. She was my last hire before the market topped out, but she busted her britches to help some of our low-end clients find affordable homes when the others on my staff were coasting with the free spend-ers, so she's the one I kept on even though things have slowed so much now that I could pretty much handle the sales by myself. We only represent buyers, not sellers, but it's been a pretty lean time for the whole industry."

Holding her thumb and index fingers almost touching, Ms. Coyne said, "Becca was that close to selling this house. It's been on the market for almost a year, waiting for the bank to set a realistic price. As soon as it dropped into their price range in January, she called the Todds. They signed the due diligence agreement the very next day and put down earnest money. Everything's been done — the repairs and the inspections — and they were due to close tomorrow.

"When we didn't hear from Becca, I stepped in to cover — did a walk-through in the morning to familiarize myself with the property and made sure that everything was in order for the closing. The Todds called back last night, though, and wanted to take one more look upstairs even though they were legally committed. Now?" She sighed. "Mrs. Todd doesn't want to have anything to do with this house even if it means losing their earnest money, and I can't really fault them, even though this is their dream house. Closer to her parents, a better school for their children."

A sturdy young woman in dark slacks, white shirt, low heels, and a windbreaker with CCSD for Colleton County Sheriff's Department stenciled on the front and back came through from the rear of the house and Dwight motioned for her to join them. Deputy Mayleen Richards had been one of the responders last night and she nodded to the agent, who gave the cinnamon-haired detective a wan smile of recognition.

"Ms. Coyne's telling me about last night," Dwight said.

The older woman shook her head. "There's really nothing more to tell. I got here just as the Todds were pulling into the driveway, about ten-thirty."

"A little late to be showing a place, wasn't it?"

"*And* it was pouring rain, but this is a step up for them and they were understandably a little nervous about taking on that much debt. Certainly she was. Two of the bedrooms upstairs have sloping dormer ceilings and she wanted to measure the height, see if their daughter's canopy bed would fit. We had started up the stairs when her husband said something about getting the bank to throw in the couch, and that's how we found the bloodstain."

Dwight raised a dubious eyebrow. "He wanted the couch?"

Ms. Coyne smiled. "Looks a little girly with those roses, doesn't it? But it's well built and Mr. Todd liked the length. He's tall as you are."

"So the first time you saw the blood was when she came in and moved the afghan?"

She frowned. "Actually, I believe he was the one who pulled it off because it was a different shade of red from the roses."

Dwight looked at Richards for confirmation. The deputy shook her head. "All I know is that Mrs. Todd said that they were taking a closer look to see if the couch would match their other furniture when they saw the blood."

"You didn't notice it when you were here earlier in the day?"

"No." Ms. Coyne pulled a crumpled pack of cigarettes from her coat pocket and held the pack briefly to her nose. "You ever smoke, Major Bryant?"

Dwight shook his head. "The surgeon general didn't have to tell me about tobacco tar. I stayed covered in that sticky black stuff every summer."

"Unfortunately, there were no tobacco farms in Pittsburgh where I grew up," she said and ruefully crammed the cigarettes

96

back into her pocket. "As I said, I did a walk-through yesterday morning after Mr. Todd called me Monday afternoon. They hadn't heard from Becca since their last time here Saturday morning. She's usually off on Mondays and her grandmother hasn't been well lately, so I thought maybe she'd run down to New Bern to check on her. But then her husband called to ask if I'd seen her. I guess that's when he reported her missing?"

Dwight nodded. "So yesterday morning was your first time in this house?"

"That's right. The Todds were Becca's clients, so normally I wouldn't have anything to do with the sale."

Dwight glanced through the notes he'd made on his pad. "Last night, Mrs. Todd told Detective Richards here that Mrs. Jowett first showed them the house in mid-January and they put in an offer on the twenty-fourth. She said they were here several times since then and that the afghan was slung over the white chair each time. The last time was around noon on Saturday. Where was it when you did your walk-through on Monday?"

Ms. Coyne's forehead creased in thought and a faraway look shadowed her eyes as she concentrated. "I'm almost certain it was draped over the end of the couch and trailed onto the floor very casually. I thought it was a nice touch."

"You told the officers that the door was locked and we've found no signs of a forced entry. Who else would have keys?"

She gestured toward the front door. "There's usually a key box hanging on the front doorknob, and you can get the letter combination to open it from the listing agent. Cubby Lee Honeycutt has an exclusive on this property and his locks are usually set to CLH. But once the Todds started the due diligence process, no other agent would show the house."

"So far as you know?"

"True. And any agent who knows Cubby Lee would also know the combination. We're supposed to ask him before we take someone through, but he's pretty loosey-goosey about it. He'd rather we show his properties to someone on the spur of the moment than risk losing a sale."

"Do you know if Becca showed the house to anyone else?"

"I'd have to check her records, but I'm pretty sure that she didn't. And certainly not since the Todds put in their offer."

"What about the Todds? Was your agency the only one representing them?"

"We'd better be. They've signed an agreement to that effect. We put in too much time and effort to have clients jumping from one agency to another. Becca's been working with the Todds for almost two months now. This was one of the first houses they looked at, because it met most of the features on their wish list and she was pretty sure the bank would eventually drop the price again. She helped them find financing and she even lined up the inspector after the bank did the repairs. Mr. Todd already did a termite check himself last Tuesday."

"The Todds own a pest control business," Richards murmured.

"Did Mrs. Jowett have any problems with the Todds?" Dwight asked.

"Not that I'm aware of."

"What about her personal life? Any problems there?"

Ms. Coyne shook her head. "I never get into an employee's private life and Becca isn't one to share intimate details anyhow. I've only met her husband twice in passing."

She hesitated.

"Something?" Dwight prompted.

"It may be my imagination, but in the last few weeks, she's dropped a few disparaging remarks about him, almost as if she's quit considering him whenever she decides to work weekends or evening."

"Well, I certainly don't mean to be the one to gossip," Ms. Coyne's secretary told Mayleen Richards an hour later, "but I'm pretty sure they have separate bedrooms. Last week I was complaining about how my husband's snoring was keeping me awake at night and she said I ought to do like she did and move him into the guest room."

"Any new man in her life?" Richards asked.

The secretary shook her head. "Not that I've heard, but she really doesn't talk about her private life much at all. Not to me anyhow."

Following up on the bit of gossip Judge Knott had passed on to Major Bryant, Richards's next stop was at the Cut 'n' Curl, which was where she got her own hair done. She was directed to Charlaine Schulz, the woman who did Rebecca Jowett's hair and who had the station next to Mayleen's own beautician.

"She was in here just this past Wednesday to get her split ends trimmed and have her roots touched up," Charlaine told her. "Not that she has any gray — she's only thirty-four — but her natural color's a mousy brown, so the roots need regular work."

In the picture Dave Jowett had given them when he reported her missing on Monday, Becca Jowett had brown eyes and long dark brown hair that fell in loose swirls around an attractive oval face.

"When I washed her hair, I saw she had a fresh hickey right about here." Charlaine had beautiful skin that seemed to glow from within as she touched a spot on her smooth neck halfway between her left ear and her collarbone. "She wasn't happy about it either when I started to tease her. I said, 'I guess he likes to mark his territory, huh?' and she made a face and said, 'First and last time. From now on, this territory's off-limits to him.' "

"Was she talking about her husband?"

"What do you think, honey?"

"Do you know who the man was?"

Charlaine shook her head. "She never names names."

"But she does talk about men she's been with?"

"Not in so many words. Just enough to let me know she's been cheating on poor Dave for two or three years now."

"You know him?"

"Oh sure. We were in school together."

"Does he know about her cheating?"

"Not from me he doesn't. I did ask her last year if she was going to leave him and she just laughed and said she couldn't afford to as long as the real estate market was so bad." The hairdresser paused. "You know, though, she did say that it looked like things might have bottomed out and be ready to take an upswing, so it wouldn't have surprised me if they'd split up in the next few months. What do you think, Mayleen? You reckon she's still alive?"

They were finished with the house by noon. The only additional bit of information gained was from scuff marks and light scratches where something heavy had been pulled across the newly refinished wood floor of the living room from the couch to the front door.

"Probably the body wrapped in a tarp or something," Denning said.

From there to the driveway, a driveway screened by two large fir trees and several tall azalea bushes, was only a few steps.

A second canvass of the neighborhood added nothing to their knowledge of what had happened there Saturday night, which was the last time anyone could definitely say they had seen Rebecca Jowett. That particular someone lived directly across the street and had a clear view when the light went on over the Jowetts' front door around seven that evening. He had seen Becca Jowett come out, zip up her jacket, and adjust her earmuffs against the chill winter air, then watched as she used the porch railing to do a few leg stretches before she sprinted down the street and out of sight.

"Sounds like he takes a right neighborly interest in her," Sheriff Bo Poole told Dwight when they met for lunch. He waved aside the menu the waitress offered and said, "Just bring me a bowl of chili and a glass of sweet tea, please."

"Same here," Dwight said. "Only make mine coffee instead of tea."

He drained the glass of ice water in front of him before telling his boss, "Yeah, McLamb said he admitted man-to-man that she turned him on."

"But?"

"It's Colonel Gessner, Bo."

"Oh," said the sheriff, and there-but-for-the-grace-of-God was in that one syllable. Three days before that Marine officer was due to rotate home from Afghanistan, he had caught a sniper bullet in his lower spine.

"What about the blood on that couch? You gonna ask for a DNA test?"

Dwight shook his head. "Waste of money right now, wouldn't you say? It's the same blood type as the missing woman. Denning says that it's so deep into the couch padding that she probably bled out right there and the cotton sucked it up like a sponge. He doesn't think anyone could have lost that much blood and still be alive."

Their chili arrived and both men crumbled packets of crackers into the steaming bowls before digging in.

"Denning found semen stains on the couch, too," Dwight said, "but no point in asking for the test till we find a body or can link someone to the scene. For what it's worth, he thinks one stain is somewhat older than the other and that the fresher one's no more than a week old. The components haven't broken down much. I've got McLamb chasing down the origin of the couch. Cubby Lee borrows things from a store out on the bypass whenever he needs to stage a house."

"Stage a house? What's that mean?"

Dwight laughed. "Make it look like someone lives there. It's good advertising for the store, and if the buyers want to keep some of the furniture, the store will give 'em a good price. The people who were going to buy the house wanted that couch till they saw all the blood."

The waitress refilled Bo's glass of iced tea and he thanked her with old-fashioned courtesy while Dwight continued to bring him up to speed on the investigation. As they scraped the last of the chili from their bowls, he said, "You talked to the husband yet?"

Dwight checked the clock above the sandwich shop's main counter. "I better get moving. He's due over at the office any minute now."

"Do I need an attorney?" Dave Jowett asked when Dwight inquired if he objected to having their interview recorded.

"I don't know," Dwight said mildly. "Do you?"

"I'm not stupid," Jowett said. "I know that when someone goes missing, the spouse is always the first suspect. So maybe I do need a lawyer." He paused and gave a wry grin. "Except that the lawyer I know best is Rob."

Dwight smiled back. "I think my brother only handles civil matters. Look, Mr. Jowett —"

"Dave," he said.

He sat at the interview table across from Dwight and Mayleen Richards while another deputy fiddled with the video camera.

Bo had hoped to squeeze enough money out of the county commissioners to set up a more modern system, but they had frozen his budget for the fourth year in a row and recording equipment ranked far below replacing worn-out patrol cars.

Like Rob, Dave Jowett was two years younger than Dwight. Back in high school, a two-year age difference meant that they had run in different crowds. Jowett had developed early male-pattern baldness and did not try to hide it with a toupee or elaborate comb-overs. What you saw was what you got, Dwight decided: an average-looking man comfortable with advancing middle age, but still in good shape.

"Look, Dave," Dwight said. "We're not looking to jam you up here and you're certainly not under arrest. We only want to have a record of your weekend. If there's a question you don't want to answer, just say so. You're free to stop talking at any point and to ask for an attorney. Okay?"

"Fair enough," said Jowett and leaned forward with his hands clasped on the table in front of him. "Fire away."

"When did you last see your wife?"

"Around three o'clock Friday afternoon. Some friends and I flew down to Shreveport for the weekend and Becca came out to say hey to the guy that picked me up, but it was starting to rain, so she saw us off from the porch."

He gave them their names and phone numbers, which Richards wrote down for later confirmation, along with their takeoff time in a private plane from the county's small airport.

"Was that the last time you spoke to her?"

He nodded. "I tried to call her Sunday afternoon to say I'd be home after dark, but it rang three times, then went straight to her voice mail."

"Was this usual?"

Dave Jowett nodded. "She keeps her phone on vibrate if she's with a client or in a meeting." He took a deep breath, then added, "And let's face it. Sometimes she just wouldn't answer if it was someone she didn't want to bother with."

"Like you?"

He shrugged. "Your wife pick up every time you call?"

"Nope," Dwight said.

Mayleen Richards suppressed a grin. She knew how it drove her boss nuts that the judge insisted that her phone was for her convenience and not anyone else's and that it stayed in her purse switched off more often than in her pocket switched on.

"So when exactly did you miss her?"

"Not until Monday morning." He explained that he and five other friends had formed a tight bond in college when they discovered they all had February birthdays. They continued to get together every year for a rotating birthday bash. "Even though we live at opposite ends of the country, three of them have their own planes and one of them will swing by for Brendan and me. Last year, it was Denver, this year, Shreveport. Brendan drove us out to Colleton International on Friday," he said, using the tag that local wits had hung on the small airstrip, "and he dropped me off around six-thirty Sunday night."

"Brendan?"

"Brendan Rehon." He spelled the name for Richards and gave her a Raleigh address.

"He come inside?" Dwight asked.

Jowett shook his head. "We were both pretty beat."

"Any sign of your wife?"

"The lights were on, like she'd just stepped out. I tried her phone a couple of times while I fixed myself a sandwich, and then I just fell into bed. Didn't turn over till the alarm went off at six. When I went downstairs, I saw that the lights were still on and her bed hadn't been slept in."

He hesitated, looked embarrassed, then said, "No big secret that we have separate bedrooms. She says it's my snoring, but . . . I don't know. I guess it's just a matter of time till we call it quits."

"Is there someone else?"

"Not for me. For her?" Jowett gave a palms-up gesture. "They say the husband's always the last to know. I tried her cell phone again, then called her mother, a couple of her friends, her office. I even spoke to the neighbors, but no one's seen her since Saturday, so that's when I called you people. Her purse is still on the dining table. Her cosmetic bag's still in the bathroom. All the suitcases are in our storage closet. I don't know if any clothes are missing, but her running shoes are gone and Shep Gessner — he's our neighbor across the street — Shep says he saw her go running Saturday night. How could she just disappear off the streets of Dobbs, Dwight? Where is she? Her mother's going crazy and her sister —"

Before Dwight could answer, Jowett's phone rang. He looked at the screen. "Her sister," he said, and immediately held the phone to his ear. "Yeah, Jen? Any word? . . . Huh? Where?"

A minute later, he clicked off and glared

at the two officers. "Someone told her sister that y'all found blood in a house Becca was showing. When were you going to tell me that my wife's been killed?"

CHAPTER 8

The majority of wild mammals do not succumb to predators. Instead, they die from diseases, starvation, parasites, fights over mates, competition, accidents, or some combination of these.

— The Turkey Vulture Society

Sigrid Harald — Wednesday afternoon
"— and the porcelain clock came from Gilead, too. English. Probably 1840. More of Matilda Louise's frivolous tastes. She almost bankrupted the family, building and furnishing Gilead. I'm told that her husband could deny her nothing."

Sigrid glanced at the dainty little clock that graced the mantel in her grandmother's bedroom, then entered its description on her laptop: *approx. 10' tall, pale green and white porcelain, sprigged with pink and yellow flowers, English ca. 1840.* "Does it still work?" she asked.

"I have no idea," Mrs. Lattimore said. "It did the last time I wound it, but that must have been thirty years ago. I much prefer my electric alarm clock." She lay back against the pillows that let her sit upright in the old four-poster bed and looked at the lighted dial on the bedside stand. "Is that everything?"

"What about the rug?" The oriental pattern looked bright and unfaded.

"No value," her grandmother said. "I bought it on sale for less than four hundred dollars in the nineteen-nineties."

Sigrid dutifully listed it and gestured to three small leather and wood cases ranged on some shelves beneath the window. "Anything in those jewelry boxes?"

"A few pearls and garnets," Mrs. Lattimore said. "Mostly it's just costume things. Before we start on the jewelry, though, perhaps you can go to the bank and bring me whatever's in my box? There's a Tiffany brooch that Mother always meant for Ferrabee to have, along with an onyx signet ring I'd like to give to Martin as well. It belonged to my father. And I suppose I ought to go ahead and give the diamond pieces to Elizabeth and Mary. Heaven knows they've hinted for them enough times these last few years. Unless . . . do you think

Anne — ?"

"Earrings, perhaps," Sigrid said. "I've never seen her wear anything else except her wedding ring."

"You either?"

Sigrid shrugged and Mrs. Lattimore shook her head ruefully. Small gold studs gleamed in the younger woman's ears. Hard to imagine diamonds and sapphires dangling there. At least the child now wore colors. Instead of the shapeless beige and black clothes that once filled her closet, she had finally begun to dress in the rich jewel tones Mrs. Lattimore had urged on her from girlhood. Today's cardigan was a vibrant turquoise over black slacks and a silk top patterned in deep blues and greens. With her dark hair cut short, lipstick, and a smudge of mascara, this odd duckling had morphed into — if not a swan, certainly into a woman who could hold her own among the more conventionally beautiful women of the family.

Remembering a pair of relatively simple emerald earrings in her bank box, Mrs. Lattimore smiled at this granddaughter she had come to value more than ever in the last month. With Sigrid she didn't have to sugarcoat her condition or keep up a pretense of being pain-free. Sigrid didn't fuss or moan or avoid the subject of impending death.

"Tired?" Sigrid asked now, closing her laptop.

"A little, but on the whole I'm rather enjoying this. It's giving me a feeling of lightness. Only two more rooms to go. All my life I've had the weight of these possessions on my shoulders, keeping them safe for the next generation, worrying about breakages or scratches. You must have hated visiting here when you were a child. It probably felt like visiting a museum."

"At times," Sigrid agreed. "But the rules were clear, and when the other cousins were here, you didn't seem to mind what we did outside or up in the attic playroom."

"And when there were no cousins? When your mother dumped you on me for your school holidays and went wandering off to the four corners of the earth?"

"She was working, Grandmother. She had to take those assignments."

"But?"

"But I didn't think you liked me very much because I was so homely."

"You were never homely, honey. I just thought you weren't trying."

Sigrid smiled. "I wasn't. I didn't see the point."

There was a moment of silence as Jane Lattimore closed her eyes and waited for a wave of pain to subside. According to the clock, Chloe Adams was due to arrive with her next pills in eleven minutes and she was determined to last till then.

With her eyes still closed, she said, "Was he good to you?"

"Nauman?"

"Yes." She opened her eyes and said, "I think he was good *for* you, but *to* you?"

Sigrid was silent. Oscar Nauman had exploded into her life, shaken up her habits, and made love to her as no one ever had. Then he'd died in a car crash and left her his entire estate — a house in Connecticut and a body of work that had made him one of the leading artists of the twentieth century while he was still young enough to enjoy it. He had also left her more desolate than she could ever have imagined and his loss was a continuing ache. Despite all the changes that short year had brought, she had not overcome the reserve that made it difficult for her to speak of her most private feelings.

"Yes," she said at last.

Mrs. Lattimore did not press her for more. She merely said, "Good."

"What about Grandfather?" Sigrid crossed

to the chest on the other side of the bed and lifted the small silver-framed photograph of a young man standing with one arm around the neck of the bronze deer that guarded the side lawn downstairs. "You've never talked about him. At least not to me. And you never remarried."

"When people ask, I usually say that once you've dwelled in Eden, you don't care for suburbia." She gave a wry smile and reached for the picture in Sigrid's hand. "Does that sound too fanciful?"

"Did Eden come before he died or after?"

Mrs. Lattimore's cool eyes warmed with amusement. "I always knew you were my most intelligent grandchild. You're the first to ask me that." She looked down at the photograph. "I adored him. I went from my father's house directly to this house when I was nineteen years old. I never lived alone, I never worked for wages, and I never had my own money. I only had to ask to be given anything I wanted."

She paused.

"But you always had to ask?" Sigrid said, filling in the pause.

Her grandmother nodded. "Benjamin was witty, charming, attentive, and, so far as I know, utterly faithful, but he went to his grave believing that if you put your wife up on a pedestal, she should never step down and try to be your equal. As much as I loved him, I had no desire to yoke myself to another man of his generation and upbringing."

She handed the picture back to Sigrid. "Would you have married your artist had he lived?"

"Probably not," Sigrid said, setting the picture so that her grandmother could see it with a turn of her head. "He was larger than life in so many ways. He took up so much space. And I *had* lived alone."

They looked up as Chloe Adams entered the bedroom with a lunch tray and the pills that dulled the worst of the pain.

She was followed by Anne Harald, whose cheeks were red from the chilly February wind. She still wore her fleece-lined jacket and boots and her lips were cold when she bent to kiss her mother. "How are you feeling?" she asked, automatically trying to fluff the pillows and straighten the covers.

"I'm fine," Mrs. Lattimore said, patiently bearing her daughter's attempts to make her more comfortable. "I've spent the morning boring Sigrid to death. Why don't you take her out to lunch and show her the wonders of Cotton Grove?" She waved a thin hand toward the nightstand. "The key to my safety deposit box is in the top drawer if you're passing the bank. I'll call and tell them to expect you."

"Bank?" Anne asked.

"Sigrid knows." She swallowed the pills, then lay back against the pillows and closed her eyes. "Y'all go on now. Chloe will take care of me."

Helplessly, Anne allowed herself to be shepherded from the room. As the door closed, they heard the nurse say, "You may not be hungry, Miss Jane, but you know you have to take a little bit of food with those pills."

Anne paused at the top of the stairs and looked down at the wide entrance hall, lined with antique chests and gilt-framed portraits.

"Thanks for doing the inventory, honey." Tears glistened in her eyes and turned them the color of unpolished pewter. "I don't think I could bear it. She's being so brave about leaving all this."

"Not a problem," Sigrid said. "I'm glad I could do it for her and I like hearing the family stories attached to the pieces."

Privately, she thought her grandmother was very wise in trying to make her coming death easier on her three daughters. "They say you never know someone until you share an inheritance with them," she had told Sigrid. "Some of these things are quite valuable and I don't want my girls to wind up squabbling over them."

She had held up her hand when Sigrid started to protest that Anne would never squabble. "I'm not talking about your mother," she had said dryly.

Once everything in the house was described and listed on Sigrid's laptop, her plan was to give a copy to two appraisers and hire them to price each item. Sigrid was surprised to hear that one of the appraisers was Deborah Knott's brother, the owner of an auction house over in Dobbs, the county seat. The other was a Grayson Gallery in Raleigh. The lower appraisal would be the base value and the total figure would be split among the three daughters. At that point, Anne and her sisters could take what they wanted, but the monetary value of their choices would be deducted from their third. If two of them wanted the same object, then they would have to bid on it, and again, the winning bid would be deducted from their third. Whatever remained in the house would be sold, as would the house itself, and the proceeds split three ways.

"Your Aunt Elizabeth wanted to know what would happen if Mary made her bid ten thousand for a sideboard appraised at five," Mrs. Lattimore had said when she explained her plans to Sigrid. "She was not happy to hear that this meant she had ten thousand less to bid with unless she wanted to pay her sisters twenty-five hundred each."

Sigrid had laughed and Mrs. Lattimore looked pleased. "I do hope you'll come back for the fun, honey."

"I wouldn't miss it," Sigrid assured her.

Anne had received a phone call from Dwight Bryant's mother before breakfast and had left the house before Sigrid came down.

"Where have you been all morning and what did Mrs. Bryant want?" Sigrid asked now as she buckled her seat belt and Anne turned the ignition key of Mrs. Lattimore's Lincoln.

"You know she's the principal of West Colleton High School?"

Sigrid nodded.

"She wanted me to look at some photographs one of her students had taken and I made the mistake of saying they showed talent." Anne fastened her own seat belt and turned the heater fan on high. "Next thing I knew, I was sitting in Deborah Knott's courtroom and had volunteered to help a youth minister structure the kid's community service."

"You did *what?*"

"That woman is a force of nature," Anne said with a rueful shake of her head. "She could probably sell scuba lessons to Eskimos."

Sigrid was shaking her own head as her mother described Jeremy Harper and how he had been charged with trespassing.

"An airfield for rendition flights?"

"Yeah, that surprised me, too," her mother said as she drove through the tall iron gate and turned onto the street. "But I guess they have to be somewhere. We're not very far from Fort Bragg, you know. And Blackwater did have its beginning up in the northeast part of the state."

"I thought that was disbanded."

"Who knows?" Anne said cynically. "I long ago quit trusting what the CIA tells us."

"You're not going to get involved with that, are you?"

"Don't worry, honey. My days of reporting on dangerous situations are over. I'm way too old for it. Somalia was my swan song. It cured me of thinking I was invulnerable." She shivered, remembering how close she'd been to coming home in a body bag. "I've promised Mac that I'll do only human interest stories and cute babies from here on out."

It had been awkward when Sigrid first learned that her former boss and her mother were seeing each other. His retirement had made the new relationship easier to take; and, mirabile dictu, after years of restlessly changing apartments more often than most women rearranged their furniture, Anne had settled into Mac's place and showed no signs of ever moving again.

"Barbecue or shrimp and grits?" Anne asked, slowing the car to a crawl along Cotton Grove's main street.

Sigrid was amused by how quickly her mother went native each time she returned to her hometown. In Manhattan, she was an adventurous gourmet who delighted in sampling the ethnic cuisines of the city's many cultures. Down here, it was chili dogs with coleslaw, fried chicken and buttermilk biscuits drenched in redeye gravy.

"Salad," Sigrid said firmly.

"Good idea," Anne said. "I haven't had any of The Rosebud's chicken salad since I got back. They use toasted pecans and lots of Duke's mayonnaise."

Sighing, Sigrid followed her mother into

the tearoom next to a hardware store.

Over lunch, Anne told her about the community service options she and Richard Williams had discussed for the boy. "Of course, Deborah Knott was the judge who sentenced him, and she has to approve. And we have to get Jeremy on board, too. He's so hung up on the airstrip and who the planes are ferrying in and out of the country that it may be hard to get him to do something more mundane. He thinks that proving who's changing fuselage numbers would be a national service, not just community."

"Are his pictures any good?" Sigrid asked.

"Not bad for high school," Anne said, spearing a toasted pecan half with her fork. "He has a good eye for details, but he's all over the map when it comes to knowing the focus of the story he's trying to tell with his camera."

"So what have you and this youth minister come up with?"

"Well, Jeremy says he wants to be a photojournalist, so I thought that I could talk to him about that, maybe rope Martin in to show him how you can earn a living taking noncontroversial pictures."

"He's what? Seventeen? Eighteen? And his brother was killed in Afghanistan?"

Anne nodded.

"You think he's going to be distracted by birds as long as there are wars and people shooting at each other?"

"Probably not," Anne agreed. "That's why Richard suggested that we take him to a disabled vets' center and have him document the stories of local veterans. He thinks it might help with Jeremy's grief over losing his brother. But Martin could still give him some tips. Did you look at the book he gave Mother? Unless he manipulated the images, he must have been on a mountaintop with a really powerful telephoto lens to get some of those shots, looking down on those birds in flight."

She glanced at her watch. "Want to ride out there with me?"

"Out where?"

"To the old farmhouse where Martin's staying. I haven't been there in years, but I think I can still find it. It's not far from Gilead and you've never seen that place either, have you?"

"As long as we're back before the bank closes," Sigrid said.

CHAPTER 9

Vultures prefer to eat fairly fresh meat.
— The Turkey Vulture Society

Major Dwight Bryant — Wednesday afternoon (continued)

"Yes, we have found blood," Dwight admitted to an angry Dave Jowett, "but until we have a sample of your wife's DNA to test it against, we can't know for sure that it's her blood."

"Who else's would it be?" the man asked as his anger gave way to apprehension and the beginning of grief. "My God, she *is* dead, isn't she?"

"It was a lot of blood," the big deputy said quietly. "Be a real coincidence if it isn't hers what with her missing and all, but coincidences do happen."

He nodded to Mayleen Richards, who leafed through the file folder on the table and pulled out a form.

Dwight handed it to Jowett. "This gives us permission to search your house."

"Search my house? Why? The blood was in that other house, not ours."

"But there might be clues that will help us identify who she was meeting."

When Jowett hesitated, Dwight leaned toward him and said, "Right now, we don't have enough to get a formal search warrant, but if you make us wait until we do, you're giving whoever's responsible more time to cover their tracks."

Dave Jowett reached into the breast pocket of his jacket and pulled out a pen. "Where do I sign?"

"Is there a computer at your house?"

"Yes, but Becca never uses it. She gets all her mail on her iPhone and uses her iPad for everything else." He finished filling in the blanks, then signed and dated the form.

"One more thing, sir," Richards said.

She was turning a faint pink and Dwight realized that she was about to say something embarrassing despite her experience here on the force.

Seeing the gleam of amusement in her boss's eyes, Mayleen lifted her chin with determination. "When did you and your wife last have sex?"

Outraged, Jowett glared at her.

"It's for purposes of elimination," she said, stubbornly holding her ground and looking him squarely in the face.

"Along with the blood, we found semen stains on the couch," Dwight told him.

Now it was Dave Jowett who looked embarrassed. "Not since New Year's Eve." Completely deflated now, he dropped his eyes and added, "I guess she'd drunk enough champagne to give me pity sex."

While Dwight turned to other matters that required his attention, Richards gathered up a team that included Percy Denning and Detective Raeford McLamb, and they headed over to the Jowett home, where Dave Jowett let them in. He gave them his cell phone number and said, "I'm going over to her mother's. Lock up when you're finished."

They put on latex gloves and spread out through the house, where they quickly identified Rebecca Jowett's bedroom. From the toiletries they found, Mayleen realized that not only did Dave Jowett sleep in the guest bedroom, but he had also been relegated to the guest bathroom.

Mentally crossing her fingers, she immediately went to the laundry hamper in the master bath.

"Bingo!" she crowed to Denning, who was right beside her.

The hamper was three-fourths full, indicating that the missing woman was not someone whose clothes went into the washer downstairs the same day that she took them off. Underpants and bras were tangled in with shirts and ankle socks.

While an assistant recorded everything with a digital video camera, Denning carefully laid the clothes out on the bathroom floor as if documenting layers from an archaeological dig. Near the top of the hamper was a lace-trimmed bikini brief with stains that made Denning smile when he hooked them out with a gloved finger. "Looks like postcoital vaginal leakage to me," he said and carefully transferred it to a separate evidence bag. The other undergarments were also bagged and labeled. At the very bottom were a similarly stained pair of underpants.

They checked the medicine cabinet and the bedside drawers, but except for birth control pills, the only drugs they found were over-the-counter items.

Her iPad was on the dining table next to her purse, and a quick check of her electronic calendar showed all of her appointments for the year. For Saturday, there were two midday appointments.

In addition to the Todds, Becca Jowett appeared to be actively involved with two other clients, and she had evidently planned to meet with one of them Sunday afternoon to show a house out in the country.

Farther down, in the 5:30 slot, was the notation "Reid S." and an exclamation mark.

McLamb was examining the missing woman's purse and wallet and Mayleen showed him the calendar. "What do you think, Ray? Reid Stephenson?"

"The attorney? Could be." He grinned. "They say he lights up a lot of women's lives."

Richards copied off the names before sliding the device into another evidence bag.

"Too bad she took her phone with her," he said and patted his own phone that was clipped to his belt. "We're all walking around with almost everything worth knowing about us right here."

As Dave Jowett had told them, the computer in their downstairs office appeared to be used solely by him. Apparently he was a trusting soul because nothing was password-protected, not even his email.

The few messages to or from his wife were the usual innocuous reminders about household matters, appointments, and social engagements. Considering the state of the Jowett marriage, they were surprised to see references to so many of those. Most seemed to be family-related. Both Jowetts were from the county and both sets of parents still lived nearby. There were events for various relatives — "Don't forget your mom's birthday on Wednesday," read one recent message signed "B."

Another was, "Jen wants to know if we can come over for bridge tomorrow night."

There were also dinners with Dave Jowett's business associates — "Please don't forget that Dale's wife is a Tea Party conservative, so no smug liberal comments, okay?" or "I've told the Krongards you had a four-bedroom house on your books and they sounded interested. You might want to have a few pictures on your iPhone when we meet them for drinks tonight."

All were signed "xoxo, Dave."

"Poor guy," Richards said. "I guess old habits die hard."

Her own phone rang, and Major Bryant's name appeared on the screen.

"Is Denning still there?" her boss asked.

"Yessir."

"Good. Sounds like we've found Rebecca Jowett's body."

CHAPTER 10

The turkey vulture has a highly developed
sense of smell, a rare ability among birds.
In one study . . . they quickly found (usually
within a day) many chicken carcasses
placed under the forest canopy, and some
of these were even hidden from view with
dried leaves.

— The Turkey Vulture Society

*Major Dwight Bryant — Wednesday afternoon
(continued)*
Dwight had almost forgotten about this
dead-end dirt-and-gravel road near where
he had grown up and still lived. If asked, he
would have said it had probably disappeared
under the wheels of bulldozers and cement
trucks when G. Hooks Talton bought up
most of the land on the south side of
Possum Creek and built Grayson Village to
spite Kezzie Knott, Deborah's father.

The incident still brought grins to the

faces of those in the know. That a wily old ex-bootlegger with a sixth-grade education had outfoxed a multimillionaire with a full stable of attorneys who hadn't bothered to read the fine print on the deeds to the farms they thought they were secretly buying up was still good for a laugh over sausage and biscuit breakfasts in any of the gas-and-grub eateries that still survived around Cotton Grove.

He must have zipped past this narrow unpaved road dozens of times since the big NutriGood grocery store opened, but he'd had no cause to turn onto it in years. Back when he was a teenager, this had been a makeout spot for randy teenagers. In fact, now that he was remembering, it was here in the backseat of his first car, an old Mercury, that he and Patty Sue Milledge had both lost their virginity. Patty Sue was a surgical nurse at WakeMed now, married and the mother of teenagers; and although they never mentioned that night again, they always hugged each other whenever their paths crossed at weddings and funerals and class reunions.

He briefly wondered if Deborah had ever parked here after a movie or a ball game; if there were a male equivalent to Patty Sue still in the area.

A single patrol car parked beside the turnoff brought his mind back to the present. He lowered his window to speak to the young officer who held a roll of yellow tape and gestured to the rough track that led through a thick stand of trees.

"Everybody's down there, Major," he said. "The crime scene van got here about fifteen minutes ago."

"Thanks, son. Just make sure we don't get any sightseers till we're finished."

"Yessir!"

Twigs scraped the sides of his truck as he followed the nearly nonexistent lane. As he oriented himself, he soon realized that he was paralleling a berm that separated this end of Grayson Village and its manicured lawns from wiregrass, sandspurs, and the volunteer pines that had sprung up in what used to be a cotton field. The lane sloped down and he knew that he must be approaching Possum Creek, but the young pines were so thick that he was only a few yards away before he finally spotted the county's crime scene van and a couple of squad cars.

Mayleen Richards came over to meet him as he got out of the truck and zipped up his heavy jacket.

"She's down there." The tip of her nose

was pink and her breath came in little puffs of steam when she spoke. "We're just waiting for the ME."

The bank dropped off sharply into a gully that ran along the creek, and a section of the track was cordoned off.

"That where she went over?" he asked.

"Denning thinks so," she said. "The leaves and grass look like they were trampled there."

In past years, before the county began maintaining waste disposal sites, this had evidently been a popular dumping place. A roll of rotten carpeting lay next to a rusty refrigerator and a broken toilet. Other household appliances were strewn along the creek bank. Black plastic garbage bags had long ago been torn open by foraging animals, the disposable diapers, aluminum pie plates, and pizza boxes spilled out and left to decay amid glass bottles and tin cans that were nearly obscured by years of grapevines and dead leaves. The slender body of a woman dressed in a dark blue warm-up suit and running shoes lay at the near edge of the gully, half covered by a filthy mildewed mattress.

"I don't know how she got found," Richards said. She thumbed her cell phone to show him pictures of the scene before they disturbed it. "She was totally hidden by that mattress. Who called it in, sir?"

"Faye said it was from an unlisted number. She thought the voice was male and not from around here, but she couldn't keep him on the line long enough to talk him into IDing himself."

Richards smiled. If Faye Myers, their gossipy gregarious dispatcher, couldn't dislodge the name, no one could.

Down below, Denning and his assistant were documenting the scene as best they could without further disturbing the body. As they waited a blue jay flew by and crows called to each other from some trees on the other side of the creek. Despite the recent rain, it had been a fairly dry winter and the creek looked a little lower than in winters past.

A few minutes later, the EMS truck arrived on the heels of the ME, who clambered down into the gully and quickly went through the formality of confirming what they pretty much knew already.

"Pulpy head wound, no signs of rigor, advancing decomposition," he said. "Last seen around seven o'clock Saturday? Yeah, that could be about right. Underneath that mattress and next to the dirt? Temperatures above freezing every night since then? Yeah,

I'd say dead about three days. They'll open her up over in Chapel Hill, but I doubt they'll get it any closer than that."

He climbed back up and stood shaking his head as the deputies below lifted the mattress away from the body. "It's the Jowett woman, isn't it? Never met her myself, but my sister lives next door to her parents. They've been sick with worry. Gonna be a sad time for them."

Grabbing hold of a three-foot oak sapling for support, Dwight worked his way down to the dump site and looked into Rebecca Jowett's chilled white face. Her hair was matted with blood and he could tell that blowflies had found the wound, but everything else looked normal. Odd the way death always relaxed the muscles and wiped away every emotion. No matter how the person died, whether peacefully in bed or in a violent shooting, he had never seen any frowns or grimaces of fear or pain on the faces of the dead, only a smooth disinterested neutrality.

"Finding anything?" he asked Denning.

The deputy shook his head in frustration. "Absolutely nothing, Major."

He pointed to the edge of the drop-off secured with yellow crime scene tape. "We think she was probably rolled off there and then the mattress pulled over her. Except for the body itself, everything else looks like it's been here for months."

"No shoe tracks around the body?"

"Just the tip of one. I took pictures but there's not enough to go on. No tread mark and some big bird must have landed on top of it. Crow or buzzard probably."

Both men looked up. Sure enough, three or four of the big birds were drifting on the thermals in wide lazy circles overhead.

"I don't suppose anyone thought to look for tire tracks before y'all drove over them?"

"Wrong, Major. Mayleen and Ray and I, we stopped to check a couple of times on the way back in. Pine straw's pretty thick and any tire marks would have been washed away in last night's rain. You can see our own tracks, though."

"So whoever found the body and reported it must have walked over." He turned to Ray McLamb and said, "Do a canvass of the houses there along the back. Maybe it was someone out walking his dog or kids playing. And ask about any activity over this way during the weekend — lights at night, the sound of a vehicle. You know the drill."

He climbed back up and told the EMS crew that they could transport the body, then noticed that the trail continued along the creek bank. He got in his truck and followed it a few hundred feet. It circled around another thick stand of slash pines before opening up into a half-abandoned pasture. There was that concrete slab Deborah had told him about and there, too, in the distance was the tenant house.

He drove back to the dump, gestured for Mayleen to join him, and called the dispatcher. "Hey, Faye. How 'bout you play me back the call you got on this body."

After listening closely, he said, "Now play it again for Mayleen," and handed her his phone.

When she had thanked the dispatcher and ended the call, Dwight said, "Did that sound like a British accent to you?"

CHAPTER 11

A group of vultures is called a "Venue."
Vultures circling in the air are a "Kettle."
— The Turkey Vulture Society

Sigrid Harald — Wednesday afternoon (continued)

It was nearing three o'clock before Sigrid and Anne finished eating and were ready to head out of town for the farm where Martin Crawford was camped.

"Anne? Anne Lattimore? Oh my goodness!" a matronly gray-haired woman exclaimed as they were paying their lunch tab. "I swear, you haven't changed a bit since high school! Well, maybe a little bit of snow on the roof, but nothing on the waist."

The woman patted her own ample waist and enfolded Anne in a hug before she could sidestep it. The face was vaguely familiar, but high school was more than forty years in Anne's past and she had not attended any of the reunions. Nevertheless, she made herself smile as if in delight and say, "How lovely to see you again after all this time! You've met my daughter, haven't you?"

From attending exhibits of her mother's photographs, Sigrid realized that Anne didn't have a clue as to this woman's name, but she recognized her cue and dutifully stepped forward with her hand extended. "Hello, I'm Sigrid Harald and you are — ?"

"Mavis Trogden," the woman said, beaming. "Mavis Rainey, that was. Your mom and I were in the same homeroom the whole four years of high school."

She signaled to a short stout woman who had preceded her into the tearoom to claim a table near the back. "Alice Jean, look who's here! Anne Lattimore!"

Several minutes of "Remember when?" and "Here's a picture of my oldest grandchild" passed before Anne could disentangle herself gracefully.

"Maybe we should go ahead and stop by the bank while we're this close," Sigrid said when they were finally out the door.

The bank was on the next block and it was a replay of the tearoom, this time with a gray-haired executive who came out of his office to take Anne's hand with shy pleasure, before turning to Sigrid. "You cannot know what a crush I had on this girl when I was sixteen."

"Ah, Bobby," Anne said, automatically dimpling. "If only you'd said something back then."

He shook his head. "No, you were always out of my league. And then you went off to New York to study photography the day after graduation and never looked back, but I've followed your career, Anne — the Pulitzer, your exhibit at the art museum, that gut-wrenching story you did on poor Somalia a few years ago before it was on the news every night. What a life you've led!"

Eventually, he escorted them back to Mrs. Lattimore's box. He seemed to know about her condition but was restrained in his sympathy. "One of the old guard," he said with a slow shake of his head. "We'll not see her like again, I'm afraid."

Anne had brought along a canvas tote and they soon transferred everything from the box. The only thing they opened was a velvet jeweler's bag that was heavier than expected. When Sigrid loosened the drawstrings and looked inside, she saw a handful of gold coins. "Can't wait to hear the story that goes with these."

"Don't look at me," her mother said as

she closed the box and slid it back into its slot. "I never saw them before."

The bank executive was in conference with someone else when they emerged from the vault area and they managed to get back to the car and lock the tote bag in the trunk without being waylaid again.

With Anne behind the wheel, they drove out of town on Old Highway 48, then turned onto a nearly deserted secondary road that took them through a part of the county that was still mostly farms.

Here in February, the fields had a locked-down air as if waiting for spring rains and warm sunshine. The ditchbanks were scruffy with dead weeds and the occasional litter of plastic soda bottles, beer cans, and plastic bags half hidden by the dry brown leaves.

Although she could discuss blood spatter patterns and blunt trauma wounds knowledgeably, Sigrid Harald was, as a rule, oblivious to nature and its cycles. She knew that the sun and the moon rose in the east and set in the west and that water usually flowed downhill, that winter required heavier clothing than summer, that daylight lengthened in the spring and shortened in the fall, ergo the nuisance of daylight saving time. If pressed, she could distinguish a rose from a daisy and a fir tree from an oak, and she could even recognize magnolias because one grew in her grandmother's front yard. Its branches spread out from the base of the trunk and continued upward for sixty feet. She knew that the thick leathery leaves stayed green year round and were made into wreaths and garlands at Christmastime, even though the huge white blossoms of summer were unsuitable for indoor bouquets.

As far as she was concerned a more intimate knowledge of nature seemed superfluous. Anything else could be Googled. Wasn't that what the Internet was for?

But she was very much aware of her mother's deepening sadness as Grandmother Lattimore's condition deteriorated day by day; so when Anne remarked on the beauty of a bare-twigged tree silhouetted against the winter sky, she was willing to keep the conversational ball rolling. "Is that an oak or a maple?"

"Oak," said Anne, who could even distinguish the pines, which all looked alike to Sigrid.

"What about those?" Sigrid asked when they passed a group of trees shrouded in gray, dead-looking vines. "Grapevines or poison oak?"

"Neither. That's kudzu. Did I forward you that picture that someone sent me last summer? The vine that went up a light pole and then leafed out at the top and along the wires on either side?"

"The one they said looked like Christ on the cross?"

"That's the one."

Sigrid smiled. "I guess if they can see the head of Jesus on a grilled cheese sandwich, why not on a power pole?"

"Don't laugh. This is our heritage," Anne said. "And speaking of our heritage . . ."

She slowed and turned into the drive of a large white house, then came to a stop as soon as the car was off the pavement. The driveway continued on past tall magnolias and ancient oaks and curved up to a set of tall fluted columns that ended in Doric scrolls.

"Tara?" Sigrid asked dryly.

"Gilead," her mother answered. "Your grandmother could say when our Gilberts branched off from the ones who inherited the place. I think it was her grandfather who was the younger son. He got money while his brother got Gilead, back before the Civil War."

"Who owns it now?"

"Kate Bryant's adopted daughter."

"Really? How did that happen?"

"It's a long and complicated story and I forget most of the details. Get Kate to tell you if you're interested.* Short version: Mary Pat's mother was a Gilbert and the house was falling to pieces when she married a man with a ton of money. He restored it as a wedding present."

"Some present," Sigrid said.

"Both died before Mary Pat was four," Anne said sadly. "Kate was the child's closest relative through the father's side, which is why she was given custody. Everything's in trust for the little girl, including Gilead."

"Poor kid," Sigrid said.

Anne shook her head in wry amusement. "Not everyone considers a large inheritance a burden, honey."

She backed out of the drive onto the road again, drove about a hundred feet, then turned left into a rough dirt lane that cut through fields green with winter rye.

"Are you sure you know where you're going?" Sigrid asked as they bumped over the rutted track.

"Sorry, but this is the only way I know how to get to the Ferrabee place."

The lane dipped down past a boxy wooden

* See *Bloody Kin.*

structure and Anne explained that they were now on Kate's farm. "This used to be a packhouse, but Kate's converted it into a studio for her fabric designs."

There was no sign of Kate and the lane continued straight through the far side of the wide yard to exit onto another road. Anne pointed to a smaller white farmhouse off to the right. "That's where Rob and Dwight's mother lives."

She made a left, then a right that took them through stands of head-high pines that were planted in uniform rows. "This used to be all tobacco," she said. "Now it's pulpwood. Not much has changed on this side of the creek, though."

As they passed a mailbox, she gestured to a well-tended lane that was lined with a double row of young bare-branched trees. Sigrid realized that a house probably lay somewhere beyond those thicker trees.

"I think Dwight and Deborah live down there," her mother said.

Sigrid twisted in her seat to look back, but nothing could be seen of a house. "Why do I have the impression that Deborah comes from a large family?"

"Because she does," said Anne. "Ten or twelve brothers, all older, and she was the only girl."

The thought of sharing a house with that many brothers made Sigrid feel slightly claustrophobic. "Did you know them when you were growing up?"

"I knew who the boys were, but they went to school out here in the country and I was at the school in town. Besides, the older ones dropped out of school early and the others were younger than me. I think we're distantly related to Deborah through her mother, but most of her brothers are from her father's first marriage. He was a bootlegger, you know."

"What?"

Before Anne could elaborate, they came to a stop sign and she looked around in surprise at a cluster of unfamiliar buildings that had sprouted in what used to be soybean fields. There was a gas station directly opposite them. Behind it was a large parking lot that fronted a NutriGood grocery store. An Italian restaurant, a hardware store, and some smaller shops lined the left side of the lot. "What the hell's a strip mall doing way out here?" Anne asked.

Cars zipped back and forth and Sigrid smiled. "Look at all the rooftops over there. Sorry, Mother, but I don't think this is 'way out' anymore."

On a corner to the left of them, tasteful

signage indicated that the houses that could be glimpsed behind the expensively landscaped berms were part of Grayson Village. A smaller sign, equally tasteful, discreetly announced that homes were available "from the low 450's."

Anne waited for a gap in the flow of traffic and sped across the intersection. After a mile or two, she shook her head, perplexed. "I don't recognize anything. Maybe I should have taken a left back there."

Suiting action to words, she executed a U-turn, and soon they were back on the busier road. She glimpsed a fingerpost and slowed to read it aloud. "Four miles to Highway Forty-Eight. Okay, this is right. And there's the road!"

She flipped her left-turn signal and cut the Lincoln in front of an oncoming vehicle so quickly that Sigrid cried, "Watch out!" and braced for impact.

"Sorry, honey."

Almost immediately, they heard the wail of a siren and, glancing behind them, saw a patrol car, its blue lights flashing.

"Oh, hell," Anne sighed and pulled onto the shoulder.

Before she could switch off the engine, the car shot around them, kicking up gravel and even a little dust despite last night's rain. A moment later, a second patrol car passed them, its siren wailing, too.

When the way behind was clear, Anne eased back onto the road and followed. "What do you suppose that's all about?"

They rounded two more curves and came upon a cluster of official vehicles, all lights flashing. A tall uniformed trooper guarded the entrance to a rough track that branched away to the left from the dirt road. It had been cordoned off with yellow crime scene tape.

Sigrid frowned as her mother slowed to a stop beside one of the squad cars. "Is this the Ferrabee place?"

"No, that's on down further, but see that kid with the camera? Jeremy Harper."

With her foot on the brake and the engine running, she rolled down her window and called to the boy, who loped over as soon as he recognized her. To Sigrid, he resembled an early Dr. Who, right down to his skinny height, an exuberance of fuzzy blond curls, and that long striped scarf.

"I'm not trying to get past the tape, Ms. Harald, honest," he said in one of the deepest bass voices Sigrid had ever heard. She stared in fascination that such a voice could come out of such a long thin neck. He had a camera case slung over one shoulder and an expensive-looking digital camera around his neck.

"Good," Anne said sternly. "Why are you even here?"

"Somebody called in a dead body about an hour ago. I heard it on my scanner."

"You have a scanner?" Sigrid asked.

"Didn't I tell you that Jeremy's a reporter, too?" Anne said. "This is my daughter, Jeremy. She's a homicide detective in New York."

"Wow! You gonna help with this investigation?"

"No, she's not," Anne said, "and neither are you." She glanced at her watch. "Aren't you supposed to be in Dobbs right now, prepping with Richard Williams for your first session with the disabled vets?"

"I was almost there when I remembered something I'd forgotten at school," he said, wrapping that striped scarf tighter around his neck. His nose and his bare ears had turned a bright red in the chill wind that whipped up the hill.

He gave a sheepish grin as his new mentor gave him a jaundiced look. "Okay, I heard the call for more backup, and since it was so close to where we used to live, I thought I'd just run back and —"

His eyes dropped before Anne's steady

150

gaze. "Okay, okay. I guess I'm going."

Anne waited until the boy got into an old blue Toyota and drove off in the opposite direction, then took her foot off the brake and continued on down the road. The road itself ended in yet another of those ubiquitous lanes that Sigrid was beginning to know and dislike.

"You do remember that this is a Lincoln *Town* Car and not a tank?" she said as tree branches brushed their windows.

"Something bigger's already been back and forth here," Anne said. "See the broken twigs?"

"You never mentioned that you were a Girl Scout," Sigrid muttered, sinking back into the cushioned seat.

Anne laughed. "Oh, honey, there's a whole bunch of stuff I never mentioned."

The brush gave way to an open pasture. To the left, a banged-up black truck was parked beside a wooden tenant house badly in need of paint. The house sat on a slight rise and the land sloped down from it to a line of trees and bushes in the far distance.

"That must be the buzzard table Deborah told us about," Anne said, pointing to the ruins of an old foundation a few yards from the creek.

She drove on over to the house, but before

151

they reached it, Martin Crawford emerged from inside and waited for them on the porch.

"Sorry I didn't call before coming," Anne said in cheerful greeting, "but we forgot to exchange numbers last night. Hey, you shaved off your beard!"

"I told you it came and went with the seasons," he said. "Hullo, Sigrid. Did you come to see the vultures? I'm afraid they're not here right now."

He pointed back the way they had come. High above the treetops, they could see four of the big creatures circling around and around.

"They seem to have found something over there that interests them more than my squirrels. But do come in. I've just put the pot on for tea."

CHAPTER 12

Circling vultures often indicate the presence of a carcass.
— The Turkey Vulture Society

Sigrid Harald — Wednesday afternoon (continued)

The old Ferrabee tenant house was typical of the living quarters a landowner might provide a sharecropper family in the thirties, forties, and fifties. It would have had electricity, but no running water or indoor plumbing and certainly no central heating. Martin Crawford gave Anne and Sigrid a quick tour to show how he had weather-stripped the doors and windows and layered threadbare carpets over the cracks in the floor. Mrs. Lattimore had invited him to rummage in her attic for pieces of cast-off furniture — the carpets, three mismatched chairs, a badly scarred and water-stained oak kitchen table, and a bookshelf. A few kitchen utensils and a single-bed mattress to put under his sleeping bag came from a thrift store in Cotton Grove, as did the kerosene lanterns. There were four rooms, but he was using only three: the kitchen, a bedroom, and the front room. A potbellied stove in the front room was enough to keep those three rooms warm and cozy.

The table was more than six feet long. Camera cases, a laptop, and several file folders littered the near end. He shifted a pile of photography magazines and news journals from two of the chairs and invited them to join him at the table.

When they told him that a woman's body had been found nearby, he said, "Do they know who she was?"

"We haven't heard, but according to the local newspaper, a Realtor went missing Saturday," Sigrid said.

Talk turned to other matters while Martin added more tea to the pot, brought out a tin of shortbread, and opened the door of the little iron stove so that the dancing flames could be seen.

"You've made yourself very comfortable here," Anne said, "but Mother still doesn't understand why you can't stay with her and drive back and forth to photograph your vultures."

"This is luxury living compared to some of the places I've slept in," he told her as the teapot and biscuit tin went around. He described camping in the high Andes to photograph condors, of being stalked by a leopard while trying to get a shot of lammergeiers in the Elburz Mountains.

Anne countered with a mud hut in Ethiopia and a yurt in Mongolia.

And Sigrid sat quietly watching both of them as they compared notes and tried to decide where they might have overlapped in the past. She had interviewed so many criminals in her career that she had gone on automatic alert the first time their cousin's eyes flicked from Anne's face to hers, as if to see how she was taking it before flicking back again to Anne's. Without his beard, his own face seemed more expressive than before.

"My father was stationed in Islamabad for a couple of years. That's the closest I ever came to Mongolia, so it must have been Peru," Martin said at last. "I forget when, though."

Sigrid wanted to shout, *"Don't tell him!"* But with no good reason to explain why, she kept silent; and when Anne supplied the year and the month, Martin nodded in agreement.

"That sounds correct. I do remember that it was May."

Like hell you do, Sigrid thought. But why would he lie about something so innocuous?

"What about So— ?" Before Anne could complete her question, her teacup somehow collided with the pot Martin was holding out and hot tea splashed on her trouser leg while the pot went flying.

Her teacup shattered but the teapot landed on the pile of magazines and survived its fall.

"Oh, Martin, I'm so sorry," Anne said, picking up the pieces of the broken cup.

"No, no. My fault entirely." He hurried to the kitchen and came back with a roll of paper towels for Anne to dry herself off with. "Fortunately, the carpets aren't Persian."

Which led to talk of Iran and how stupid the United States and Great Britain had been to orchestrate the overthrow of the democratically elected Mossadegh and replace him with a dictatorial shah.

"You think we could have had a secular Muslim state there like Turkey?" Anne asked.

"Probably. That's what my father always thought." He sighed. "But enough about politics. I have some wonderful photographs of Medina. Were you ever there? Let me show you."

He swiveled his chair around to open the laptop on the table and the two women pulled their own chairs closer. Once they were past the novelty of an Arabic keyboard, the pictures had Anne oohing and ahhing over some of the effects he had achieved and how his pictures of village life captured the ebb and flow of the culture.

"This is exactly what I'm hoping Jeremy can learn," she told Sigrid, her eyes snapping with excitement.

"Jeremy?" he asked.

She described her morning in court and how Deborah Knott had consented to a community service plan she hoped to put together with a youth minister in Dobbs. "Would you talk to him, too, Martin? Show him some of your work? Please?"

He raised a doubtful eyebrow. "Talk to him about the poverty-stricken life of a freelance ornithologist?"

"About making a living with words and a camera without breaking the law. If we hadn't come along just now, I have a feeling he would have found a way to sneak through the woods to where the body is. Deborah went pretty easy on him this morning, but if he keeps pushing the boundaries, she could send him to jail for violating his probation, right, Sigrid?"

Sigrid rather doubted it would come to that, but she nodded anyhow, knowing Anne thought it would strengthen her appeal for help.

"Well . . ." he said.

"Great! Give me your phone number so I can call you. Maybe we can set something up for tomorrow and —" Movement through the front window caught her eye. "More company, Martin. A police car."

There was a tap of the horn — a way of announcing oneself that country people still used — then someone emerged from the squad car.

Sigrid's chair gave her an unobstructed view of the yard. "It's Dwight Bryant," she said. "He probably wants to know if you saw anything over there."

As Dwight and Mayleen Richards stepped up onto the porch, Martin Crawford opened the door for them.

"Bryant," he said, holding out his hand to shake. "Good to see you again. It didn't quite register last night that you're a police officer. Come in, come in. I'm afraid I'm a bit short on chairs, though."

As Dwight introduced his deputy to the

others, Martin gestured for her to take his chair and refused to take her no for an answer. He closed his laptop and pushed the clutter down to the far end of the long sturdy table.

"I think it will support both of us," he told Dwight; but as he backed up to the table and started to press down with his arms to hoist himself up, they saw an involuntary grimace of pain. Embarrassed, he settled for leaning against the table.

Concerned, Anne said, "Are you okay?"

"I'm fine. Really. Took a bad tumble last year and broke both arms. Fell down the stairs in my own house. Would you believe it? Slipped on a loose tread. I keep forgetting that they haven't completely healed."

Another lie? Sigrid wondered. In her experience, people deviating from the truth tended to give more information than was needed. She glanced at Dwight Bryant, who was leaning against the doorframe. His face showed nothing more than polite sympathy.

"I'd offer you some tea, but I only have three cups." Martin smiled at Anne. "Actually, I seem to be down to two at the moment. I shall have to see about getting more."

"That's okay," Dwight said. "We can't stay. We've discovered the body of a missing woman on the other side of those woods there and wondered if you could tell us anything about it?"

"A missing woman? I'm afraid not. As you know, I was away last night until after ten and I went straight to bed when I returned."

"We think she may have been put there three or four nights ago. We're hoping to find someone who saw car lights at an odd time or noticed an unfamiliar vehicle on the road. It's a dead end and you're probably the only one using it much on a regular basis."

Martin Crawford shook his head. "Sorry, Bryant. I'm a stranger here myself so I wouldn't know who did or didn't belong. For what it's worth, when your wife and her nephew stopped by yesterday, they were my first visitors in the two months I've been here. I have heard some young chaps larking up and down the road on their quads, and they did try to come through here a few weeks ago, but I told them they were trespassing and sent them packing. Can't have my vultures scared away, you see."

"The thing is," Dwight said, continuing as if the other man hadn't spoken, "someone called it in around two this afternoon. An anonymous man. Sounded like he had an accent very much like yours."

"Oh?"

"Was it you?"

"Anonymous, you said?"

"That's right."

"Probably someone who wanted to be helpful but didn't want to become involved, wouldn't you say? From the size and grandeur of that housing estate, surely one or two of her majesty's subjects might live there and have telephones?"

"Would you mind if we looked at the call record on yours?" Dwight asked bluntly.

"Actually, I bloody well would," Martin said. He was at least four inches shorter than Dwight but he drew himself up pugnaciously. "I'm not used to having my veracity questioned."

"Martin," Anne said softly, and he turned to her with a what-the-hell? shrug of his shoulders and a sheepish smile.

"Quite right, my dear." He went into the closed and unheated bedroom and returned with two cell phones. One was the latest iPhone, the other was a cheap throwaway. "I haven't used either of them in several days. This one's for overseas calls and this disposable toy is for local calls to the library and Aunt Jane. It costs too much to use my regular mobile here in the States."

He selected the outgoing call option on

both phones and handed one to Dwight and the other to Mayleen Richards.

It took them only a moment to see that he had told the truth.

"I apologize, Crawford," Dwight said, returning the phones. "It's just that when I saw the buzzards kettling above the body, I thought maybe they made you curious enough to go over and take a look."

"Quite all right. I expect it goes with the job." He laid the phones on the table and turned toward the kitchen. "Now, I can't offer you tea, but I do have an extra glass if you'd like a spot of something else?"

"Another time," Dwight said. "Right now, we have to get back to Dobbs. I have to tell the woman's husband that she's been found."

Sigrid watched him go with torn loyalties.

Martin Crawford might be family, but Dwight Bryant was a fellow law officer.

When her cousin had given them a brief tour of the house earlier, there had been an open satchel on the floor beside his sleeping bag. He had immediately directed their eyes to the north wall papered in old newspapers to keep out the worst of the winter chill. Most of them dated back 30 years and Anne had marveled at some of the headlines. When Sigrid looked again at the satchel, a

162

pillow lay on top of it, hiding the four or five throwaway phones she had glimpsed before.

None of her business, she told herself. If Martin was the one who had made that call, he had acted responsibly. He wouldn't be the first person who preferred not to get involved with murder.

"What did Dwight mean when he said the buzzards were kettling?" Anne asked.

"It's a fanciful way of describing the way they move up and down when they circle over prey. It reminds people of air bubbles in a pot of boiling water." Martin smiled. "Speaking of which, shall I make us another pot of tea?"

CHAPTER 13

Turkey vultures not only find food individually when foraging, but also may notice when other vultures in flight begin to descend to food and then follow those vultures to the food source.
　　　　　　　— The Turkey Vulture Society

Late that afternoon, my clerk, Frances Warren, leaned in to tell me that Rebecca Jowett's body had been found. "Out near where y'all live," she said, but that was as much as she knew.

My calendar turned out to be more packed than expected, thanks to the inefficiency of our current DA, so there was no time to go chasing down rumors if we hoped to get through everything. Happily, Frances kept all the paperwork moving and together we reached the last case just as the hands on the courtroom clock passed five.

It was a he-said-she-said bar brawl involving a young white woman, her current black boyfriend, and her white exboyfriend, and I had heard all I needed to when the door of my courtroom opened and a little boy with a backpack hanging from one shoulder entered and slipped into the last row of benches. He gave me a snaggletoothed smile and held up a book to let me know he was going to sit there and read until I was finished.

Cal.

I smiled back at him and quickly disposed of those three. A night in jail had calmed them all down, and from the way she was flouncing and smirking and tossing her long hair back from her face every few minutes, I suspected that the young woman was rather pleased to be the object of hot desire for two good-looking men. Indeed, she had probably incited them. Nevertheless, they were the ones who had thrown the punches and broken some glassware, although she seemed to have done her bit to keep the fight going. I gave them each three days, with credit for time served and the rest to be suspended on the usual conditions. They were to make restitution of seventy-five dollars to the bar owner for the breakages. (He was asking for two hundred even though I knew from past testimony that seventy-five dollars would buy five or six dozen bar glasses at Sam's Club.)

At this point, I paused and looked at the white bar owner, who is in court at least once a month to testify about similar occurrences. "If you like, sir, I can order them to stay away from your premises."

"Naw, that's okay," he said. "Long as they behave theirselves, they can come on back."

"That's your decision," I told him, "but I'm putting you on notice now that if you or any of your customers are back here anytime soon, I might be forced to see about shutting you down for maintaining a public nuisance."

He started to protest, but I held up my hand for silence.

"Every time you or your patrons wind up here in court, it costs the taxpayers money, and you've used up more than your share of tax dollars these last few months. If you can't maintain order, we'll have to see who can."

I turned back to the first three. "Pay the clerk in the hall on your way out and you're free to go."

"We each got to pay seventy-five for them broken glasses?" the young woman asked.

"No, twenty-five apiece, but you each do have to pay court costs. The clerk will work out a payment schedule if you don't have the cash on you."

I winked at the bailiff and gave a crisp formal tap of my gavel. "Court adjourned, Mr. Overby."

"All rise," he said solemnly even though Cal was the only one still seated on the benches. My stepson came immediately to his feet.

"This court is now adjourned," Overby said, then smiled. "Hey there, Cal! How's it going?"

"Fine," he said shyly as he came forward.

Frances greeted him by name as well.

Dwight is well liked around the courthouse, and in the year that Cal has lived with us, he's become familiar to a lot of the people who work here and they would spoil him if they could. Part of it is the usual brownnosing. After all, I *am* a judge and Dwight is Sheriff Bo Poole's chief deputy. But Cal's a nice kid, quiet, polite to his elders, and doesn't try to take advantage of our positions.

Overby held the door behind the bench for Frances and her files and would have held it for me, but I gestured for him not to wait because Cal had left his backpack and jacket on the bench.

As he came back up to the bar, he looked

around the modern room with its pale blue walls and its bleached oak furnishings. There's a big gilt seal of state on the wall behind my blue leather chair, with an American flag on one side and a North Carolina flag on the other. Otherwise, the room is quite plain. "Is this where Mary Pat and Jake got adopted?"

"No," I said. "That was in the old courtroom. Want to see it?"

"Sure."

We stopped by my office so that I could drop off my robe and pick up my parka, then crossed over to the older wing.

The main courtroom is still used for superior court trials and for swearing-in ceremonies or whenever else the participants wish to invoke the power and stone-footed majesty of the law. Twice as big as the other courtrooms, the cavernous space is paneled in dark oak and the raked floor is carpeted in deep red wool. Acanthus leaves are carved into the plaster medallions on the high vaulted ceiling and pierced brass lanterns hang down from the center of each on long black cords above solid oak benches. They cast a golden glow over the courtroom.

Most adoptions are just a matter of filing the correct forms, which the clerk of the court checks to see that all the hoops have been jumped through, but Kate and Rob got him to make a nice little ceremony out of signing the final form, and they did it here.

"It looks like church," Cal said in a hushed voice.

"It does, doesn't it?" I said, feeling a bit proprietary.

I had been sworn in here, my daddy holding the Bible on which I took my oath, with all my kinfolks looking on (and taking up a good quarter of the benches). I still get goose bumps thinking about all that these venerable walls have witnessed over the past hundred years.

"Mary Pat said it felt a little bit like getting married."

"What about Jake?"

He shrugged. "I don't think he cared. Besides, Aunt Kate's his real mother — his biological mother," he elucidated in case I was confused. (There had been much discussion of "real," "biological," and "adoptive" during the whole adoption process last summer.) "And he's been calling Uncle Rob Dad ever since he could talk."

"So where's your own dad?" I asked, glancing at my watch. "Are you riding home with him or me?"

"With you. He said tell you he'd be home by seven." He cut his eyes up at me with a mischievous grin. "He also said he'd have told you himself if you'd had your phone on."

I fumbled in my parka pocket and found my phone. "It was on," I said. "See?"

"But it was in your office. And your door was locked. And I bet it was on vibrate."

I laughed and called Dwight back. My call went straight to his voice mail. "Got your message and your son," I said. "See you at seven."

My friend Portland had given me a ride out to Will's place at lunchtime, so my car was waiting for us in my parking spot across from the courthouse.

Cal slid into the front seat beside me and dropped his backpack on the floor behind us.

As he talked about school and how Dwight had picked him up early, I realized that he hadn't wondered why Dwight was out that way. Cal's certainly aware of what we do for a living, but we try to keep the worst from him and I could understand that Dwight wouldn't want him to know why he'd had to wait in the squad car while his dad went in to talk to some man.

On the other hand, he's no dummy.

"There were a lot of cars at that house," he said, "but I don't think it was a party."

"Probably not," I agreed.

"Did somebody get killed?"

"I'm afraid so, honey."

"Somebody's mom?" he asked in a small voice.

"No, I don't think she had any children."

"That's good."

There was a pensive look on his face. I never know whether it's the right thing to talk about Jonna or not, but Dwight and I had agreed we would try not to make it awkward for Cal to speak of her. I reached over and gave his hand a quick squeeze. "You're thinking about your mother, aren't you?"

He nodded. "When she got killed, there were all those cars at Grandmother's house."

"That's because so many people loved her and were sorry she died."

We rode in silence for a few minutes. The sun sank closer to the horizon, turning the bare-leaved twigs and branches into delicate wrought-iron tracery against the orange-and-blue stained glass of the sky.

Cal sighed. "The thing is . . . sometimes I can't remember what she looked like."

Before I could speak, he said, "I mean, I

have her picture in my room, and there's that album we brought back, but sometimes it doesn't feel real. I try to remember what it was like up in Virginia, but it sort of gets tangled up with here."

Embarrassed, he brushed away the involuntary tears that filled his eyes and turned away from me to stare out the side window.

"You're afraid that you're going to forget her?"

He didn't answer but I saw his head nod.

"Cal, I know it doesn't seem fair to your mother, but it *is* natural. That's what time does for all of us. If everything stayed fresh and sharp, we wouldn't be able to get on with our lives. I know how much it hurt when she died, because I remember how bad it was when my own mother died, but if we didn't let time smooth away some of those memories, we wouldn't be able to get up in the morning. You'll always be sorry she died, but you won't ever completely forget her, so you don't have to feel guilty because some of the memories get mixed up. Wherever her spirit is, she knows you still love her."

Miraculously, it must have been the right thing to say, because by the time we got home, he was himself again.

We let Bandit out and he lit the fire

Dwight had laid that morning. Our cleaning woman had been there that day so the house was shining, the laundry folded and put away, and supper would be the spinach lasagna we hadn't eaten last night. While I changed into jeans and comfortable shoes, Cal reviewed his spelling words and I called them out to him. The drill was i-before-e words and he got most of them right the first time through. After that, he picked up *The Hobbit* and asked if we could read another chapter. We had gone through all the Harry Potter books by Christmas and my sister-in-law Barbara, who runs the county library system, had assured me that Cal would understand *The Lord of the Rings* if we read it together.

Neither Dwight nor I are huge on books, and neither of us had read the Tolkien saga, but I had discovered that I liked reading aloud and I liked it that Cal snuggled next to me on the couch to follow along with the words. Even Dwight got caught up in the adventure and would come in to listen if he was home. I could say that both of them took after Dwight's mother, who always had two or three books going on her bedside table, but I knew that it was Jonna who had read to Cal from the time he was a baby.

There was much about Dwight's first wife

that was less than admirable, things I hoped Cal would never learn, but when he leaned against me, too absorbed in the story I was reading aloud to pull away if I put my arm around him, I always sent her a mental thank-you.

The lasagna was nicely browned along the edges and the aroma of basil, garlic, and tomato sauce filled the house when Dwight got home so shortly after seven that he could claim he was on time.

"Hello, my precioussss," Cal hissed as he set the table.

Dwight laughed and caught him up in a bear hug that ended with Cal slung over his shoulder as they headed off to the bathroom to wash up. "What did I miss, buddy? Does Gollum know that Bilbo has the ring?"

Cal's recap of the chapter Dwight had missed carried us through supper.

It wasn't till Cal was in bed with Bandit curled up beside him that I could finally ask Dwight about Rebecca Jowett and hear how she had been found across the creek from the farm on a trash dump, less than a mile from us as the crow flies.

"Or as a buzzard flies," Dwight said sourly.

He was convinced that Martin Crawford was the one who had found the body and called it in. "No way would somebody studying buzzard habits not walk over that way to see why they were kettling."

"But if he showed you his phone?"

"He could have erased the call as soon as he made it."

"He probably just doesn't want to get involved," I said soothingly. "A stranger in a strange land? At least he called. *If* he called."

"All the same, there's something off about that man. And I think Sigrid feels it, too."

"Sigrid?"

"Yeah, she and her mother were at Martin's when Mayleen and I got there. She doesn't say much, but I get the impression that nothing important gets by her."

CHAPTER 14

Male and female turkey vultures are identical in appearance.
— The Turkey Vulture Society

Major Dwight Bryant — Thursday morning
"Thank you for coming in," Dwight said, extending a hand to Wes Todd and his wife, Ginger. "This shouldn't take too long. We do understand that time is money."

"Not as much as it used to be," Mrs. Todd said with a self-conscious laugh. "So many people are behind in their mortgage payments, they don't worry about termites or carpenter ants." She wore a billed cap with a cutout and an adjustable plastic band in the back. Her flaming red hair, the color of maple leaves in October, was pulled away from her heart-shaped face in a long ponytail that protruded from the cutout and bounced against her shoulders whenever she moved her head. "We've laid off some workers and I've had to get back out in the field myself because there's not enough office work to keep me busy all day."

"It's just temporary till the economy picks up," Wes Todd said, as if nettled by her comment on the state of their business.

When they shook hands, Dwight noticed that Mrs. Todd's were almost as callused as her husband's. Despite her slim build and hesitant smile, this was a woman who probably helped haul extension ladders in and out of their trucks and who could drill through concrete foundations to get at termite nests.

She took one of the chairs at the table in the interview room and undid the zipper of her jacket. Like her husband's, it was sturdy brown canvas with the words "Todd Pest Control" and a local phone number stitched in orange on the back. They both wore brown canvas coveralls and work boots, too, but while those work clothes made her husband look competent and strong and ready to face anything from coons and bats to mice and hornets, she looked more like a tagalong tomboy who would cringe from a garter snake.

"Now, honey," her husband said, taking charge, "they don't want to hear about our business. They want to hear what we know about Becca Jowett, right, Bryant?" His dismissive man-to-man tone made Dwight glad he'd sent Mayleen Richards out to interview the dead woman's mother and sister this morning. Todd's attitude would have had her hackles rising.

Mrs. Todd didn't seem to mind his patronizing words. She was more worried about the video camera that was pointing in her direction. She fluffed her ponytail, then clasped her hands in front of her on the table, both feet firmly on the floor.

Dwight explained that Deputy McLamb would video the interview and assured them that they could stop it at any time if they felt they were about to say something incriminating.

Ginger Todd's eyes widened. "Incriminating? Wes?" She looked at her husband anxiously.

He teetered between annoyance and embarrassment. "God, Ginger, as many of those stupid *CSI* shows as you watch, you've got to know that they question everybody when someone gets murdered. They don't think we had anything to do with it. It's just routine, right?"

"Right," Dwight said with a reassuring smile for Mrs. Todd. "We're trying to get a feel for what Mrs. Jowett was like, whether you noticed anything that might help us learn who did this to her. For instance, when did you-all meet?"

Ginger Todd relaxed enough to tell how they had sat at the same table with Paula Coyne and Rebecca at a Chamber of Commerce lunch last fall. "I said something about needing a bigger house now that our daughter's getting too old to share a room with her brother anymore."

"That's all Ginger had to say," Todd said with a rueful smile. "Becca jumped right on it. She was one sharp lady. Told us that the housing market had probably bottomed out and that if we were ever going to get a bigger house in a better neighborhood with a good school for the kids, we needed to act quick before prices started back up."

"The updated colonial on East Cleveland Street was one of the first she showed us," his wife said, "even though it was way out of our price range."

"Not *that* far out," Todd snapped. "We're not on food stamps yet."

His words made Dwight realize that this was a man who measured his worth by his bank account and what he could buy, whether or not he could actually afford it.

"It was higher than we wanted to go," his wife said stubbornly, "but it was a short sale and Becca was sure the bank would come down on it. Which they did. While we were waiting, she showed us some other places, but this one was so perfect for us."

"We lowballed the offer and the bank accepted it," Wes Todd said, now smugly proud of his business acumen. "We were supposed to close this very afternoon."

"Now we have to start looking all over again," Ginger Todd said.

Her husband gave Dwight another of those man-to-man looks. "Our lawyer says we can probably get our earnest money back because of what happened there, but Ms. Coyne says the bank's willing to cut the price another five thousand if we'll go ahead with the deal."

Mrs. Todd's face flushed as bright as her hair. "I told you, Wes. I don't care if they give us the damn house on a silver platter. I'm not living there, so forget it!"

In answer to Dwight's questions, they agreed that Becca Jowett had been friendly and helpful, "but in the end, we were a potential commission, not best friends," Ginger Todd said. "It's not like she would tell us if she was upset about anything. Although . . ."

"Yes?"

"We told you how she showed us the

house again Saturday morning so I could measure the windows?"

Dwight nodded encouragingly.

"She had such pretty long brown hair, not like my carrot top. When we were leaving, she started to zip up her coat and her hair got caught. I helped her untangle it and I saw that she had a hickey on the side of her neck. I said something about her husband being a real tiger and she looked embarrassed and, I don't know, I got the feeling maybe it wasn't her husband that gave it to her."

"Oh for God's sake, Ginger!" her husband said, looking uncomfortable.

"I'm not talking ugly about the dead, Wes. They ought to know." She turned back to Dwight and McLamb. "Such a pretty woman. It's a real shame."

When asked to say where they were Saturday night, Mrs. Todd said, "Wes got a call around six-thirty and had to go out on a job, so I took the children over to spend the night at my parents' and stayed to visit awhile. Wes got back — what time, honey? Around nine? Nine-fifteen?"

"Something like that. These days, we never say no to any job, no matter what the time," Todd said and gave them the name and address of a customer whose teenage daughter was freaking out because she was sure there were rats in the wall of her bedroom.

"She was right," he said. "There were. I baited six traps — two in the attic, two in the crawl space under the house, and two in her bedroom that I baited with her leftover cheese pizza. We caught a pregnant female with the pizza. A fat male in the crawl space went for the peanut butter."

The Kendricks were a good ten years older than the Todds, well-to-do and still on the sunny side of fifty. Their children were out of the house and the Kendricks declared themselves ready to embrace a more care-free lifestyle.

"I've had it with old houses and big yards," Paul Kendrick said. "I want to sell my riding lawnmower so I can play golf on the weekends. Let a homeowner's association do the mowing and pruning."

"And I want granite countertops and stainless steel appliances," his wife, Nita, said. "Three bedrooms, not five. Low-maintenance and no strings. We've even told our daughter she'll have to take her dog when she graduates this spring so we can pick up and go whenever we want to."

She was a small cuddly woman with a stylish, asymmetrical gray bob, a surprisingly deep laugh, and a penchant for bright red lipstick and bold colors. She wore large hoop earrings, three-inch heels, and form-fitting black slacks with a cropped red wool jacket.

Paul Kendrick looked like an ad for a man's hair-coloring product. Just under six feet tall, he had thick gray hair, a cleft chin, well-toned chest muscles beneath his sage green sweater, and the poised assurance of someone who has always known himself attractive to women.

"Too damn bad about poor Becca," he said when he and his wife entered the interview room shortly after the Todds left.

"Boyfriend or husband?" Mrs. Kendrick asked brightly.

"Excuse me?" Dwight said.

"Oh, don't mind her," Paul Kendrick said with a self-deprecating chuckle. "She thought Becca was hot for me. I can't convince her that it was all part of the woman's sales pitch — flirt with the men, flatter the women, and maybe we won't notice the chipped tiles or where the dog pissed on the carpet."

A brief look of uneasiness crossed his handsome face when he realized that the interview was to be recorded, but his wife smiled into the camera and said, "Well, of course we don't mind, but there's really not much to tell. We met Becca at a fund-raiser for Doug Woodall when he ran for governor last year, and we called her about two weeks ago when we decided to put our house on the market. She explained how she could only work as our buying agent, so we listed our house with Cubby Lee Honeycutt and she started showing us every condo and town house in Dobbs and Widdington, too. Unfortunately none of them rang our chimes. We were going to tell her that we'd about decided to look in Raleigh or Cary instead. Real estate's a little pricier there and so are the taxes, but that's where the good restaurants are and the symphony and ballet, too, for that matter. Once we sell the house and Paul retires in another five or six years, there's nothing to hold us here in Colleton County."

"When did you last speak to Mrs. Jowett?" Dwight asked.

"Last Saturday," Nita Kendrick said promptly. "She called to say there was one more town house she wanted to show us that had just come on the market, a three-bedroom end unit, just like we'd told her we wanted, but we'd already looked at another one in that neighborhood and it was a little more downscale than we wanted."

"So you didn't go take a look?"

"No."

"Actually," Paul Kendrick said sheepishly, "I did."

"What?" His wife's pretty face registered surprise.

"Saturday afternoon. You'd gone to that baby shower for the Witchger boy's wife, so when she called again and swore that unit was perfect for us, it just seemed easier to let her show it to me than turn her down altogether. I wasn't doing anything else that afternoon and she'd put in a lot of time for us."

"That was her job," Mrs. Kendrick said. Ice frosted every word.

"I know, I know, hon. But it was something to do. As soon as I walked in the place, I knew it wasn't for us and I told her so. In fact, I went ahead and told her that we were going to start looking in Raleigh."

Nita Kendrick continued to stare at him coldly and he became even more conciliatory. "She got a little bitchy about it, so I wrapped it up and left. I wasn't there a half hour, and you know I was home before you were."

To fill the awkward silence that followed, Dwight asked if Rebecca Jowett had seemed upset or preoccupied with something other than real estate.

"She seemed the same as usual to me," Mr. Kendrick said.

"Did she ever mention problems in her personal life?"

"Not really," said Mrs. Kendrick while her husband gave a negative shrug. "She did ask how I kept in shape and said she had to run several evenings a week or she'd look like Miss Piggy." She clenched her fists and flexed her forearms as if pumping hand weights. "Paul and I work out in our home gym every morning."

For such a small woman, Dwight suspected she could throw a mean punch were she so inclined.

"Just for the record, could you tell us where you were Saturday night between seven and midnight?"

Paul Kendrick started to object, but his wife stopped him with a look.

"They have to ask, darling," she said sweetly. "After all, you might have been the last one to talk to her before she disappeared, unless Major Bryant knows of someone else?"

When Dwight didn't rise to her bait, she smiled at him. "Very well. I came home from the shower a little before six with a splitting headache, so I took some aspirin and went straight up to bed. Sleep is the only thing that helps. I woke up a little before ten, and when I came down, Paul and Mitzi were gone."

"Mitzi?"

"Our daughter's spaniel," Kendrick said. "I watched a DVD, then took her out for a walk. If you don't believe me, one of our neighbors was out with their dog, too."

"Oh, I'm sure he believes you, darling," said Mrs. Kendrick. "Although you do see that if I was sound asleep, how do we know that *you* — ?"

"Not funny, Nita. She's joking, Major Bryant."

Dwight frowned at her. "Murder's not a laughing matter, Mrs. Kendrick."

"You're right," she said contritely. "I shouldn't tease. Paul and I were both in all evening. I couldn't get to sleep right away and I heard him banging around in the kitchen for at least a half hour. I even woke up for a few minutes sometime between then and ten and heard the music from one of our favorite movies, so he was home, too."

As they watched the Kendricks leave, Ray McLamb murmured to Dwight, "That's one pussy-whipped dude. Wonder how many nights he's gonna be sleeping on the couch?"

"Sorry, Dwight," Reid Stephenson said when told why he'd been invited to stop by the sheriff's department. "I was in Southern Pines Saturday night. A command performance with the parents."

Deborah's cousin and former law partner was the firm's current Stephenson, but his father, Brix Junior, remained a powerful entity even though he was retired and had technically handed his share of the partnership over to Reid. His mother sat on the boards of a half dozen charities.

"They've found another debutante for me," Reid said with a grimace. "This one breeds hunters. Tally-ho, y'all."

Dwight grinned. "All the same, ol' son, Rebecca Jowett's calendar for Saturday night says 'Reid S' with an exclamation mark beside it."

"Yeah, well, she did call and ask me if I'd like to have a drink with her. Her husband was going to be out of town and she wanted to celebrate her first sale in over two weeks. Sounded fine to me. We hadn't gotten together in a few months and she was always good for a few laughs. Then Mother called and played the guilt card, so I asked for a rain check." He shook his head. "I've felt really bad about it ever since I heard she disappeared Saturday evening. If I hadn't canceled, you reckon she'd still be alive?"

"I couldn't believe it at first," said Larry Sokoloff, a pudgy thirtysomething. "You don't expect somebody you know to get murdered, do you?"

Newly divorced and looking for a small house with enough land to let his two goldens romp freely, he had met Rebecca Jowett for the first time last week when he walked into Coyne Realty and asked about a listing in the local newspaper. "My ex-wife got the house back in Wisconsin, I got the dogs and no alimony payments. Becca was supposed to show me a place on Sunday, but she never called. I thought she'd blown me off."

He was a cardiac nurse out at the hospital and had spent Saturday night working the four-to-midnight shift in the intensive care unit. When asked about his relationship with Becca Jowett, he'd frowned. "What relationship? It was all business."

Well, yes, he admitted, she might have flirted with him a bit, "but I'm not ready to get back in the game yet. Besides, I thought she was just being Southern."

■ ■ ■ ■

Cubby Lee Honeycutt had an exclusive for the house on East Cleveland Street, "but the damn thing may never sell after this," he said gloomily as he jotted down the name of the last real estate agent to show it before the Todds put in an offer.

When questioned, that agent said, "Yes, I showed it to a couple who were moving down from New Jersey, but they wanted to add on a wing for a mother-in-law suite and the neighborhood covenants won't allow that.

"Rebecca Jowett? Sure, I knew her. Knew who she was anyhow. We weren't really friends. Just business associates. Makes you think about showing a house to strangers, doesn't it? I've never had a bad experience, but a friend of mine down in Atlanta was almost raped." She held up the cell phone in her hand and clicked the deputy's picture. "Before I go inside a house alone, I always send a picture of the client back to my office, and I make sure they know it."

A canvass of the houses that backed up to the berm separating Grayson Village from the Ferrabee tract and the old dump where the body was found had turned up nothing. No headlights shining through the thick pine trees, no sightings of people.

"A few teenagers used to ride their four-wheelers over there when the weather was nice," one homeowner told them, "but as cold and wet as it's been, I haven't seen or heard any of them since that warm weekend back in January."

They had located some of the teenagers in question. The kids knew about the dump and had picked through it. "I got the glass door off a real old washer," one of them said. "Made me a neat picture frame." But except for a cranky Englishman who'd chased them away and threatened them with trespassing, they had never seen anyone else on the deserted land.

When she returned from interviewing the dead woman's family, Mayleen Richards reported that the parents were too grief-stricken to be of much help. "They're sure the whole world loved her, that her marriage was perfect, and that no one could possibly have a reason to hurt her."

"So what else is new?" Dwight said, remembering Dave Jowett's stunned disbelief when he delivered the bad news yesterday.

"Her sister was there."

"And?"

"She seems to be real conflicted over the whole situation. She loved her sister, but she's heard the rumors and she was angry for the way Becca cheated on her husband. From some of the things she said, I get the feeling that she might have feelings for him."

"She have an alibi?"

"She and a friend share an apartment and both of them were in and out the whole weekend."

"Hey, boss," said McLamb, who had been studying the large map of the county that hung on the wall of the squad room. "That address the Todd guy gave you. The place with the rats?"

"Yeah?"

"It's in the Creekside development on the other side of that new grocery store out near you. Less than a mile from where the body was dumped."

"Rats?" asked Richards.

Dwight briefed her on the people he had interviewed that morning. "Oh, and we got the preliminary results of the autopsy. They can't say for sure when she died, but it was around an hour after eating at least one stalk of celery with what they think was pimento cheese. I don't suppose you looked in her refrigerator?"

"No, but want me to call her husband and see?"

Dwight nodded. "And then you and Ray go out and see if you can find out when Mr. Todd got there to set his rat traps and exactly how long it took him."

"You got it, boss," Raeford McLamb said. He glanced at the clock. Almost lunchtime. "Whatcha feel like having for lunch, Mayleen? A slaw dog or hamburger?"

"Tacos," she told him with a happy smile.

CHAPTER 15

Vultures have excellent eyesight, but, like
most other birds, they have poor vision in
the dark.

— The Turkey Vulture Society

The clock at the rear of my courtroom
showed two minutes past noon and the
orange juice and scrambled eggs I'd had for
breakfast over five hours ago was long since
gone. I had virtuously skipped the bacon
and buttered toast I'd made for Dwight and
Cal, so instead of misdemeanor felonies and
supervised probations, my mind was wandering over to Sue's Soup 'n' Sandwich
Shop across the street from the courthouse.
Mushroom and barley soup. Grilled cheese
on whole wheat.

While Julie Walsh, who was prosecuting
today's calendar, pulled the shuck on the
next case, I mentally turned the pages of
the café's menu. Thursday's soup of the day

is always cream of broccoli with a heavy sprinkle of bacon. Or what about Sue's stuffed potatoes? Cheese, bacon, chopped onions.

A door opened in the wall behind me and a clerk handed my clerk a note that she passed up to me. I opened it to see Dwight's familiar scrawl: "Lunch in my office in 15 minutes?"

I scrawled back, "Make it 10," and caught the eye of the ADA. "Ms. Walsh?"

"Sorry, Your Honor. Call Ruben Oliver."

Oliver had light brown skin and shoulder-length black curls. At first I thought he was African American until he spoke and I heard the Latino accent. Twenty-four, charged with misdemeanor larceny and resisting arrest. After taking a beer from the Quick Stop's cooler, he had given the clerk the finger and strolled out of the store. Gothic black letters and symbols on his fingers spelled out the name of a gang down in Fayetteville, one that was not active in our county so far as I knew.

The clerk's testimony was brief and to the point. As was that of the police officer who had responded to the call and had to chase Mr. Oliver through a parking lot and down an alley. I had no doubt that Oliver was guilty as charged. When I questioned him about his tattoos, he swore he was no longer in a gang and wanted to start his life over in Durham, where he had relatives.

"But aren't those gang symbols on your fingers?" I asked.

He grudgingly admitted that they were and said he wished he'd never had them put on.

"If you really want to get rid of them," I said, "there's a doctor here in town who'll remove gang tattoos for free."

He thought about it a minute, then shook his head; but after I had pronounced him guilty and told him the penalties, he pushed back his hair and pulled down the collar of his shirt. There in vertical black letters on the side of his neck was the name "Estrella."

"That doctor — can he get rid of this bitch's name for me?"

"Sorry," I said and remanded him to the jailor. "This court will be in recess until one-thirty."

"All rise," said the bailiff.

Downstairs, Dwight immediately closed the door to his office and gave me the long slow kiss we had forfeited this morning so as not to embarrass Cal. I put my arms around his neck and pressed my body against his, giving myself up to the sensual pleasure of his mouth, his hands, the smell of his skin.

"Too bad your office is so small," I said when the kiss reluctantly ended. "We could really use a couch in here."

He laughed and pushed aside the papers on his desk to clear a space for the salads he'd sent out for. Tuna for me, steak for him. He's never going to give up red meat altogether, but he does try to humor me with more green veggies. Last year, that salad would have been charbroiled hamburgers and a double order of french fries.

"I hope this doesn't mean you won't be home for supper," I said.

"Nope. Not unless something breaks in this Jowett case, and I'm not holding my breath." He handed me a can of tomato juice and snapped off the plastic lids of our salads.

"Rough morning?" I shook the can hard, then popped the top and inserted a straw.

"Just that my two prime suspects seem to have solid alibis," he said gloomily.

While we ate, he told me what they'd learned about Rebecca Jowett — how she was reputed to be promiscuous and how the lingerie in her laundry hamper seemed to confirm it. "That hairdresser you told me about? She told Mayleen that she had a fresh hickey on her neck last Wednesday and it was still faintly visible when we found her. We're pretty sure Dave didn't give it to her. Anyhow, he was in Louisiana all weekend."

He described Wesley Todd, a macho type, and Paul Kendrick, who appeared more than strong enough to move a slender corpse. "We've sent her underpants out for DNA testing. See if the semen on them matches the couch. We're also sending the foam cups both men used when I interviewed them. So far as we've learned, they seem to be the only men she's been involved with who fit the time frame for that love bite." He paused and grinned at me. "Unless we count your Don Juan cousin."

"Reid?"

"He was supposed to have drinks with her that night, but he got ordered to Southern Pines instead."

Remembering Reid's exasperation with his parents' determination to see him settle down, I had to laugh. "The debutante with her own breeding stable? Yeah, he told me about that." I took another swallow of my tomato juice. "But why would Todd or Kendrick kill her? Rough sex that got out of hand?"

Dwight shrugged and uncapped a bottle of water, his choice of on-duty beverage when he's OD'd on coffee. "Whatever the motive, it's no good without opportunity. Becca Jowett's neighbor says she left the house around seven and the autopsy puts her time of death about an hour or so after eating some celery and pimento cheese. I suppose Kendrick could have sneaked out while his wife was sleeping off a headache, but she was pretty detailed about the early part of the evening."

"Any tomato juice in her stomach?" I asked, hoisting my can. "Could she have stopped off somewhere for a Bloody Mary?"

"With a side order of pimento cheese?"

"You're right. That sounds like a light snack out of her own refrigerator. So that would mean she couldn't have been killed much after eight?"

"I'm guessing eight-thirty at the latest. At which time, Wesley Todd was setting out rat traps in the Creekside subdivision and Paul Kendrick was banging pots and pans in his kitchen if we can believe their wives."

"But if she ate the celery earlier than seven . . . ?" I frowned in concentration. "What if Todd drove down East Cleveland Street on his way out of town, saw her going into the house alone, and stopped his truck — it *was* a truck, wasn't it?"

"I guess," said Dwight. "We'll have to check."

"So he stops his truck, goes in with her. They fight for some reason. He kills her and slings her in the back of his truck and covers her up with a tarp or something. Then he goes on to the client's house, sets his traps, and dumps the body on his way home." Even as I spoke, I saw the big hole in my theory. "Only there wasn't much of a moon that night, so how would he have known how to find that dead-end drop-off in the dark?"

He grinned. "Probably the same way I would, and don't tell me you never parked out there with some horny teenager either."

"Moi?" I said, knowing that my own grin was an admission of guilt. "Did Todd grow up over that way?"

"Not sure. He may be one of those Todds who used to farm some of the Creech land on Old Forty-Eight."

Dwight lifted a forkful of cubed steak and butter crunch lettuce and paused with it in midair. "If he did, that scenario of yours might work. Becca Jowett told the hairdresser that she didn't like it that rough and that whoever marked her wasn't going to get another try. So he sees her going into the house, thinks he'll have a little romp before going out to catch rats, she refuses, he flies off the handle, and bang! He's got a dead woman bleeding out on the couch. He stashes her in the truck, pulls the afghan over the bloodstain, and the rest is like you said."

He carried the fork to his mouth and I could almost see his mind working as he chewed and swallowed. "And you know something else? Ms. Coyne told me that he was the one who drew attention to that couch. *And* he was the one who whipped off that afghan. They were supposed to close today, so if they hadn't found the blood, they would have handed over their check. Now that it's known the murder took place there, they're balking at going through with it, and they may even get their earnest money back, but once their check was deposited, the bank could probably string it out for who knows how long?"

With Dwight eager to get a search warrant for Wes Todd's truck, we didn't linger over the rest of our lunch and I went back upstairs a little early to find Anne Harald and Richard Williams waiting to show me the community service plan they had worked out for Jeremy Harper.

Among Richard's many interests are gardening and flowers. Winter or summer, there's almost always something blooming in his and Carolyn's yard, and even in the throes of February he had put together a small vase for my desk: a fistful of fragrant daphne blossoms mixed with cedar and boxwood, the whole thing no bigger than a baseball.

"Lovely," I said, lifting it to my nose and breathing in the clean, sweet aroma. "So tell me what you plan for the Harper boy."

They quickly laid it out for me.

Richard was a volunteer for the disabled vets' chapter in town. "Mostly I just sit and listen to them," he said. "They want to tell their stories, to make sense of what they've gone through. We have an old man who lost an arm and a foot at Iwo Jima and a Marine who had his spinal cord severed in Afghanistan."

Anne said, "We think Jeremy can use his camera and computer skills to put together an essay about their views on war and why it was worth the sacrifice, maybe even get their views on torture and whether or not they think it works. It could be an article that one of the service magazines would want to run."

"You've spoken to them about it?" I asked. "And they've agreed?"

"They're looking forward to it," Richard said.

"And Jeremy's on board with this, too?"

"I think so. Of course, Anne's sweetened the pot a little."

"Oh?"

She nodded. "My cousin Martin that you met Tuesday night? He's agreed to talk to Jeremy about some of the interesting places his cameras have taken him."

"And Anne's giving him a tutorial in how to ask tactful questions," Richard said.

"That won't take too much time from your mother, will it?" I asked.

Anne gave a wry smile. "She and Sigrid are making an inventory of the house and I'm in the way."

That surprised me. "I should think you'd know more about what things are than Sigrid."

"I do," Anne said, and for a moment her blue-gray eyes misted over. "That's part of the problem. Sigrid can look at them more objectively than I can."

I suppose "objective" is a kinder word than "cold." I was more drawn to Anne's warmth, but if I were dying and saying goodbye to things I'd held dear, cool objectivity might not wear me down like teary-eyed emotion.

I added a note to Jeremy Harper's file. "This sounds good to me," I said. "Just make sure one of you documents his hours."

CHAPTER 16

Its primary form of defense is regurgitating semi-digested meat, a foul-smelling substance that deters most creatures.
— The Turkey Vulture Society

Major Dwight Bryant — Thursday afternoon
When Dwight and Ray McLamb, followed by Percy Denning in his van, pulled into the parking lot of Todd Pest Control, the door to the office was locked, but a flat cardboard clock face with moveable hands indicated that someone would be back at two. As it was now 2:00 on the dot, they leaned against the side of the van to enjoy the warmth of the February sun and to talk about Carolina's chances at the ACC basketball tournament next month. Despite the cool air and the diesel fumes as a semi ground its gears and eased away from the traffic light on the corner, it felt good to be outside.

At 2:04, a beige pickup with bright orange lettering pulled in beside them and Wesley Todd got out of the cab, accompanied by one of his workers. Both wore the company's brown coveralls and jacket. Todd handed the man some keys and gestured for him to go on inside before walking over to them.

"Help you, Major?" he asked warily, squinting in the bright sunlight.

"I hope so," Dwight told him. "We'd like to search your truck if you don't mind."

"Search my truck? Why?" He bristled as Denning and McLamb moved around to the rear and began to lower the tailgate. "What the hell y'all think you're doing? You're damn right I mind."

"Actually, we have a search warrant, Mr. Todd," Dwight said, pulling it from his jacket pocket. "Rebecca Jowett's body was transported from the house on East Cleveland to that dump site over near the Creekside subdivision where you were on Saturday night. We're wondering if your truck was used."

"You think *I* killed Becca?"

"You tell me, sir. You were having sex with her, weren't you?"

"Go to hell!"

Todd's big hands clenched into fists, but

before he could land the punch, Dwight caught his arm and twisted it back. McLamb hurried over and together they pinned the man into submission.

"Whoa, now," Dwight said, loosening his hold on Todd. "How 'bout you back that mule up and let's start over again."

They released him and Todd stood there rubbing his elbow where it had been wrenched. Still angry, he straightened the billed cap that had been pushed sideways in the scuffle and said, "I don't know where you got the idea I —"

"We found semen stains on that long couch you liked so much," Dwight told him bluntly. "And more stains on Mrs. Jowett's underwear. We've sent them to the SBI for DNA analysis, along with the cup you drank from in my office this morning. You willing to bet we won't get a match?"

Todd held his belligerence a moment longer, then backed down. "Okay. Yeah. We had a thing going there for a while, but that doesn't mean I killed her. We both knew it was just a fling."

His anger changed to a half-sheepish, half-smug look of masculine cockiness. "That husband of hers was a weenie and she was ready for a real man. She came on to me first and she liked what I had to offer."

"Except you got a little too rough?" Dwight asked.

"That little nip on her neck? Hell, man, that was just a goodbye present. I've got a good marriage and I'm not about to mess it up for some little fancy-pants who thought she could play with fire and not get her fingers burned. And listen, you're not going to say anything about this to my wife, are you? I'll be honest with you, okay? Yeah, I boned her, but it was over."

"You're saying *you* dumped *her*? That's not what she said."

"Huh? She talked about me?"

"Not by name," Dwight admitted. "But once we realized it was probably you? DNA doesn't lie, you know."

McLamb had gone back to searching the truck with Denning, who had finished with the cab. Now he looked over to Dwight and said, "No tarp."

"Tarp?" asked Todd. "Why would I carry a tarp?"

Both men walked around to the back of the long-bed utility truck. Side racks held an extension ladder and a stepladder. The back of the truck itself held buckets of chemicals with hazardous warnings, a sprayer, traps of various sizes, and other pieces of equipment.

"Ah," said Denning. "Missed it before."

Crammed up under the utility toolbox behind some coils of plastic tubing was a roll of heavy clear plastic sheeting.

"When did you last use any of it?" Dwight asked.

"Three weeks ago," Todd answered. "The Dik-a-Doo Motel out on the bypass. One of the outside rooms got bedbugs and we had to seal off the door and window and fumigate the place."

"We're going to have to take that," Dwight said.

Wes Todd glanced at his watch and then at the glass door of the office, where his employee could be seen looking out in curiosity. "My wife's due back here any minute, so could y'all just take what you want and leave? You know how women are. She sees you here, she's gonna want to know why, and now I've got to go make sure Salvador there don't mention y'all either. I'm asking you, man-to-man. Don't tell her about me and Becca, okay?"

"We won't. Unless it turns out you've been lying about what you did Saturday night. Just don't leave the area."

"Surprise, darling!" Paul Kendrick said, handing his wife a shiny brochure and an envelope with two airline tickets to Puerto Vallarta.

Nita opened it with the tips of her perfectly manicured fingernails and frowned. "What's this?"

"A Valentine present. I've rented us a little hacienda in Sayulita for the rest of the month."

"Sayulita?"

"Don't you remember? The Grebers stayed there last year and loved it and you said it sounded heavenly. A pool comes with the house. *And* a maid. We can be sunning ourselves and drinking margaritas day after tomorrow."

"Saturday?" Even though three weeks in Mexico implied more than the usual peace offering, she decided to be generous. After all, the little slut was dead. "I'll have to run in to Raleigh this afternoon. I don't have a thing to wear. You'll need to see about boarding the dog and get someone to keep an eye on the house."

"I don't have a thing to wear" usually meant a twelve-hundred-dollar shopping spree; but even with the tickets and the rental cost, if it kept Nita from asking more questions or consulting an attorney, he knew he was getting out cheaply.

By the time they got back, the police

would have pinned someone else for Rebecca Jowett's murder or else the investigation would have moved to the back burner. Either way, they surely wouldn't care where he was Saturday night.

"From there, I moved on to Chiclayo, then up into the mountains above Chota, where I found these nestlings — *Sarcoramphus papa* — and their parents." Martin Crawford clicked his mouse and a soaring vista of rocky crags, blue skies, and a pair of adult king vultures filled the screen of his laptop. They had bright orange patches on their heads and their black-tipped white wings spanned five feet.

It was a gorgeous picture.

Just like the other fifty or sixty gorgeous pictures he had showed them, thought Jeremy Harper, who was starting to be bored out of his skull. With Anne's cousin in the middle, he had been forced to sit shoulder to shoulder like this for almost forty-five minutes. Anne Harald had met him in the high school parking lot and led the way out here. She had promised him an interesting afternoon, and the first few slides of Peruvian fiestas with the colorfully dressed natives had been okay, but how many stupid bird pictures was he supposed to look at before he could say, "Okay, I get it," and they could move on to something better? It didn't help that a rank odor emanated from the man's clothes.

"I'm quite certain I saw those pictures I took in La Libertad just a day or two ago, Anne," he said with pedantic fussiness. "Let me see now. You were there to photograph El Diego at his house in Trujillo, correct?"

"Who's El Diego?" Jeremy asked, grateful for a change of subject.

"The greatest living Peruvian poet at the time," Anne said. She leaned forward to talk across Martin while he scrolled through one page of thumbnail vulture pictures after another so rapidly that they almost blurred. "Word was out that he was finally going to be given the Nobel Prize in Literature because his main opponent on the Nobel Committee had suddenly dropped dead. He was quite old and he had twisted his ankle while my editor was arranging the interview. Charlie — my editor — was sure that he was going to break out in waves of senility before I got there. It was a good interview, though. The man was brilliant, and he had such an expressive face that the pictures almost took themselves. A month later, the magazine ran them both as a three-page obituary."

"Huh?"

She shrugged and used her fingers to comb back the short salt-and-pepper curls that fell over her forehead. "The twisted ankle turned out to be a broken hip as well. By the time they realized and put him in the hospital . . ." She shrugged. "He got pneumonia and slipped into a coma. I was the last one to interview him."

"Wow!" said the teenager.

"Wow, indeed, young Jeremy," Martin Crawford said ponderously. "One never knows when history is going to be made. That's why you must stay alert, keep your cameras ready, and act as if this is the last bird you'll ever photograph before it goes extinct. The same with your disabled veterans. Any one of them could pop off without a moment's notice, is that not right, Anne?"

She murmured agreement, but before she could expand on her answer, Crawford said, "Now these eight pictures of a fledgling *Vultur gryphus* were taken just as it stepped up to the edge of the cliff to try its wings for the first time. Had I not been watching carefully, I would have assumed it was waiting to see a parent return with food."

Jeremy sighed and dutifully turned his eyes back to the screen. His eye was caught by one of the thumbnails at the top of the screen. Each tiny picture represented a separate file and this one looked like a Gulfstream jet.

"What's that?" he asked, pointing to the file.

"Which?" Martin moved his cursor to the top. A click of the mouse and the whole line of thumbnails was replaced by another line. He clicked a few more times, but that picture never reappeared. "Oh, dear. I'm always losing my place."

"It was a small jet," Jeremy said.

"Jet? Oh. Probably one of those puddle jumpers that one must use to get off the beaten paths. Now here's an interesting group of —"

"Could I talk to you a minute, Martin?" Anne said, interrupting him. "Outside?"

"Certainly." He pushed back his chair and handed the mouse to Jeremy. "Just keep left-clicking," he said. "I'm not sure, but this may be the file where I came across some nubile young women bathing in a river. Very naughty of me to take their pictures before they realized a man was within miles, but you may be amused."

He stood and followed Anne, who had already grabbed up her coat and opened the door, letting in a welcome wave of fresh air.

Once they were out on the porch, she turned to him and said, "What the hell's going on?"

"Going on? You asked me to speak to the lad about my work."

"You're supposed to be filling him with enthusiasm for a rewarding craft. The adventure of travel. The dollars and cents of selling an article. Instead, you're narrating a very bad travelogue and putting us both to sleep."

Her cousin looked offended and stepped onto the ground so that he could sit on the edge of the porch. The pasture that spread out and away before them was a palette of subtle browns and burnt sienna. Tufts of pale yellow broomstraw and patches of dried weeds with dead flower heads waved in the light breeze that blew up from the creek. Dark green pines swayed majestically in the distance and the pasture itself was dotted with tiny green seedlings. In another few years, those pine seedlings would reclaim this pasture if no one mowed it or built houses out here.

At the bottom of the slope, two large vultures were perched on the ruined masonry wall that stuck up from one side of that concrete slab. Two more circled overhead.

"You're acting like a caricature of a pompous British colonial," Anne told him. "I almost expect you to say, 'Pip, pip, old chap,' or 'Cheerio!' *Naughty* of you? Oh, please. If you didn't want to talk to him, why didn't you just say so?"

"I could hardly say no when I'm using your mother's hospitality to gather material for my article, now could I?"

"*No* is all you've been saying since we got here, beginning with that disgusting odor you're wearing," said Anne, who had carefully positioned herself upwind from him.

"Eau de vulture vomit?" He chuckled. "They do insist on regurgitating on me if I'm not careful when I handle them."

"You *handle* them?"

He realized instantly that he had slipped and smoothly recovered. "I've banded a couple, yes. I thought I'd leave the information with the local wildlife service in case they wish to follow up on my observations. But you're right and I apologize for my behavior. I've got a lot on my mind right now. My editor's getting impatient, so I'm hoping to wrap this part up by the weekend and get back to England to finish writing the article and edit my photographs."

Anne had dealt with enough cranky editors over the years to sympathize.

"Okay," she said. "I'll let you off the hook for Jeremy, but you have to come to dinner again before you leave. Mother has a few small family things she wants you to have."

"Done," he said.

The keyboard of Martin Crawford's laptop might have been in Arabic, but arrows are international symbols, and as soon as Crawford and Anne Harald went outside, Jeremy Harper slid the cursor to that top row of thumbnails and clicked the left arrow until he came to the file with an airplane, then clicked to open it. The screen filled with more tiny pictures and it took him a moment to realize what he was looking at.

With one eye on the computer and the other on the window that let him see the two adults, he pulled a jump drive out of his pocket and inserted it in the computer's USB port. A few more clicks and that file was copied and the jump drive back in his pocket.

When Anne Harald returned with her smelly dull cousin, he made himself look like the clueless nerdy kid they seemed to think he was, ogling the pictures of naked young women splashing in a jungle pool.

As soon as his cousin and her do-good

project left, Martin Crawford stripped off and put those befouled trousers out on the porch. With a little luck he would never have to wear them again. He filled a basin with warm water from the kettle and scrubbed himself until all the stench was gone. Dressed again in clean clothes from the skin out, he opened both the front and back doors to let cold fresh air blow through the whole house.

All credit to Anne and the boy, he thought, still surprised that they hadn't left the instant they got a whiff of him.

But he was getting careless. Not merely that slip of the tongue with Anne, but leaving his computer alone with that boy. Happily, the screen appeared to be as he'd left it, and his mail program was password-protected had Jeremy tried to open it. Nevertheless, it had been a stupid mistake.

Especially now, when everything was coming to a head.

CHAPTER 17

Turkey vultures are masters of soaring flight — which is by far the most energetically efficient form of travel. In fact, flying turkey vultures use only slightly more energy than they do when standing on the ground doing nothing.

— The Turkey Vulture Society

Thursday afternoon
Both of Jeremy Harper's grandparents and his mother worked, so the modest three-bedroom house on the edge of Dobbs was empty when he parked out front that afternoon and went straight to his bedroom.

As he waited for his PC to wake up, he shucked off his jacket, turned his cap backwards so that it would keep the frizzy silver curls out of his eyes, and unwrapped the striped scarf from his long thin neck, fuming with impatience.

It sucked that his computer was so slow.

He knew he was supposed to be grateful that his mother had scored this one when her company updated all their hardware, but jeez! Snails ran faster than this antique hunk of junk he was stuck with. He thought longingly of the Mac Pro that a friend had gotten for Christmas. All Sam did with that state-of-the-art laptop was play games and cruise the net for porn sites that hadn't been locked out by his parents. If he had that machine and a decent photo editing program — !

Fat chance of that happening anytime soon, he thought gloomily. His Burger King job barely paid for gas and car insurance. No way was he ever going to save $3,500 for a Mac and the expensive software program that would let him work magic with the pictures he took.

At last the screen stopped blinking and he clicked on the photo app. Another wait for it to load, then he slipped his jump drive into the USB port and opened the file he'd copied from Martin Crawford's computer. As he scrolled through the pictures, his curiosity deepened.

Not buzzards and definitely not Peru.

Each picture was time-stamped, beginning with Wednesday morning a week ago and ending with Monday; and most were aerial views of the Colleton County countryside. Not just anywhere in the country either, but out at the county airport. There was that little block building that acted as office and terminal and there were the hangars. And damn! Look at the clear shot of that little Gulfstream!

Each scene seemed to have been shot in bursts of three. He adjusted the focus until he could read the fuselage numbers. He jotted them down and switched over to his search engine. As part of his Patriots Against Torture activism, he kept the FAA bookmarked, and soon he was searching their database for the owner of this plane. When the name popped up and he Googled it, he was disappointed to realize it belonged to a local insurance agency and not to some shell company that might be fronting for the CIA.

The wings of a Learjet could be seen off to the side, but even at extreme magnification, he could not make out any details.

As one three-picture set after another of the airstrip and the surrounding area scrolled past, he puzzled over how Martin Crawford had taken them. Had he rented a plane and flown back and forth over the strip at a low altitude? A hot air balloon?

He flicked back to the beginning and saw three aerial views of the shack where the ornithologist was staying. The details were amazing. There was Possum Creek and Grayson Village and there was Crawford's truck parked next to something square down near the creek. Another click or two and he was looking down on a flying buzzard, the back of its ugly red head and ruff of feathers clearly visible, and there on the ground so directly beneath that only the face of the foreshortened figure was clear — Crawford himself. He seemed to be holding up some sort of small device that was pointed straight toward the camera. Cell phone?

"Holy shit!" the boy whispered to himself as the problem of viewpoint crystallized into certainty. "He's put a miniature camera on one of those damn birds!"

Why?

Jeremy leaned back in his chair to consider the implications. Clearly the device Crawford held was a remote that could trigger the shutter of the camera.

And all those pictures of the airstrip. Was the man a spy? If so, who for? What was an Englishman who used an Arabic keyboard doing here in Colleton County? Was he planning to rescue someone from one of those rendition flights or to blow up the place or what?

As one wild scenario after another filled the boy's head, one thing was becoming clearer. Here was a story a hell of a lot more interesting and potentially more profitable than interviewing wounded veterans. Only how to go about it without letting Anne Harald or Martin Crawford realize what he was up to?

Once again he went slowly through the pictures, bringing each up to its maximum magnification so that he could see every detail. And that's when he spotted them — three pictures that would surely be worth $3,500.

Thirty-five hundred? *Hell, make it 5,000,* he thought as he printed out the pictures.

The only real question was whether to make the call today or wait till morning. He ejected the jump drive, hid it where he was sure no one would ever find it, then went looking for the Colleton County phone book.

Taking a handful of the cheap throwaway cell phones from the satchel in his bedroom, Martin Crawford checked that all were still completely switched off before he put them in his jacket pocket. He had paid cash for the phones at different electronics chain stores in Raleigh, and his name was not connected with any of them. Nor had they been turned on since he drove out of Raleigh.

Before leaving the shack, he made sure that his own personal mobile was switched on and under the pillow on his bed. Modern technology was a wonderful thing, but it could also trip you up if you weren't extra careful. Cell towers could and would track a phone that was switched on even if not in use.

It wasn't much of an alibi, but better than nothing if he needed to claim that he had never left the place that evening. Not that he expected it to come to that.

Twenty minutes later, as the sun slid toward the horizon, he was seated in his nondescript black truck at a strip mall on the eastern edge of Cotton Grove, where he called a local motel that he could see from where he sat. As with so many motels around the South, this one was owned by a low-level consortium of Pakistanis.

When a clerk answered, he adopted an Egyptian accent and asked if an Alex Franklin had checked in yet.

"I'm sorry, sir. We do not have reservations for Mr. Franklin."

Crawford thanked her, broke the connection, and checked his mental list of passport aliases the man commonly used. This time he pinched his nose and used a high-pitched French accent. "Do you have a Frank Alexander staying there?"

"Yes, sir. Will I connect you?"

"No, I'll just come over when I get in. What room is he staying in?"

"So sorry, sir. I cannot be telling you that."

"Never mind. I'll call back once I fly in tonight. We're giving him a surprise party. Do you know if any of our other friends have arrived yet?"

From the clerk's voice, Crawford gathered that she was young and not too long in this country. "I am not knowing, sir. No one is saying this to me. Will you be needing a room, too, sir?"

"No, I usually stay with friends."

He ended the connection, pocketed the SIM cards from both phones, wiped his fingerprints, then crushed the two phones he had used under his foot and deposited them in trash barrels at opposite ends of the small town.

He waited a full 35 minutes before calling the motel again, and this time he used his stepmother's accent. Within minutes both were speaking Punjabi. He lent a sympathetic ear when the girl admitted that she was more homesick than she had expected to be, and a mild joke made her giggle. Two minutes later, he had extracted the room number and assured her that yes, there was indeed a surprise party of old friends in the works. She promised not to tip Mr. Alexander off.

Again he crushed the phone and tossed it in the weeds, then drove to another quiet spot where he used a wire cutter to reduce all of the three SIM cards to shreds of plastic and copper before strewing them along his route.

And then he waited.

CHAPTER 18

Many vulture species around the world live closely associated with human societies.
— The Turkey Vulture Society

Maidie Holt, Daddy's longtime house-keeper, had asked me to pick up a couple of bags of stone-ground yellow grits from the only store in Dobbs that carries that brand. The local grist mill has been in operation since the 1830s, and no commercial grits taste as flavorful. As long as I was getting them for her, I bought a bag for myself. There was a package of shrimp in the freezer that we had brought home from Harkers Island in the fall. They needed to be eaten before they got freezer burn, and shrimp and grits is an easy dish that doesn't take too much preparation. I knew I had onions, a green pepper, and half-and-half on hand, so I wouldn't have to stop at a grocery store.

The version I make calls for some sort of fancy Italian ham, but my brother Robert cures out a mean country ham with a smoky, salty flavor that can't be matched by anything from Italy and he always gives us five or six pounds of it for Christmas every year, each slice individually wrapped for the freezer.

According to him and Daddy, our winters used to be cold enough to let the legs and shoulders hang in the smokehouse all winter without spoiling. No more.

A quarter cup of Robert's ham diced and sautéed would easily substitute for pancetta, but no other brand of grits could substitute for the bags on the car seat beside me.

As I drove west out of Dobbs, it seemed to me that the days were getting noticeably longer. Time was passing much too quickly, though. Turn around twice and it would soon be summer — sandals, cotton slacks, and sleeveless dresses. What with the growth spurt Cal had taken this winter, I doubted if there was much he could still wear from last summer. Unfortunately, he likes to shop for clothes just about as much as Dwight does, but maybe I could issue a bench warrant for the two of them and haul them both out to one of the Raleigh malls this spring.

They say time is relative, and to prove it,

228

Einstein supposedly compared a minute of sitting on a red-hot stove to a minute of kissing your lover. Driving into the sunset past pine thickets and dormant fields, I wondered how Sigrid, Anne, and Mrs. Lattimore were experiencing time these days. Was it zipping past or dragging?

I turned into the lane that led to our house, then took a cutoff that would take me across the farm to the homeplace. Bare-twigged oaks and maples formed a delicate fretwork against the orange-and-purple sky, reminding me of the stained glass windows in the church where Mrs. Lattimore's funeral service would probably be held before summer. Even though Daddy's almost never sick and always gets a good report on his annual physical, Mrs. Lattimore's terminal illness made me doubly conscious of his eighty-plus years.

His old truck was parked at the back door, and without knocking, I opened the squeaky screen door, then the heavy wooden one, and walked into the kitchen where he and Maidie were. Both sat at the kitchen table and both were in their stocking feet. Maidie was taking the meat off a roasted chicken, carefully putting the skin and bones into a pot with chopped onions to make broth for pot pies. Daddy had spread a newspaper over his end of the table, and several pairs of shoes, including Maidie's, waited for his attention. Despite the pungent onions, I could smell the shoe polish he had spread on the leather, a familiar homey aroma.

I hugged them both and snitched a bit of chicken while Daddy reached in his pocket to pay me for the grits. Maidie fumbled in her own pocket and came up with only two quarters.

"Don't worry about a bag of grits," he told her. "I didn't give you no birthday present yet."

"Ain't my birthday," Maidie said, her gold tooth flashing.

"Then it must be Cletus's. Tell him happy birthday from me."

"You mean you ain't gonna get him that white Cadillac he's been wanting?"

"What'd he do with the red one I give him for Christmas?" Daddy asked in mock indignation.

I laughed. Those two have been teasing each other for most of my lifetime, long before Mother died. They tried to get me to sit down and visit, but I told them Dwight and Cal would be wanting their supper soon.

"Y'all gonna be home this evening?" Daddy asked.

"Dwight's probably already there and I'll be there myself in a few minutes. Why?"

"Nothing really. Just ain't seen Dwight to talk to this week."

"Then come on over for supper. I'm fixing shrimp and grits."

He looked at Maidie, who gave a dismissive wave of her hand. "Go on. You'll not be getting anything that good here. I was only gonna warm you up some stuff from last night."

"Well, if you're sure," he said, speaking to both of us.

"Come!" I said.

"Go!" said Maidie.

By the time Daddy joined us, Cal had finished struggling with his math homework — fractions — and Dwight had picked up the newspapers that had been scattered around the couch when I came home.

I spooned the grits into a ring on a large serving platter and now I finished thickening the creamy sauce and poured it over the pile of sautéed shrimp in the middle.

"Yum!" said Cal as he speared a shrimp on his fork.

I knew I'd find a little pile of diced green pepper on the side of his plate when supper was over, but on the whole, Cal's not a fussy eater, so I don't nag. Dwight and I have a two-bite rule. He has to eat at least two bites of everything served, but then he's free to fill up on bread and whatever else is on the table. No way am I going to lock horns in pointless food fights. He gets plenty of fruits and vegetables and it all balances out in the end.

Conversation was general at first because Dwight and I both know from long experience that Daddy will get around to saying whatever he wants to say in his own good time. We caught up on family news. Only six of my eleven brothers live out here on the farm, but two more live in Dobbs, so we stay in fairly close contact. We're not as close to the three who live out west, but Daddy said Adam had called from California a couple of nights ago.

"Everything okay with them?" I asked.

"Far as I could tell," Daddy said. "Sure didn't say nothing worth a long-distance phone call."

He's from the generation that remembers when calling out of the state cost a dime or more a minute and it bothers him to talk more than three minutes even when he's been told over and over again that there's no extra charge.

"He did say Karen's mama won't doing

too good and she may fly out here next week if somebody could meet her at RDU."

I made a mental note to email Adam's wife and ask for details of her flight.

Eventually, Cal finished eating and asked to be excused. He carried his plate over to the sink and then went into the living room to settle down in front of the TV.

Dwight split the remaining shrimp between our three plates and Daddy said, "I heared y'all know that buzzard man that's staying across the creek over yonder."

There was no point asking who he'd heard it from. Daddy's web of informants stretches across the county and not much pertaining to him or his slips past unnoticed.

"Ferrabee Gilbert's boy, right?"

"You knew her?" I asked, surprised.

"Naw, both them Gilbert girls was older'n me. I just used to see her around town once in a while 'fore she run off to Washington. Pretty little thing. Prettier'n her sister, and you know how she's still a good-looking woman. Never quite understood how come ol' Ben Lattimore turned Ferrabee loose for her. Her boy must take atter his daddy, though, 'cause I don't see none of her in him."

"You've met him?" Dwight asked.

"Well, I didn't sit down and eat supper

with him like y'all did, but yeah, I met him."
He cut a shrimp in half and I wondered if
Chloe Adams had talked to Maidie, who
has her own network of informants.

"They say he writes picture books about
buzzards?"

"That's right," I said.

"See, the thing is, I've watched him feed
them buzzards. Even seen him pick some of
'em up and put bands or something on their
legs."

I was intrigued. "The buzzards let him do
that?"

"Ain't all that unusual. Remember my
cousin Bud? He raised a buzzard chick that
got blowed outten its nest. They tame real
easy. But I ain't seen this man take no
pictures of 'em. Course now, I only watched
him a couple of times and it may be that he
goes somewheres else to take pictures. They
follow him, you know. Follow his truck anyhow."

"What's really bothering you about him,
Mr. Kezzie?" Dwight asked, cutting to the
chase.

"You know that dirt road that runs along
the back of the airport? Garrett Road?"

I didn't, but Dwight nodded.

Daddy took a forkful of grits and smeared
them in some of the sauce on his plate.

"Him and them buzzards go there almost every day it ain't raining. There or to Johnson Mill Road."

"That goes through the woods on the other side of the airport, doesn't it?" Dwight asked. "What does he do?"

"Nothing," Daddy said flatly. "Once or twice he just parks on the side and sets there. Sometimes when he hears somebody rattling down that dirt road, he'll lean back and put his hat over his eyes like he's sleeping, excepting atter they go past, he sets back up again and watches them buzzards kettling up over the truck."

He took a large swallow of his iced tea. "I heared he was out there on Garrett Road around noon today, so I rode over to take a look. He had his jack and a spare wheel laying beside the right back wheel next to the ditch, so I stopped and asked if I could be of help. He thanked me kindly and said that he could handle it, so I drove on."

"But?" Dwight asked.

"That tire won't flat, Dwight, so why was he playacting that it was? What's he doing out there?"

CHAPTER 19

Generally, turkey vultures do not kill.
— The Turkey Vulture Society

Thursday night
The knock on the door of the motel room came shortly after seven.

"Yeah?"

"Barbecue Pit," said a muffled male voice.

With his hand on the automatic in his pocket, the man inside said, "Hold it up to the peephole."

Not that he was going to look. He hated these damn things. Apocryphal or not, the story had gone around a few years back about someone being shot through the eye he'd used to see who had knocked, and he never used one if he could avoid it.

Instead, he pushed aside an edge of the window curtain and peered out.

Reassured by the familiar face of a kid who had delivered to him on his last trip and the logo on the white paper bag the kid was holding up to the peephole, he let the curtain fall, unlocked the door, and handed over a couple of bills.

"Keep the change," he said expansively.

Although the tip was barely eight percent of the bill, he planned to add his usual twenty percent to this receipt before he turned it in with the rest of his expense chits. They had deep pockets and they never questioned him about small things, but two dollars here, three dollars there — it could add up to a tidy yearly sum. He wasn't getting any younger and a man had to shore up against retirement, didn't he?

He popped the top on a can of beer that had chilled in his ice bucket, then removed the lid on the foam take-out plate and felt his mouth water as the aroma of vinegar and roasted pork reached his nose. He had been born in Texas, and grilled beef ribs drenched in a fiery tomato sauce with jalapeño cornbread on the side would always be his favorite, but the chopped pork barbecue of eastern North Carolina and its deep-fried hushpuppies sure ran Texas a close second.

He unwrapped the plastic utensils and napkins and dribbled a packet of Texas Pete over the fragrant meat before turning his attention back to the weather channel on his TV screen. They had planned for him to refuel here and fly on to Maine tonight, but a vicious little ice storm up there had closed the Bangor airport so he'd been ordered to wait it out till morning.

A secure bunkhouse occupied a corner of the hangar here, but it didn't have television and it didn't have beer and he sure as hell didn't feel like listening to the moans and curses of the prisoner he was ferrying up from Gitmo. The medic refused to give him another knockout shot till they were ready to put him back on the plane tomorrow morning. *Been up to me,* thought the man, *I'd have given him a knockout shot to the head with a monkey wrench.*

He devoured a crispy hushpuppy in one bite, then picked up the remote and clicked over to a basketball game. According to the announcer, Duke had a good chance to win the NCAA championship this year.

Shortly before ten, Martin Crawford crossed the motel parking lot and moved silently along the side to the room number the clerk had given him. He had already checked that there was no security camera on this side, only on the reception area. Nevertheless, before putting his ear to the door, he kept his hat pulled down and his scarf pulled up until he had unscrewed the overhead light-bulb with a gloved hand. From within came an announcer's excited voice and the televised roar of a sports event.

A tiny crack in the curtain let him see the whole room: a rumpled bed, a handgun on the nightstand beside it, and a glimpse of movement in the bathroom beyond.

He's getting fat and sloppy, Crawford thought to himself as he picked the lock. He was prepared to kick the door in if necessary, but to his surprise, the man had also neglected to put the safety latch on. In three steps, Crawford had crossed to the gun and dumped its clip onto the floor.

A moment later, the man walked out of the bathroom, bare-assed, still damp from his shower, toweling his hair dry.

"Guess what, Al?" Crawford said. "Your pals didn't quite kill me after all."

Chapter 20

Extremely unaggressive and non-confrontational, the turkey vulture has only rarely been documented to feed on still-living prey.

— The Turkey Vulture Society

Dwight Bryant — Friday morning

The first call came at 8:07, only minutes after Dwight got to the office and poured himself a cup of coffee.

"Major Bryant? Dwight? It's Anne Harald. I'm sorry to bother you so early, but Mrs. Harper called and she's worried. She says Jeremy didn't come home last night."

"Who?" Dwight asked.

"Jeremy Harper. One of your mother's students. He was arrested for trespassing out at the little county airport. Richard Williams and I are supposed to be monitoring his community service."

"Oh yeah, Deb'rah told me about that."

"We both left my cousin Martin's place a little after four yesterday and no one seems to have seen him since. She's called everyone she can think of. I just wondered if you'd heard anything?"

"Sorry," Dwight told her. "But teenage boys aren't noted for telling their mothers where they'll be every minute. He probably spent the night with friends and will show up at school this morning."

"Well, maybe," Anne said doubtfully. "But if you hear anything . . . ?"

"I'll call you," he promised.

Sigrid was not a morning person, but the aroma of full-bodied coffee and Martha's made-from-scratch cinnamon rolls had rousted her from bed, and she entered the dining room in time to hear the end of Anne's call to Dwight.

"The Harper boy's missing?" she asked as she filled a cup from the silver urn on the sideboard.

"His mother thinks so." Anne bit into a soft warm roll that oozed with vanilla icing. "I just hope it's teenage thoughtlessness and that he's not sticking his nose in things that don't concern him."

Following her mother's train of thought, Sigrid said, "Like that woman they found out near Martin's place?"

Anne nodded. "If he got it in his head to investigate on his own . . ."

Her voice trailed off in uncertainty and concern.

Sigrid immediately thought of the homicide Dwight and Deborah had stumbled into when they were in New York last month. A boy had gone missing in that case, too, and his mother's pain was too fresh in her mind to let her tell Anne not to worry. "Have another cinnamon bun," she said.

The second call was a 911 logged in at 10:14. An accidental death out at the Clarenden Arms Motel on Highway 48 near Cotton Grove. A man had slipped in the bathtub and managed to break his neck.

"On our way," Dwight said.

Twenty minutes later, he stood in the bathroom with the local medical examiner and stared down at the nude body of a middle-aged, well-nourished white male who looked as if he had fallen backwards into the tub while standing under the shower and hadn't moved since.

Richards came to the doorway holding a wallet in her gloved hand. "According to his driver license, he's Frank Alexander, fifty-three. From McLean, Virginia. The manager says he's a private pilot who's stayed here before."

Dwight nodded and turned back to the ME, who lived in Cotton Grove and had arrived several minutes before them. "In a fall like this," he said, "you usually just get a partial break. Looks to me like his neck snapped like a stick, almost as if he went over backwards and banged his neck on the edge of the tub without trying to break his fall. If it's between the C-2 and C-3 vertebrae, that would cause almost instant death. We'll know better when we take a look at his neck."

"Time of death?"

"Too soon to know. No rigor, but that doesn't mean much. The maid said the shower was still on when she came in to clean the room at ten. As soon as she found him, she called the manager, who turned it off. Warm water, so it's hard to get an accurate reading of his temperature. Cleanest corpse I ever saw." He gestured to a nail clipper on the sink. "One fingernail torn into the quick, the rest trimmed down to the nub. You can bag his hands, but I can guaran-damn-tee you there's nothing there."

Dwight automatically scanned the bathroom floor but saw no nail clippings. The wastebasket was empty, too, not even the usual plastic liner.

"Any defense marks?"

"None that I can see. No sign of a struggle either unless you count the torn nail, and that could have happened earlier. Right now, I'd call it an accident pure and simple."

He half turned the body so that Dwight could see where the blood had pooled in the man's buttocks. "And that reminds me. You'll be getting the report in the next couple of days on the Jowett woman."

"Any surprises?" Dwight asked as his eyes roamed the bathroom.

"Naw. What you saw was what we got. Two strong blows to the head. We found her facedown, but her butt looked just like this, too, so she was moved."

"Well, we knew she wasn't killed out there at the dump."

Dwight stepped back into the bedroom just as Deputy Richards lifted a greasy white bag from the wastebasket. The stiff paper crackled when she opened the bag with her gloved hands. "Looks like he had a couple of beers and takeout from the Pit," she said. "Want me to run by and ask?"

"We'll do that," someone said.

Dwight turned and saw a tall black man who filled the outside doorway. Two equally large white men were directly behind him.

"And you would be?" he asked mildly.

"FBI," the man said and held up his badge. "Agent Sherman Pritchard. Mr. Franklin was one of ours."

"Franklin?" Richards looked at him dubiously. "His driver license says Alexander. Frank Alexander."

Agent Pritchard just smiled. "Right. Like I said. One of ours."

Dwight's own boss edged around the big men. "Sorry, Dwight. I had a call from the AG himself. It's theirs now."

Despite the departmental budget crunch, Sheriff Bowman Poole was not one to give up jurisdiction lightly. That he was turning this over to the feds without a fight must mean that strong words had come down from above.

Acknowledging the inevitable, Dwight nodded. "Fine. You'll share the results of your investigation with us?"

"Anything pertinent?" the FBI agent said. "Absolutely."

"Don't hold your breath," Bo Poole muttered to Dwight as they headed back to their respective vehicles.

The sun was high in the sky when Martin Crawford stepped out onto the porch with a steaming mug of tea in his hand. For the first time in months, he had slept deeply, without the nightmares that had plagued him for so long. He felt as if a great heavy darkness had been lifted and left him — if not filled with cleansing light, then certainly with the possibility of that light.

He yawned and gingerly flexed his left arm. It still throbbed with pain and he wondered if he had wrenched something loose again. As soon as he got back to London, he would have to try another round of therapy, see if that would help him regain his strength. His right arm felt just fine.

He buttoned his jacket against the cold north wind and reached back inside for his hat, then walked out into the sunshine.

The vulture he had tamed circled overhead with its two mates, then gracefully floated down to the concrete slab he whimsically called his vulture table. The other two followed.

"No breakfast for you chaps this morning," he called with a cheerful salute of his mug. "Time you went back to foraging on your own."

Even as he spoke, though, he realized that something had caught their interest on the other side of the slab. One vulture had perched on the ruined brick foundation and seemed to be peering over the edge. The other two had settled on the ground. As he watched, one of them hopped closer and dipped its neck to pull at whatever it was. Puzzled, he saw the featherless head come up with something striped in colors.

It took a moment to realize he was seeing the Harper boy's scarf.

Concerned, he left his mug on the edge of the porch, hurried over to his truck, and sped across the meadow.

The vultures flew up as he circled the slab and skidded to a stop. He immediately recognized that mop of fair hair. The Harper boy lay in a heap at the base of the wall and he did not move when Crawford called his name.

No response, and when he touched that still white face, the skin was cool and clammy. Yet just before Crawford despaired for the boy's life, his fingers found the barest thread of a pulse on the side of his neck. Blood had oozed from the back of his head and matted the frizzy blond curls. He hesitated.

Move him and risk further damage, or leave him to go call for help?

Cursing because he had left his phones at the house, he swung back into the truck and tore across the meadow.

Moments later, he had called 911 and succinctly described the situation and his location. "The lad's name is Jeremy Harper. He appears to have a serious head injury."

Dwight was eight or ten miles from the old Ferrabee place and still fuming over the FBI's usurpation of that motel death when the call came in about the Harper boy. He signaled to the cruiser behind him and pulled a circle in the yard of Holy Tabernacle AME Church.

Just as they arrived at the intersection near his favorite grocery, an ambulance from Western Wake Medical Center bore down on them, siren wailing and lights flashing. Dwight figured he knew the exact location better than the driver, so he streaked around it with his own lights and siren and led them through the unpaved road to the dead end, then down the lane and across the pasture to Crawford's buzzard table, where the Englishman waited. Almost before Dwight could cut his engine, the EMS crew were out of the ambulance to work on the teenager, who lay sprawled on the ground beside the far edge of the slab, his arms thrown across his chest and his legs under his body as if he'd been dumped there feet first.

The next few minutes were organized

chaos as they loaded Jeremy Harper into the ambulance and headed back to Wake.

"How did he get here?" Dwight asked, looking across the slab. It was littered with tufts of brown fur and small dry bones that crunched beneath his feet as he walked over to the edge and looked down at where the boy had lain.

Martin Crawford shook his head. "I haven't a clue, Major. He wasn't there at sunset, when I came down to give the vultures a dead rabbit, and I didn't see any lights before I went to bed. Didn't hear any motor either. Without electricity, I usually turn in early and get up with the sun, but I wrenched my arm yesterday and it was bothering me so much that I took a couple of sleeping pills, so it was after ten before I awoke and perhaps another hour before I stepped outside and saw one of the birds come up with his scarf. I guess they thought it was some sort of fur." He shook his head. "Poor kid. I hope he makes it."

"Someone drove past your windows and you heard and saw nothing?"

"They didn't necessarily drive past the house, Major. See those trees down there? There's a rough track along the creek bank."

"So you know about that track, do you?" Dwight asked with a sardonic lift of his eyebrow. "That's how you found that woman's body, right?"

"Now, Bryant. I thought I satisfied you on that."

"Oh, you did," Dwight drawled. "You certainly did."

CHAPTER 21

While remaining on the lookout for food,
vultures are equally attuned to their fellow
vultures. They note when others' behavior
indicates the discovery of a food source,
and will flock to the area.

      — The Turkey Vulture Society

Friday morning (continued)
"Major Bryant," Deputy Richards called.
"Look!"

Between the slab and the thick young
pines, a short stretch of dead grass and
weeds clearly showed that something had
recently passed that way and bent the stems
to the ground. A vehicle had driven up to
the slab, then circled around to leave the
way it had come.

Deputy Denning had arrived with the
crime scene van before the paramedics
moved young Harper onto a stretcher; but
by then, the ground there was too thor-

oughly trampled to yield usable tracks even had there been any. Now he walked over with his camera to try and document the ones Richards had noticed. Unfortunately, there were no apparent tread marks in the grass that would help identify the tires.

"I'll backtrack, see if I find anything useful," he told Dwight and headed slowly down through the trees, carefully staying to the side, his eyes alert to any stray cigarette butt or scrap of trash that might be found.

Dwight watched pessimistically. Any tire tracks Denning might find could well be his own. He had driven through from the dump site in his own truck after Rebecca Jowett's body was found over there on Wednesday. He said the same when that officer returned with pictures from three different tires.

By then, he had called Anne Harald and asked her to let the Harper boy's mother know that her son was on his way to Western Wake. As a journalist, she immediately launched into the five Ws — who, what, when, where, why? — but he had a few Ws of his own.

"Where did he go when he left you yesterday? Who was he going to meet?"

"He didn't say, Dwight. I assumed he was going home. Back to Dobbs. He did seem in a hurry to leave, but I think that was because Martin smelled like rotten skunk. One of those buzzards had vomited on him and it was rather disgusting, to say the least."

"Did he mention any enemies? Anybody he might have fought with?"

"I only met the kid Wednesday after Deborah agreed to let us set up a community service project for him, so I barely know him and I certainly don't know who might have wanted to hurt him. Where was he found?"

"I'll get back to you," Dwight said and ended the call.

"My cousin couldn't help?" asked Martin Crawford, who had lingered within earshot.

"What about you?"

"I wish I could," the Englishman said, "but as Anne must have told you, I met the lad for the first time when she brought him by yesterday. I doubt if they were here an hour. She thought I could inspire him to build a career with his photography skills, but he seemed bored by what I had to say and I'm on a tight deadline with my article, so we agreed I couldn't help. Do you suppose this has anything to do with the dead woman?"

"Why do you say that?"

"Two bodies dumped in roughly the same

area? It would be quite a coincidence, wouldn't it?"

"Coincidences happen," Dwight said mildly. "Speaking of coincidences, would you mind explaining your interest in our little local airstrip?"

"My interest?"

"You've been spending quite a bit of time out there. The locals have seen you on several occasions."

Crawford looked puzzled. "Really? I've driven around the area to look for roadkill and to test the limits of how far the vultures will follow my truck now that they associate it and me with food, but I wasn't aware of favoring any one particular spot." He smiled and pointed overhead where a distant buzzard was only a winged dot against the sky. "That one always seems to know when I'm outside. It's rather amusing actually. I stopped to buy a few supplies at that supermarket down the road and two of them perched on the roof to wait for me to come out. I hope no one interprets that as a commentary on the freshness of the food inside."

Dwight was halfway to the hospital before he realized that Crawford had not asked what he meant when he said "speaking of coincidences."

■ ■ ■ ■

Mrs. Harper and her mother were in the ICU waiting room. Both women were anxious and distrait and neither could offer a theory as to why Jeremy had been hurt and left for dead.

"He's not a popular kid," said Marcie Harper, who was as tall and skinny as her son with a slightly tamer version of the boy's silver-blond curls. "But no one ever picked on him as long as Steve was around."

"Steve?"

"His brother," Mrs. Harper's mother said. Whereas her daughter and grandson were tall and thin, she was short and stocky, with flat dark hair worn in a modified mullet. "He was killed in Iraq three years ago."

Boxes of tissues were scattered around the room and Mrs. Harper blindly reached for one. "Jeremy's all I have left." Tears rolled down her cheek. "I can't bear to lose him, too."

"Marcie?"

Although the women were dressed in tailored office clothes — Dwight later learned they both worked for the state in adjacent government buildings behind the capitol — the man who diffidently approached wore khaki trousers and shirt and a denim windbreaker with his name and the logo of an oil company stitched on the left breast pocket. Mid-forties, with thinning brown hair, he paused a few feet away as if unsure of his welcome.

"They just called me," he said. "Is he going to be all right?"

Mrs. Harper's mother bristled protectively. "Like you care, Frank?"

"He's my son, too, Ida," he said quietly and turned to his ex-wife. "Marcie?"

"They don't know," she said, her voice breaking. "They're working on him, but they haven't told us anything yet. His head — he could be paralyzed or permanently brain-damaged . . . oh, Frank!"

He opened his arms to her and she went without hesitation, weeping on his shoulder as he held her tightly.

Dwight left them and asked a nurse to direct him to the hospital's security chief. After explaining the situation, he said, "We don't know why someone wanted to kill him, we don't even know *if* they did. It could still be an accident and the person panicked and dumped him, thinking he was dead."

The security chief saw where Dwight was going. "You're asking us to keep an eye on him on the off chance that someone will try to finish the job?"

Dwight nodded.

"Don't worry, Major. Long as he's in ICU, only family members will be able to get in and he'll be under someone's eye all the time."

When he got back to the waiting room, the Harper family had been joined by Richard Williams, whose calm good humor comforted Jeremy's grandmother, who still seemed to resent her ex-son-in-law's presence.

An anxious Anne Harald was there, too, and she pounced on Dwight immediately. "Was this something to do with his trouble out at that rendition airport?"

Until then, he had almost pushed the incident at the Clarenden Motel to one side of his mind. Even though there was no way she could have heard about that pilot's death, Anne's question brought it front and center and she seemed to sense the difference.

"Does it?" she pressed him.

"I don't know," he answered, "but it's certainly something to think about."

He left his card with the Harpers and asked them to call if they thought of anything, no matter how trivial, that might explain the attack on Jeremy.

A half hour later, he was seated in the principal's office at West Colleton High.

His mother was distressed to hear about the attack on one of her students, but she had her secretary pull his records and she sent for the yearbook advisor who had worked with Jeremy most closely.

Neither woman could suggest a reason for anyone to hurt Jeremy.

"He doesn't have a lot of friends, but I can't say he has any enemies either," said the advisor, who had once sat behind Dwight in freshman algebra. "As your mom told you, his brother's camera seemed to give him focus, no pun intended."

"Freshman year was hard on him," Emily Bryant said. "His brother's death, his parents' divorce, losing their house here and having to move over to Dobbs. He blamed his dad for everything even though the poor man got downsized from his office job and was out of work for months. I think he was still coming to terms with all that."

Dwight's former classmate nodded. "Like most kids, there's never enough money for all the electronic toys they think they need. He was particularly hot to get a more powerful computer with the latest software for editing his pictures, and once his father

258

found a job, Jeremy thought he ought to make good on all the missed child-support payments by buying him one."

Yes, they knew about his affiliation with Patriots Against Torture and they did not question the sincerity of his commitment, but all he had done was march and protest. His arrest for trespassing was the most confrontational thing he'd done, and even that carried no personal animus for anyone unless it was Deputy Tub Greene, another of Miss Emily's former students.

"Tub does like wearing that uniform," she said dryly.

Back at the office, Dwight sent for Tub Greene. While he waited, he dispatched a deputy to talk to the PAT people over in Kinston and had McLamb brief him on the status of Rebecca Jowett's murder.

"No progress," McLamb said. "We're still waiting on the DNA results. Wesley Todd's alibi checks out. He set traps out there in Creekside Saturday night and the first set of traps were retrieved early the next morning."

"First set?" Dwight asked.

"Yeah, his wife set out fresh ones Sunday morning and caught two more, according to the customer. Right now, they're rat-free and ready to give a testimonial to the Todds for prompt and efficient service."

"What about Becca Jowett's other client, Paul Kendrick?"

"Again, nothing to link him till we get the DNA tests back. He may have screwed her, and his wife's alibi for him is flimsy, but I think it's sincere."

At least Richards was able to tell him that Deputy Sam Dalton had made an arrest in the arson case on their plate. As they had suspected, the property owner was upside down on his mortgage and had torched the place for the insurance.

Tub Greene seemed bewildered by Dwight's request to account for his movements from four o'clock the afternoon before, but he answered promptly that he had gone off duty at four, then he and his girlfriend had driven over to Chapel Hill for dinner and the ball game. He did turn a little pink when saying that it had been a late night.

Dwight grinned. "Like till daybreak?"

"Will that be all, Major?" Tub asked, turning even redder.

Bo Poole passed by his open door as Greene was leaving.

"You eat yet?" the sheriff asked.

Dwight looked at his watch. Nearly 2:30. No wonder his stomach was rumbling. He should have taken his mother up on her offer of a tray from the school's cafeteria.

They drove over to a chicken place and Dwight finished briefing his boss as they sat at a Formica-topped table with a basket of biscuits and fried chicken between them.

"Your turn now, Bo," he said to the small-sized man with the outsized personality. "How come the attorney general turned that accident over to the FBI?"

"Why's the sky blue? Why's water wet?" Bo said. "It is what it is, Dwight. We all know the CIA calls the shots out there at the airstrip. It stinks that they send men to be tortured overseas, but the AG can't buck them any more than I can buck him. Ours not to reason why they don't want us investigating an accidental death."

He dipped his biscuit in his side dish of gravy and looked at Dwight with shrewd brown eyes. "Unless it's not an accident?"

"Our ME thinks his neck was broken here." Dwight touched the back of his own neck, high on the nape. "Takes a hell of a concentrated force to do that, Bo."

"He could have fallen on the side of the tub."

"True. Except that he was lying on his

261

back as if he'd fallen straight back. You saw the way that tub sloped down. Hard to land on your neck with that much force. You might bang your head, but your arms and shoulders would normally break your fall."

"What else?" Bo asked.

"He had one torn fingernail and the rest of them were cut down to the quick and looked like they'd been scrubbed with his toothbrush or something, but I didn't see any nail clippings and the plastic liner from the bathroom wastebasket was gone."

"Somebody making sure there was nothing under the dead man's nails that could tie him to the scene?"

"Or he could have given himself a manicure in front of the TV with all the clippings buried in the rug," Dwight said. "We'll never get a chance to look for ourselves, and I doubt if Agent Pritchard's gonna tell us."

Bo Poole leaned back in his chair and his wise brown eyes crinkled with cynical amusement. "Well, now, there's more than one way to rob a henhouse, ol' son. And I bet we both know a few black snakes. You talked to Terry Wilson lately?"

"A couple of weeks ago, but he's SBI, Bo, not federal."

"And you think he don't know any of them?"

"Wouldn't hurt to ask," Dwight agreed.

Back in his office, Dwight put in a call to his longtime friend. He and Terry Wilson were old fishing buddies from when he first came back to the county and Mr. Kezzie invited them out to try their luck with his bass. It was inevitable that Deborah would meet him, too. Just as inevitably Terry made a play for her, since everyone, including Deborah herself, assumed that Dwight felt only a brotherly affection for her. He'd been forced to watch their flirtation and to show no emotion when she confided to him that it might be getting serious.

In the end, Deborah realized that Terry's son and his job would always come first. "And I don't want to come third," she told Dwight. "He's fun to hang out with, but he's not marriage material."

Terry took the rejection philosophically. "Hell, Dwight. After three divorces and two broken engagements, this ain't the first time a woman's told me no. Probably not the last time either. Tell you one thing, though — I've bought my last diamond ring."

"You bought Deborah a diamond?"

"Well, naw, but I was thinking about it till

I saw what Lee's first year at State was costing me."

After that Deborah treated Terry like yet another brother and the three of them stayed friends. Terry still came out to the farm to fish with Mr. Kezzie and Cal even called him Uncle Terry as if he were Rob or one of the Knott brothers.

"Hey there," Terry said when he recognized Dwight's voice. "Guess what? I just bought me a diamond ring."

"Huh?"

"Yeah, I know I said never again, but we've been living together almost as long as you and Deborah, so —"

"You and K.C.?"

"Well, who the hell else would it be?" he asked indignantly.

K.C. Massengill was a sexy little blonde, one of the SBI's best narcotics agents until she was promoted to a division head and an office job around the same time that Terry came in off the streets. Dwight remembered Deborah's glee when she told him that Terry had moved into K.C.'s house out at Lake Jordan and how K.C. had shrugged and said, "He's probably only interested in my bass boat."

"Y'all settin' a date or is she just in it for

the jewelry?"

"Right now, we're looking at the last Saturday in June, after Lee's graduation. You know what they say, Dwight — fourth time lucky. You and Deborah be sure and save the date."

Dwight congratulated him, then asked if he'd heard about the death out at the Clarenden Motel.

He hadn't, but after listening to as many of the details as Dwight could give him, Terry promised to see what he could learn. "It may be on into next week 'fore I can tell you anything."

"That's okay."

"Pritchard's a tightass, but why do you care if he takes over? Less work for you guys."

"I just like to know what's going on under my nose," Dwight said.

And why, he wondered after hanging up, was it under his nose anyhow? Why Colleton County?

According to an in-depth story in the *New York Times,* a story that he'd heard confirmed in sub rosa conversations, the usual scenario for small jets had them flying from Gitmo to here for refueling, then from here to Bangor and back again. In Maine, it was said that prisoners were put on a larger plane and flown to Shannon, Ireland. From there, the destination would be to some hellhole that wasn't hampered by human rights watchdogs.

Despite the *Times* story, most people around the county neither knew nor cared about those flights, so who in Cotton Grove would want the man dead? Maybe he and the ME were overthinking the whole thing. Maybe it really was an accident.

On the other hand, Bo was right. They did know people. And not just local SBI agents.

Dwight reached for the phone again. His Army Intelligence days were several years in his past, but he had kept in touch with a couple of former colleagues who could ask discreet questions through back channels. At least he might learn who this so-called Frank Alexander of McLean, Virginia, really was, see if he had any ties to the area, just in case it turned out to be a private killing and nothing to do with what he did for a living.

Maybe it was a jealous husband. Or a scorned mistress. Hell, it could even be somebody pissed off because he'd quit supplying them with Cuban cigars.

CHAPTER 22

Both parents share the responsibilities of
incubating and caring for the brood.
— The Turkey Vulture Society

The weekend started off uneventfully.
Dwight and Cal were home before me on
Friday, and as soon as I opened the garage
door to the kitchen and smelled sage and
onions, I knew that Dwight had started
roasting the two chickens I'd buttered and
seasoned the night before. Roast chicken
for supper tonight, hot chicken sandwiches
tomorrow night, and if there were any
scraps left over, chicken pot pies on Sunday,
with lots of peas and carrots under the crust.

Dwight poured me a bourbon, heavy on
the Pepsi, to go with his beer, and we took
our time over the meal while discussing our
plans for the weekend. They mostly consisted of no plans and our phones did not
ring once. Cal talked us into a game of crazy

eights after supper, then two chapters of *The Hobbit* before he started yawning and got ready for bed.

When I asked Dwight how his investigations were going, he told me about the maybe not so accidental death out at the Clarenden Motel and how the FBI had claimed jurisdiction because the victim was a pilot and, quote, "one of theirs," meaning that he was possibly connected with those rendition flights.

I had heard about the attack on Jeremy Harper from Richard Williams.

"The doctors told Richard that he could be in a coma for two weeks until they get the swelling down," I said as I finished loading the dishwasher. "Was he hurt because he tried to take pictures of those airplanes?"

"Too soon to know, shug. He was left near where we found Rebecca Jowett's body, so yes, it could be related to her death. On the other hand, he did spend an hour out there with Anne Harald and Martin Crawford yesterday."

I followed him over to the couch with my coffee. "Did you tell Crawford he's been seen loitering around the airport?"

"Yep, and he claims it's a total co-incidence. He says he was only experimenting with those buzzards, seeing how far they would follow him."

"You believe him?"

Again that noncommittal shrug as he reached for one of the seed catalogs that had begun to pile up on the coffee table. "What kind of corn you want this year? Silver Queen or Seneca Chief?"

"Seneca Chief," I said promptly. "Yellow over white? No contest. But it's too early to plant."

"Yeah, but Seth's putting together an order for family and I need to let him know what we want."

I laughed. *"We?"*

We had agreed last year that he would keep our garden small, because I don't like to spend my summer weekends freezing and canning vegetables. All the same I wound up with several quarts of tomato puree for spaghetti sauce and more than a few packages of corn and butter beans.

"Haywood and Robert are coming over tomorrow morning to disk in the garden and run a few rows for garden peas. Time we got them in the ground. February's half gone."

"We do not need a *few* rows," I said. "One row will be plenty."

"Not if you give away as many as you did last year." He grinned, knowing full well that my generosity was so I wouldn't have to shell and freeze them.

On the other hand, our kitchen gardens tend to be communal. My sisters-in-law will come pick whatever we don't want, just as we'll raid their late tomatoes and okra if we forget to keep ours watered through the heat of summer.

We were up fairly early the next morning, but my brother Haywood arrived on one of the big farm tractors even earlier. While Cal rode his bike down to the road to fetch the newspaper, Dwight started a pot of coffee and I made sausage patties to go with waffles. Isabel has asked us all not to feed him, but Haywood always assumes we've fixed enough for him, and as soon as he got a whiff of that sausage, heavily seasoned with sage, he climbed down off the tractor, washed up at the kitchen sink, and sat right down at the table in happy anticipation.

I doubled the waffle batter and added extra patties to my black iron skillet.

"Bel only set out cereal and fruit this morning," Haywood said, beaming when the waffles began coming off the iron. He slathered on the butter and added a pool of maple syrup. "A man cain't go all morning on just cereal and fruit."

Cal finished his waffle in record time and went outside to clamber up on Haywood's tractor. While we ate, Mayleen Richards called. She had spoken to Jeremy Harper's doctor minutes before.

"No change in his condition," Dwight told me when he'd hung up, "but it looks as if whoever did it caught him off guard. The doctor says he was probably hit twice, just like Rebecca Jowett. No defense marks on his hands or arms. He told her that if the second blow had landed on the same spot, he'd be dead now. All the same, it's still too soon to know how much permanent damage there'll be. The good sign is that neither his hands or feet are drawn up like they'd be if he was paralyzed."

I topped off his coffee and he cut into a second waffle as Haywood was finishing off his third.

Minutes later, another deputy called to report that Jeremy Harper's blue Toyota had been found in the NutriGood parking lot only a few miles away.

I half expected Dwight to go running over, but he told the officer to question all the clerks there once the stores opened and to keep him informed. When he saw my look of surprise, he grinned and said, "Well, you're always telling me I have good people and that I need to trust 'em to run with the ball."

"And besides," said Haywood, "you got them peas to plant."

Three more cups of coffee later (and another round of waffles for Haywood), our brother Robert pulled up on a smaller tractor rigged with plows to run rows.

"You was supposed to be done disking by now," he scolded Haywood, "but here you set, feeding your face. Bel's right. You're just digging your grave with your teeth."

Since Robert's not exactly a beanpole either, Haywood didn't pay him any mind. He climbed back up on the John Deere and headed out to the garden site. I handed Robert up a mug of coffee with a spoonful of the honey he likes and he told me that his wife Doris planned to take their grandson to see *The Lion King* that afternoon. "She says she'll take Cal and Mary Pat and little Jake, too, if y'all pay for their tickets and popcorn."

"What do you think?" I asked Cal when we were in the car to pick up the other two for the day to give Kate a break.

He gave me a big thumbs-up. Despite computer games and DVDs, all three children are entranced by the big screen.

Or maybe it's the popcorn.

■ ■ ■ ■

We got back to the house in time to wave goodbye to Robert, who had finished running precise, ruler-straight rows where Haywood had disked. I love the smell of new-turned dirt, and soon I had a hoe in my hands, too. Dwight and I each took a row and sent the children ahead of us to drop two peas into the furrows at a time, three or four inches apart, then he and I used our hoes to cover them and firm the soil.

Despite the cool air, it felt good to be out working in the sunshine. Dwight pruned dead branches from the azaleas and other flowering shrubs, and the children and I piled them for a bonfire. Then the kids washed up and finished working on their valentines for Monday while I made lunch.

Doris picked up Cal and his cousins in time for the two o'clock matinee. After a morning out in the fresh air, Dwight turned on a ball game and stretched out on the couch. I sat down in a nearby lounge chair with a basket of clean laundry and we watched Carolina run up and down the court while I folded T-shirts and underwear.

I meant to rest my eyes for only a minute, but I must have drifted off, because it was halftime before I opened them again, and Dwight was sound asleep. I quietly put away the folded clothes and went out to the kitchen to make a salad to go with the hot chicken sandwiches I planned for supper.

He woke up when the kids came back and sat up yawning. "Want me to run them over to Kate's?"

"No, I'll do it. You watch the rest of the game."

Instead of heading toward the garage with us, Cal sat down on the couch beside Dwight and I realized that he and Mary Pat must have butted heads over something, because they didn't bother to tell each other goodbye.

Mary Pat claimed the front seat as her right now that she was almost ten, while Jake buckled himself onto the booster seat that the state requires and that he'd have to keep using for another couple of years, to his chagrin.

"You and Cal have a fight?" I asked when we were under way.

She shrugged and didn't respond, but Jake said, "She called Cal a scairdy cat."

"Shut up, Jake," she said tightly.

"Scared of what?" I asked.

"Nothing," she muttered.

"He's too scared to —"

Before Jake could tell, she rounded on him. "I mean it, Jake. *Shut up!*"

"I don't think your mom would appreciate that kind of talk," I told her.

We rode in silence till we reached the end of our drive and were out on the hardtop, then she looked at me and said, "How come you won't adopt Cal?"

I was so startled by her question that I almost ran off the road.

"What?"

"He thought you'd adopt him when Mom and Dad adopted Jake and me, but you didn't and now he's too scared to ask you why. Don't you love him?"

"Well, of course I do."

"Then how come?"

"I didn't know he wanted me to," I managed to say. "Are you sure he does?"

She gave a firm nod and I heard murmured agreement from Jake.

"And he wants to call you Mom, not Deborah. Like Jake and me call Aunt Kate and Uncle Rob Mom and Dad now."

"Do they know about this?" I asked.

She shook her small head. "Cal made us promise not to tell them, but he never said I couldn't tell you."

Even though I was shaken to the core, I was still amused by the way she could split

275

hairs like a budding lawyer.

"I hope you'll both keep that promise a little longer," I said.

That evening, after Dwight had tucked Cal in for the night, I went down to his room alone and sat on the edge of his bed. I hadn't felt this nervous and unsure of myself since the night Dwight proposed.

Enough light spilled in from the hall for me to see Cal's puzzled expression as he looked up from his pillow. Bandit lifted his furry head from the other side of the bed, then settled back beside Cal with a doggy snuffle.

Fingers crossed that I could come up with the right words, I smoothed his hair and said, "Mary Pat told me why she called you a scairdy cat."

He seemed to freeze, then pulled the covers up to his chin with his fists clutched in the quilt. "She's a big blabbermouth," he blurted angrily.

"But is she right, honey? Do you want me to adopt you?"

He pulled the covers even tighter and gave a shrug so like one of Dwight's that I wanted to hug him then and there. "I don't care," he muttered.

I put my hand on one of his clenched fists.

"Adoption's a serious thing, Cal. I love you and I'd really like to be your legal mother, not just your stepmother, but you have to want it, too."

He didn't say anything, just looked at me wide-eyed.

I made myself smile. "Of course, there are drawbacks. You won't be able to say you don't have to mind me because I'm not your mother."

That almost got an answering smile from him as we both remembered that incident from last summer, and I felt a slight easing of tension in his fist.

"And you don't have to stop loving your first mother either. Look at how many new people you've learned to love this year — Granddaddy, all your new uncles and aunts and cousins. That doesn't make you love Dad or Grandma less, does it?"

He shook his head solemnly.

"So you think about it," I said, "and if this is something you really want, we can talk to Dad about it in the morning, okay?"

Silence.

"Okay," he whispered at last.

Breakfast was awkward the next morning even though Dwight was clueless and I tried to act normally. Cal talked to Bandit and avoided my eyes. Finally, I went into the bedroom, did my hair, and got dressed.

When I came back out, Dwight frowned. "I thought we were skipping church today."

"You and Cal are, but I haven't seen Aunt Zell and Uncle Ash in over a week, so I thought I'd go to church with them this morning."

Relieved, he settled back with the Sunday papers while I put on my coat and found my car keys, then paused as I opened the door to the garage. "Besides," I said, "Cal has something he wants to talk to you about."

Cal gave me a stricken look, but before either of them could speak, I was out of there.

With my phone switched off.

When Mother died, I quit talking to Daddy and all my brothers except Seth, dropped out of college, and ran off the rails for a while. Too much tequila let me almost kill the car jockey I briefly married, and I headed for New York. When I finally came home, it was to Aunt Zell's house in Dobbs, not the farm. They had turned part of their second floor into a self-contained apartment for Uncle Ash's mother and it had sat vacant since her death. Aunt Zell had never given up on me, and because Uncle Ash was still out on the road as a buyer for one of the large tobacco companies, they both assured me I would be the one doing them a favor if I moved in and kept Aunt Zell company.

Aunt Zell is like Mother with the edges smoothed off — a "good woman" as opposed to a "good ol' gal" — and she seemed happy to see me when I pulled into their drive just as she and Uncle Ash were setting out for church.

She could always read me like a book, but her only comment as she tucked her arm in mine was, "Your menfolk aren't with you?"

The minister's text for the sermon was Psalm 118:24: "This is the day which the Lord hath made; we will rejoice and be glad in it."

I took that as a good sign. All the same, a whole flock of swallowtails were doing barrel rolls through my chest when I drove down the long winding lane to our house. As soon as I neared the closed doors of the garage, though, I started laughing. In leftover red paint, a crudely lettered banner stretched across the whole width:

CONGRATULATIONS, NEW
MOM!!

IT'S A BOUNCING BABY, HALF-GROWN, SON!!!

CHAPTER 23

In deserts, or areas with rocky soils or insufficient fuel for cremation, disposal of human remains by vultures may be the best and cleanest option.

— The Turkey Vulture Society

Major Dwight Bryant — Monday morning
Next morning when Dwight drove Cal down to the road to meet the school bus, Cal said, "Can I tell Mary Pat and Jake that she's going to adopt me?"

"*She?* She who?"

Cal's brown eyes sparkled with mischief. "Judge Knott," he said, gurgling with laughter.

Until Deborah mentioned it yesterday, Dwight had not noticed that Cal had quit using her name unless there was absolutely no way to avoid it.

But when Deborah told him he could start calling her Mom if he wanted to, that didn't seem to come easily either, so she had laughed and turned it into a game. She made him say "Mom" ten times in a row, then pelted him with questions that he had to answer "Yes, Mom" or "No, Mom."

"And you have to say 'Son, son, son,' " he told her, which sent her reeling around the house in silly introductions that left him in giggles.

"Mister Bandit, have you met my son?"

"Major Bryant, I'd like you to meet my son."

To her own reflection in the mirror: "Hey, I hear you have a son now."

She downloaded the simple three-page adoption form — *Petition for Adoption of a Minor Child (Stepparent)* — and Dwight had looked at it in disbelief. "That's it?"

"You wish. We're in for at least one home visit and evaluation by Social Services and God knows what else. But we can drop this off at Ellis Glover's office tomorrow, get the ball rolling. If we're lucky, we could be official by April or May."

"That long?" Cal was dismayed.

"It'll be worth the wait," Dwight said. "If I know your new family, they'll have a big pig-picking to celebrate."

"And lots of sparklers," Deborah promised, her blue eyes shining.

■ ■ ■ ■

"Talk to you a minute, boss?" Mayleen Richards said.

When she first joined the department, Richards was a farm-bred, sturdily built young woman from Black Creek with freckles across her prominent nose and cinnamon brown hair. After dumping both her dull marriage and her equally boring job in the Research Triangle, she had pestered Bo Poole till he took her on. Now she lived in a one-bedroom apartment over a garage on the outskirts of Dobbs and was estranged from her conservative family, who were appalled that she had taken a Mexican lover, even though Miguel Diaz owned a flourishing landscaping business and was an American citizen. Originally hired for her computer skills, she had worked her way up to detective, and she and Raeford McLamb were now Dwight's most trusted deputies.

"Sure," Dwight said. "What's up?"

"Mike threw a fiesta this weekend and I got to talking with one of his cousins. She told me that she works out at the Clarenden, the four-to-midnight shift. I know we've been warned off, but she was on duty Thursday evening with another woman. Jasmeet. I guess she's Pakistani or Indian. Anyhow, this Jasmeet told Mike's cousin that at least two men called Thursday evening to ask if a Frank Alexander was registered. The first one didn't want to be connected to the room because he said he and some friends were going to surprise him. But he did want to know the room number, which she didn't give him. The second man was from the same place she is and spoke her language, so when he seemed to know about the surprise party and asked for the room number she gave it to him even though that's against the rules."

"A surprise party, hmm?"

"Yes, sir. Mike's cousin doesn't want to get her friend in trouble, but she thought somebody ought to know. And after they heard that the FBI was calling him Alexander Franklin, Jasmeet said she thought somebody had called earlier asking for that name."

"Alexander Franklin, Frank Alexander. Interesting. Mike's cousin wouldn't happen to know what language this Jasmeet speaks, would she?"

"Poon-something?" Mayleen asked doubtfully.

"Punjabi?"

"Yeah, that's it."

"Did Jasmeet tell the FBI?"

"I don't think so. Mike's cousin says she's afraid of what their boss would say if he found out, so if you pass it on, could you leave out the part about her telling the room number?"

"You know I can't make that promise, but don't worry about it. I'm sure the feds are gonna solve this without our help."

"Right," she said, and started to leave when something caught Dwight's eye.

"You say Mike threw a fiesta this weekend? Wouldn't have anything to do with that rock on your finger, would it?"

Even though she had suddenly flushed a bright red, she looked down at a diamond solitaire that was at least a three-quarter carat and wiggled her fingers. "What? This ol' thing?"

"Your family finally come around?"

She grimaced and shook her head. "Never gonna happen, I'm afraid, so I told Mike we might as well quit waiting. We're thinking Easter and I'll need to put in for some time off because he wants to take me to Mexico and meet the rest of his family."

They were interrupted by Ray McLamb, who came bounding in, dapper and sleek with the pencil-thin mustache he had recently grown. His brown face was creased with laughter as he grabbed Richards in a bear hug and swung her around even though she was almost as tall as he and could probably spot him a few pounds. "Congratulations, girlfriend!" he said. "Want us to throw you a bridal shower?"

She laughed. "Been there, done that. Got more crock pots and silver picture frames than I'll ever use. Oh, and I forgot to tell you, Major: I called the hospital this morning. Mrs. Harper thinks he tried to squeeze her hand when she spoke to him."

"Hope she's right," Dwight said.

"But we still don't know if he's connected to the Jowett murder or that pilot's, do we?" asked McLamb, getting serious.

"Or neither," Dwight told them. "And I don't think he's going to be able to tell us himself anytime soon, so that's our first priority. Why don't you go back and talk to the real estate agent, the Todds, and the Kendricks? See if they've remembered anything useful. And ask if any of them knew Jeremy Harper or had a connection to the airfield. Talk to Richard Williams, too. Maybe the kid confided in him."

"What do you want me to do?" Richards asked.

"How about you get on the computer and see what you can dig up on that group that organized the demonstration out at the airport. When she tried his case last week, my wife says he testified that they don't have a physical headquarters, just an Internet site. Dalton didn't have much luck in Kinston, so see where the links take you."

He reached for his phone as they left. It was still his most useful tool in any investigation, especially since the hiring freeze had left the department at least three people short. Too soon to ask Terry if he'd learned anything, but he did connect with the SBI lab to ask where they were on the DNA samples they'd submitted.

"I moved it to the front of the line for you, Major," the lab tech said, "and I'd appreciate it if you'd tell Special Agent Massengill just how helpful I was."

Dwight chuckled. "You got it, son."

"I won't be able to send you the written report for another day or two, but unofficially, we got two matches."

"Two?"

"She was a busy little beaver, Major. Semen on the first pair of pants matches sample number two. On the second pair, sample number one. Number one was also on that upholstery sample. There was another stain on that upholstery, but it's a lot older and doesn't match with either of the two men."

Dwight carried his notes down to the crime scene lab that Deputy Denning had set up and told him the results. "Remind me of the sequence," he said.

Denning pulled up the file on his computer screen and a picture appeared of the contents of Rebecca Jowett's laundry hamper, laid out on the floor in the order in which they had been retrieved.

"Number two is Paul Kendrick; number one is Wesley Todd. So here's where we found Kendrick's semen," Denning said, pointing to a lacy item that had come from near the top of the hamper. "Down here at the bottom, Wesley Todd."

"So she got it on with both clients about a week apart?" Dwight asked. "First Todd and then Kendrick?"

"That's what it looks like," Denning agreed.

"Kendrick did say she showed him a condo on Saturday afternoon."

Denning grinned. "Wasn't all she showed him, was it?"

He clicked his mouse a few more times till he came to pictures of the tire tracks he'd found Friday morning. "Two of 'em are yours, Major, but this one isn't."

The picture showed a crisp ripple pattern.

"Unfortunately, it's a common make and too new to show an individualized wear pattern. But see over here? Looks like a roofing nail's embedded there, so if we found the right tire, we could tie it to that lane."

Dwight's cell phone rang as he walked back down the hall. It was their medical examiner. "Thought you'd like to know the autopsy results on that motel death."

"They let you attend the autopsy?"

"Get real, Dwight. But professional courtesy still means something in my field, and I've seen the preliminary report. Like I thought, the spinal cord was severely damaged near the top of the spine, between C-3 and C-4. That means spinal shock and almost instantaneous death. He had a minor scratch on the back of the neck and one very light bruise, but he died too quickly for significant bruises to form."

"What about that scratch?"

"Just a shallow tearing of the epidermis. Approximately two centimeters long, no more than two millimeters wide. And he could have done it himself earlier. Oh, and absolutely nothing under his fingernails."

"Are they calling it an accident or murder?"

"Right now, it's labeled a suspicious death."

"I don't suppose they named any suspicious names?"

"Not that my friend's heard."

"He give you a time of death?"

"Well, a barbecue plate with slaw and a side order of extra hushpuppies was delivered a little after seven Thursday evening and he died about two or three hours after eating it. Assuming he finished it off right away, that would put the TOD between nine and eleven. Unless, of course, he waited for everything to get cold."

"Not hardly likely, is it?" Dwight said.

He spent the rest of the morning catching up on paperwork, then met Deborah up in Ellis Glover's office at noon. Tall and thin and completely bald except for a tonsure of straight white hair that circled a dome as shiny as any ivory billiard ball, their clerk of court had hooded eyes and ascetic straight lips. Give him a monk's robe and he could have stepped out of a medieval painting, but he was all smiles today as he showed Dwight where to sign the consent to adoption form.

Afterwards, as they walked out into the sunshine, Deborah said, "What do you feel like eating?"

"Anything but barbecue," Dwight said.

By late afternoon, reports were starting to roll in. Mayleen had contacted various PAT members from around the Triangle who had been at the demonstration where Jeremy Harper was arrested. They all expressed surprise and concern to hear he'd been attacked, but could offer no valid reasons why. As far as she could gather, none of them were particularly close to the boy. They approved his enthusiasm for ending torture, but thought he went off half-cocked in his advocacy of more militant action. "He brought a bolt cutter to one demonstration, for God's sake," said one PAT member. "He wanted us to cut a hole in the chain-link fence and storm one of the hangars. Like there were any prisoners being held there. It's just a refueling stop, not a terminus."

"They did have one funny story, though," Mayleen said. "Jeremy was right about how they change the registration numbers on the fuselage, only sometimes they're not as clever as they think they are. They sent me pictures of a Learjet with one set of numbers on the left side and an entirely different set of numbers freshly stenciled on the other side."

■ ■ ■ ■

"Sorry, Major," Ray McLamb said, "but Ms. Coyne couldn't give us anything more, and neither the mother or the sister ever heard her mention the airfield except to say that's where Mr. Jowett flew out of on a private plane Friday night. Rebecca Jowett was never out there so far as they know and the husband says the same thing."

He flipped through his notepad. "Todd was out on a call, but Mrs. Todd was there and she walked us through how long it would take to set those traps in the house and up in the attic. How they had to find where the rats got in and seal up the holes. Did you know that female rats can get pregnant at three and a half weeks?"

"Never thought about it," Dwight said.

"Of course, they only live about a year in the wild," McLamb said, "so I guess they have to get an early start. Not like a damn crow that can live twenty years."

Dwight grinned, having heard his deputy's annual rant about how crows stripped the pear tree in his backyard.

"And all the times check out?"

"Yessir. She said he left the house around six-thirty Saturday night. She took the children over to her mother's to spend the night and he drove straight out to the client's house. That checks. The client says he got there around seven and spent at least an hour and a half setting the traps and looking for rat holes. According to Mrs. Todd, he got home a little after nine."

"What about Kendrick?"

"Now that's an interesting problem. He and his wife flew to Mexico this weekend."

"They did?" Dwight frowned and leaned back in his padded chair.

"A neighbor gave me their daughter's phone number and she was really ticked about it. Seems Kendrick called her and told her she had to come get her dog. That he was taking her mother to Mexico for Valentine's Day, only they aren't due back till the end of the month."

"Some Valentine present," said Dwight. "Well, we can wait, but if he's not back by the first of March, we might have to issue a fugitive warrant on him."

"Speaking of Valentine presents, is it okay if I take off now?" McLamb asked. "I forgot to buy Lillie anything and I'll be in the doghouse the rest of the week if I don't show up with something." He paused in the doorway. "How'd it get to be that men have to buy the valentines and the anniversary cards?"

"Damned if I know," Dwight said, secure in the knowledge that he had it covered.

He slid on his jacket, picked up his hat, and was reaching for the light switch when his desk phone rang.

To his surprise, it was one of his old Intelligence buddies. "Your dead pilot? Yeah, he's CIA all right. Up until last year, he was stationed at Shannon. Then he was yanked back here and reassigned to the flying equivalent of a desk job."

"What happened? What'd he do?"

"I don't have any details. No names either. Sorry, pal. All I know is that there was a scuffle on a flight to Warsaw last spring where he was copilot. His story was that the prisoner somehow got loose and killed an agent who was hitching a ride back to the UK. All my source could tell me is that both bodies were cremated in Berlin without an autopsy or any official investigation. It wasn't the first time he'd been involved in something like this where the prisoner somehow got loose and wound up dead, but this was the first time another agent died. For what it's worth, nobody's shedding any tears over this guy's death. I hear it's going to go down as an accident pure and simple.

Hope you don't have a problem with that."

"Hope I don't either," Dwight said. He thanked his friend and sat back in his chair, his mind teeming with one wild scenario after another. No matter how he tried to put the pieces of the two deaths together, they seemed totally unrelated, with the Harper boy their only common denominator.

Was it a coincidence that he'd been left halfway between Crawford's house and the site where they'd found Rebecca Jowett's body?

Despite Crawford's innocent-sounding explanation, he and Jeremy had both been interested in the airfield and the dead man was a CIA pilot making a layover there, something he'd done before according to what the motel manager told Mayleen before the FBI showed up and took over.

So where did Martin Crawford and his interest in the airfield fit in?

Martin Crawford had reported Becca Jowett's body. He'd found the boy, too.

Another coincidence? Like —

Well, damn! he thought.

The other night Crawford had mentioned that his stepmother was Pakistani. Dwight swiveled around to his computer and quickly Googled Pakistan. As he'd thought: one of the major languages of that country was Punjabi, the native language of that clerk Jasmeet out at the Clarenden.

An ornithologist?

Like hell.

More like MI6.

Yes, Crawford had written books on the subject and no doubt he led informative bird tours. In Dwight's experience, good spies usually had a real expertise in some area or other: archaeology, primitive art, engineering, sociology — anything that would explain why an average-looking, innocuous man might be bumbling around in a foreign country.

He reached for his phone again and was soon talking to his sister-in-law. "Kate?"

"Hey, Dwight. Cal just told us his news. That's so great."

"Thanks, but that's not why I called."

"You're going to be late picking him up?"

"No, I was wondering if you'd do me a big favor."

"Sure, what is it?"

"Could you invite Deborah and me to supper tonight? Along with Sigrid and Anne and their cousin? And make it sound as if it's your idea, not mine?"

"Are you serious?"

"I know it's short notice, but —"

"Dwight, you do know it's Valentine's

Day, don't you?"

"Oh, damn! I'm sorry, Kate. I guess you and Rob already made plans?"

"Actually, we didn't, but we're an old married couple. You and Deborah are still newlyweds. Aren't you taking her out to dinner?"

"Nope. Lucky for me, she doesn't seem to care about Valentine's Day."

Kate laughed. "Okay, you bring the beer and I'll see if I can round up the others."

As he left the parking lot, Deputy McLamb remembered that he was supposed to interview Richard Williams, the Methodist youth minister who was mentoring Jeremy Harper. On the off chance that he would be at home this late in the day, McLamb parked in front of the house on a side street a few blocks from the church and was gratified when Williams himself came to the door.

"Well, hey there, Ray," he said jovially, reaching for the younger man's hand and pulling him into the house. "Carolyn, look who's here! It's Sister Alice McLamb's grandson."

Stunned, McLamb said, "You remember me? It's been over twenty years."

"I never forget the good kids," Williams said. "Besides, I see your grandmother at least twice a year and she always talks about you and shows me the pictures of you and your children."

He led McLamb into the dining room, where his wife was tying red bows on a dozen or more white milk-glass bud vases. Each vase held three red carnations and some greenery. The table was littered with flowers, stems, stray leaves, and snippets of red ribbon. Several sheets of heart-shaped stickers waited to be stuck on the trailing ends of the ribbons.

Carolyn Williams welcomed him with a warm smile. She had a long attractive face topped with soft gray curls cut very short.

"Don't mind the mess," she apologized. "We're just finishing up the last of the Valentine flowers for the geriatric ward out at the hospital."

As a child, McLamb had often attended his grandmother's AME church here in Dobbs. Several times a year, Williams would come over to hold storytelling sessions for the children. McLamb's favorites featured a character the youth minister had invented: Herman the Worm, who wiggled his way into all sorts of adventures. He would tuck the tip of his tongue down between his lower lip and teeth so that "Herman" spoke with a very thick accent that children found irresistibly funny.

"Do you need to speak privately?" Mrs. Williams asked.

"No, I'm just backtracking on the Harper boy. We wondered if he said anything, anything at all that might help us understand why someone tried to kill him?"

Williams smoothed back his rumpled white hair. "I'm sorry, Ray. He was bitter about his brother's death and his parents' divorce, and he really wanted to shut down that airfield, but on a personal level?" He shook his head.

"If you do think of anything," McLamb said.

"Of course. Now, can't we give you a glass of tea or a cookie?"

McLamb shook his head. "Thanks, but y'all need to finish up and I need to get to a florist before it closes."

"For your wife?" Carolyn Williams asked.

He nodded.

Husband and wife exchanged glances and Richard Williams thrust one of the bud vases in his hands.

McLamb breathed in their spicy scent. "Oh, I couldn't."

"Thure you can," the older man said in his Herman voice. He pulled a "Be Mine" heart-shaped sticker off the sheet and stuck it on the collar of McLamb's jacket. "Abby Balentime's Day!"

Normally when he got to Kate and Rob's house to pick up Cal, Dwight would just tap his horn, open the truck door for his son, and wave to Kate or the nanny. Today, he got out of the truck and reached for the doorbell just as Cal pulled it open, one arm in his jacket, his backpack slung over the other shoulder and clutching a folder made of red construction paper that was leaking shiny valentines.

Kate followed him down the hall and helped him pick them up. "Sorry, Dwight. We didn't hear your horn."

"I didn't blow it," he said.

She handed Cal a half dozen cards and smiled at her brother-in-law. "Anne and Sigrid are up for tonight. In fact, Anne sounded happy to be able to talk to you face-to-face. She's feeling guilty about the Harper boy."

"What about Crawford?"

"I left him a message on his voice mail, but I haven't heard back yet. I told them all seven o'clock."

"Thanks, Kate."

"If you can't find a sitter, bring Cal back with you and he can spend the night here."

CHAPTER 24

There are a few reports of the species killing live prey, but such reports are rare.
— The Turkey Vulture Society

February 14 has never been a big deal for me since the year Mason Faircloth gave Caroline Atherton a dollar valentine with a satin heart on it, while the one he stuck in my construction-paper mailbox came from a package of "25 for $2.50" with their one-size-fits-all sentiments. I was nine years old and my heart was broken.

Mother didn't laugh at me when she found me in tears after school, but she did go through all the cards I'd gotten and made me stop and think about the hand-made ones. "These are the ones that came from the heart," she told me. "Not the Hallmark ones."

As far as she was concerned, birthdays, weddings, funerals, and Christmas were the only legitimate occasions for sending cards, and then only to people who didn't live under her roof. Even Mother's Day was a commercial ploy to guilt people into spending money.

It's made me cynical about the public display of roses and tulips that arrive at the courthouse on birthdays, anniversaries, and Valentine's Day. I suspect that more than one woman orders them for herself so that everyone will think she has a romantic husband.

All the same, I admit that I bought a couple of chocolate éclairs sprinkled with red candy hearts for Dwight and Cal, and I was delighted with the valentine Cal made for us with "Dad and Mom" spelled out in red crayon on the front.

I was less delighted to hear that Dwight had accepted an invitation to Kate and Rob's for supper with Sigrid and her mother, even though he sweetened the announcement with a new charm for my silver bracelet: the silhouette of a boy's head, engraved with Cal's initials and the date of his birth.

"Your idea or Kate's?" I asked.

"The bracelet or supper?"

"Both."

"Mine. Sorry."

"Still baiting your hooks?"

"Can't catch anything if you don't have a line in the water," he admitted. "And it won't hurt to have another professional's eye on the cork. Sigrid did say she wanted to see how we ran things down here."

I immediately started calling around the farm for a babysitter and got lucky on my first try. My brother Zach's daughter Emma agreed to come over, and her brother Lee said he wasn't doing anything either, so if there was going to be free pizza . . .

In the end, it cost us two large pizzas, because Emma called back within the hour to say Seth's daughter Jess and Andrew's Ruth wanted to come, too. Wherever two or three of the kids are gathered, more of my nieces and nephews are sure to turn up. Evidently the tribal grapevine was working just fine, because I was able to tell Cal, "They said they'd be happy to stay with their new cousin."

We were the first to get to Rob and Kate's and she was apologetic. "Sorry, Dwight, but Martin Crawford begged off and I didn't know how much you wanted me to push it."

"That's okay," he told her.

Sigrid and Anne blew in about two minutes later, red-cheeked and hair tousled by the wind. We shed our heavy coats and soon sat down to an informal supper of Rob's hearty beef stew with a few bottles of Dwight's homemade ale, perfect for a cold winter's night.

"I don't normally like beer, but this is quite good," Sigrid said, wiping the foam from her upper lip. She was as relaxed as we'd yet seen her, but the death watch was starting to wear on both of them.

"Grandmother doesn't seem to be in too much pain. The doctor's put her on an intravenous pump with a mixture of something that makes her sleep a lot."

"My sisters are flying in the end of the week," said Anne, who was further worried that something she had said or done might have led to the attack on Jeremy Harper. "I spoke to Mrs. Harper this afternoon. She says he tried to squeeze her hand and that his eyelids fluttered a little. I don't know if it's wishful thinking or he really is starting to come around."

"Where's your investigation going?" Sigrid asked with professional interest. "Any leads?"

"Not really," Dwight said. "We found his Toyota over by the NutriGood store on Saturday morning. "Unfortunately, no one seems to know when it was parked there."

"Could he have gone straight there after leaving us on Thursday, or do you think somebody else drove it there later?" Anne asked.

"No telling, but we've asked the media to run our hotline number in case anyone noticed. The steering wheel wasn't wiped and it's covered with his fingerprints."

Anne sprinkled pepper on her stew and described some of the adventures she'd had over the years, adventures she'd told the Harper boy about. "I wanted to give him a sense of the opportunities out there if he was persistent and determined. Now I'm wondering if I gave him an unrealistic view of how willing some people are to answer awkward questions."

Sigrid took another swallow of beer. "I know Martin found him near where that real estate woman was dumped, but is there any real connection?"

"Not that we've found, and believe me, we've looked."

"What about your cousin?" I asked.

Anne made a rueful face. "I'm afraid he was no help at all. He showed us some pictures and talked about tracking vultures, and Jeremy found it about as exciting as watching paint dry. To be fair, though, he's on a tight deadline and his editor's bugging him to finish the article."

She broke off a piece of her crusty whole wheat roll and buttered it. "He wants to get it finished before he flies back to England."

"He's leaving?" Sigrid asked, looking a little surprised.

"If you don't mind my asking," Dwight said, including Sigrid in his question, "how much do y'all know about him?"

"What do you mean?" Anne asked.

"Well, the other night, you said you hadn't seen him since y'all were kids, and it was almost like Sigrid never even knew he existed. You sure he's who he says he is?"

Anne frowned. "Well of course, he is," she said. "Who else would he be?"

"Just askin'," Dwight drawled.

"I may not have been in touch with him, but Mother certainly was. Not with Martin himself, perhaps, but she and his stepmother exchange Christmas cards and pictures every year. Of course it's Martin."

Sigrid had been watching Dwight's face, and now she leaned forward to say, "Something about him bothers you, Dwight?"

He nodded, then looked around the table. "What I say stays here, okay? A man died out at the Clarenden Motel Thursday night. They're calling it an accident, so the news media haven't paid much attention to it, but I'm thinking it looks more like murder."

Anne was bewildered. "What does that have to do with Martin?"

"Maybe nothing, but he's been seen loitering in the area of the airstrip and the dead man was a pilot. Not that they're admitting it."

Sigrid's gray eyes sharpened with interest. "Who's 'they'?"

"The FBI. A field agent showed up about a half hour after we did and claimed jurisdiction. I reached out to some of my old Intelligence buddies and they say he does some of those rendition flights between Guantanamo Bay and Maine that they try to pretend don't happen. I checked the weather reports and Maine was iced in Thursday night, so he had to stay over. The maid found him in the tub with the shower on next morning. It was supposed to look as if he slipped and broke his neck in the fall, but our ME thinks he was murdered."

Rob and Kate had been following the conversation as if watching a tennis match between the two of them.

"Someone snapped his neck?" Sigrid asked. "How could they call it an accident? Doesn't that leave bruises?"

"Not necessarily," Dwight said. "Not if it

happens too fast for the blood vessels to react."

Rob looked at Dwight in something between morbid fascination and awe. "*You* could do that?"

"In theory, yes," Dwight admitted. "If you're asking if I ever did, the answer's no."

"It isn't just theory," Anne said quietly. "I saw it done."

We all stared at her.

"In Somalia," she said. "Almost twenty years ago."

We listened, fascinated as she told us about going into Mogadishu with some UN peacekeepers on a humanitarian trip. "Conditions were horrendous, but it was supposed to be safe as long as we were careful. That's where I took the picture that won me my second Pulitzer."

She described how she had gone to one of the outlying camps with a couple of truckloads of food and medical supplies and how they were ambushed and everyone killed except a fellow journalist.

"I was sure they were going to kill us, too, especially when two rough-looking Arabs came into the hut. Instead, one of them distracted our guard and then the other one came up behind him and broke his neck."

With a few graceful motions, she pantomimed reaching up under the guard's arm, then locking her hands on the back of his neck to force his head forward and down in a strong sharp yank. "I'll never forget the sound the bones in his neck made when they cracked. He was dead before he hit the ground."

She took a deep breath as if to dispel the memory. "They sneaked us out in burkas and got us back to the city. The man that killed the guard even saved one of my cameras. The one with the Pulitzer picture. He — *Oh sweet Jesus!*"

All the blood drained from her face as she broke off and looked at Sigrid in shock.

"What?" Sigrid asked in alarm.

"Martin," Anne whispered. "That Arab was Martin."

She gripped the edge of the table with both hands as if to steady herself. I pushed her water glass closer while the others pelted her with exclamations and questions.

She swallowed some water and we watched the color slowly return to her lovely face.

"Are you sure, Mother?" Sigrid asked.

"Remember when he came to dinner last week and I asked him if we'd met before? How he looked familiar, but I couldn't place him? And when we saw him the next day, he'd shaved off his beard. I remember noticing that Arab's eyes. Martin's eyes. I'm positive it was him."

"But why wouldn't he have told you who he was?" Kate asked.

"If he was in deep cover, it could've compromised his mission," Dwight said. "Sounds to me like he took a serious risk to rescue you."

"Deep cover?" Sigrid frowned. "He's a spy? CIA?"

"I'm thinking more like MI6. The real MI6, not James Bond."

"But he's an ornithologist," I protested. "He writes books, leads bird tours."

"Perfect cover," Dwight said. "Professional spies often have degrees in specialized fields — something that gives them a legitimate reason to be in a foreign country. Stinking buzzards make as good a reason as anything else."

There was shocked silence as his words sank in, then Sigrid said, "Dwight, there's something I didn't tell you when you asked Martin if he'd been the one to call in the body of that dead woman."

She seemed slightly embarrassed. "I'm a police officer. I know better, but it really didn't seem important at the time."

"What didn't?" Dwight asked.

"You asked to see his phones and he showed you two of them. But he had at least a half dozen more in a satchel in his bedroom."

She described how Crawford had diverted their attention with the old newspapers plastered on the wall while he covered up the phones.

"I was pretty sure he'd reported the body, but I honestly thought he denied it because he just didn't want to get involved in a homicide investigation."

Anne appeared bewildered. "I never even noticed."

"You also didn't notice that you told him the dates you were in Peru so that he could claim that's when he was there, too," Sigrid said.

Anne leaned back in her chair and looked at Dwight with troubled eyes. "Did Martin kill that pilot? Why? And why hurt Jeremy?"

"Whoa, now," Dwight said. "Let's don't go jumping to conclusions here. Just because you think he might have killed a guard twenty years ago doesn't mean that he's the one who did that pilot yesterday. And don't forget that Crawford's the one who found the Harper kid and reported it in time to save his life."

(*"That's right!"* said the preacher, who likes

311

to think the best of people.)

(*"Unless,"* said the cynical pragmatist, who often thinks the worst, *"he felt that the boy might never regain consciousness and that calling for medical help would automatically shift suspicion away from him."*)

Anne still seemed shaken by her memories. "I don't *think* Martin killed that guard, Dwight. I know he did. But in all these years, he's never gotten in touch. Never let me know. Never let me thank him. Why?"

"If he's still working in covert ops, it would be too dangerous," Dwight said.

"Working here?" Anne frowned.

"We won't know till we ask him, and even then? Who knows?"

"He might really be working on a legitimate article," I said helpfully. "Don't spies have to keep their cover stories current?"

"It's all so hard to reconcile," Anne said.

"Let's forget about him for a moment and go back to your time with Jeremy," Dwight said.

"I told you." Anne gave an impatient shake of her head as if to clear away confused memories and emotions. "Your mom showed me some of his work and made such a strong case for him that I couldn't say no. Besides, I'm not all that good in a sickroom and I was driving Mother crazy. I thought it would give me something to do. My first meeting with him was immediately after Deborah turned him over to Richard Williams and me. We found an empty conference room there in the courthouse and talked about that disabled veterans' group that Richard works with. He seemed willing enough to give Richard's suggestions a try, and he was supposed to meet with them after school, but when Sigrid and I drove out to Martin's so I could ask him to help — that must have been right when the body of that real estate agent was found — Jeremy was there with his camera, trying to get a closer look."

She broke off another piece of her roll, then laid it back on her plate. "I sent him on his way and Richard did say he showed up at the vet center. A little late, but there, so he didn't come back and sneak in. At least not then."

She pulled off another bit of the hard roll and it crumbled in her fingers. She didn't seem to notice. "Maybe he went back the next day after we met with Martin? That close, wouldn't he have driven down that other lane and checked it out?"

"Maybe," Dwight said. He opened a second quart bottle of beer and topped off our glasses. "Tell me about his visit with

Crawford."

"There's really not much to tell. Martin was wearing some clothes that those buzzards had vomited on when he was banding it. Talk about gross! Then he was deliberately boring because he really didn't want to help with Jeremy. I told you. He just showed us picture after picture of vultures. Vultures flying, vultures feeding, vultures roosting in treetops."

"How did Jeremy react?"

"Polite, but by about the sixtieth or seventieth picture, he had run out of things to ask about focus or lenses. Martin could have told so many interesting things — organizing tour groups, the contacts he needed to make, lining up hotels and mountain guides, but no, it was one damn bird after another. We were both ready to pack it in and I was so furious with Martin that we went out on the porch and I jumped all over him. That's when he admitted he really didn't want to help but he couldn't refuse when he was using Mother's hospitality to write his article."

Her slender fingers absentmindedly shredded another corner of her roll.

"And nothing was said or happened that might link to Rebecca Jowett's death or to the airfield?"

"No." She frowned. "Oh, wait! You know when you're clicking through photo files, how those little thumbnails of different files will run along the top of the screen?"

Dwight nodded encouragingly.

"One of them showed a small jet. Jeremy spotted it and asked about it, but when Martin tried to go back to it, he couldn't find the file. Which seemed rather odd to me then. Makes perfect sense now. He told Jeremy it was one of those puddle jumpers that fly between small cities and immediately changed the subject. That's when I made him go outside with me so I could find out what was going on."

"How long were you out there?" Sigrid asked.

"I don't know. Five minutes? Six?" She wrinkled her nose. "His clothes stank so badly, I wasn't in any hurry to go back in and sit down next to him, I can tell you that."

We smiled and Dwight said, "So y'all left Jeremy alone with Crawford's computer?"

"Plenty of time for a tech-savvy kid to find that file," I said. "If he had a jump drive —"

"Two or three of them," Anne said. "He doesn't have a laptop or an iPad, so he uses those memory sticks to move data from his PC at home to the school's computer."

We kicked it around some more, wondering what the picture of a plane might mean. Anne had seen it only for a moment or two before Martin made it disappear, but from her sketchy description of the number of windows, Dwight said, "Probably a six-passenger Learjet. The kind of plane our man with the broken neck flew."

CHAPTER 25

Scavengers in flight can view large areas at once and also keep their eyes on other scavengers.

— The Turkey Vulture Society

Our impromptu supper party broke up around 9:30 and Dwight was silent on the short drive home. I knew he had to be thinking of all that Anne and Sigrid had told him, and I thought I knew where he'd wind up with those thoughts. Sure enough, when we reached the house, he did not cut off the engine.

"I'll be back in about an hour," he said.

"I'm coming with you."

"No you're not."

"Dammit, Dwight! If you think I'm going to let you go alone to meet with someone who can kill with his bare hands, you can think again. Just let me check on the kids, see if they can stay another hour, okay?"

I got out, leaving the truck door open. "And if you drive off without me, I'll roust out Bo Poole and half your deputies, I mean it, Dwight."

He wasn't happy, but he did wait while I went inside. Cal was already asleep and the kids were watching a scary movie that wouldn't end till eleven, so they were willing to stay. Especially when I mentioned that there was a half gallon of Rocky Road ice cream hidden in the freezer under packages of peas. I made a quick detour back through the garage to get my .38 out of the locked toolbox in the trunk of my car. Daddy had given it to me back when I was still in private practice and driving all over that part of the state alone at night. Dwight made me get a permit once he realized I wasn't going to give it up, but I probably don't get it out more than once a year.

I tucked it into the deep pocket of my coat, a three-quarter-length car coat of thick black wool. What Dwight didn't know wouldn't hurt either one of us.

He was still frowning when I got back in the truck, and immediately started laying down conditions.

"I won't speak unless spoken to," I promised. "But let's keep some space between us, just in case."

For some reason, this amused him. "I really don't think he's likely to rush us or try anything physical."

He described how Crawford had been unable to hoist himself up onto a table a few days earlier. "He *says* he fell down some stairs last year and broke both arms."

I heard the slight emphasis on *says*. "You don't think so?"

"Oh, I'm pretty sure his arms were broken," Dwight said grimly. "He certainly doesn't seem to have a lot of strength in the left one. But I doubt if he got hurt falling down some stairs."

"So he couldn't have been the one who broke that pilot's neck?"

"Ordinarily, I'd say no, but we don't know how badly he wanted the man dead. Assuming he did."

"But he's a spy?"

"He could be. Or an ex-spy."

"Shouldn't you tell the FBI?"

By the dashboard lights, I saw Dwight's wry smile. "After they've made it very clear that they don't want my help? If they haven't tumbled to his interest in the airport, why should I tell them?"

"You'd let someone get away with murder before you'd swallow your pride?"

"It's not always black and white, shug."

I thought about that and what it could mean as we turned at the NutriGood intersection. The lights from a gas station at the edge of the highway beamed a dozen bright lights in every direction, polluting the darkness and washing out the stars. Why our county commissioners can't make developers reduce the wattage on their lights and aim them downward is something I'll never understand. They just look at me blankly when I corner one of them and ask.

When we reached the dirt-and-gravel road that led to the old Ferrabee place, I said, "You've never talked to me about when you were in Army Intelligence."

"Sure I have."

"You've talked about Germany, but not what you actually did there."

He didn't answer.

"Or why you got out."

"Jonna hated the Army. She hated it as an enlisted man's wife and she kept on hating it even after I was commissioned and started getting promoted."

"So you got out because of her?"

He shrugged. "She thought it would save our marriage."

"You're evading the question," I said quietly.

He didn't answer until we reached the end

of the road, where he stopped the truck, cut the headlights, and half turned to me in his seat. "Let's just say that I got to a level where I didn't like what I was seeing and I didn't want to do the things I was going to be asked to do."

"But you've stayed in touch with some of the people who stayed in."

"Yes."

"And they've told you something about the dead man. More than what you've told Anne and Sigrid."

"Yes."

"Things you're not going to tell me?"

"Let it go, honey."

There's a time to push and there's a time to back off.

"Okay," I said.

He put the truck in gear, flicked on the lights, and we drove down to the old farmhouse. Crawford's truck was parked out front, but there was no sign of light through the windows. Dwight pulled up only inches away from the porch and tapped the horn two or three times, then opened the door so that anyone inside the house could see by the interior cab light who we were.

A few minutes later, the door opened and Martin Crawford stepped out onto the porch. He was fully dressed in his heavy black jacket with his hat pulled low on his forehead as he peered out at us warily. "Bryant?"

"Sorry if we woke you, Crawford," he said, one foot on the ground, the other on the edge of the floorboard, "but I need to talk to you, ask you a few questions."

"They can't wait till morning?"

The moon was about halfway to full, and when Dwight doused the lights, the stars overhead blazed out of the velvety sky. To the west, beyond the trees, we could see a faint glow of the lights from that service station, but the rest of the sky was pricked with twinkling points. Despite the moon, it was such a clear, high-pressure evening that I could even see the Milky Way swirling through the winter constellations. A cold wind blew up from the creek, though, and I hunched deeper into my wool coat as the cab's heat was sucked away.

Crawford closed the door behind him and eased himself down to sit on the edge of the porch only a couple of feet away from Dwight.

"We had supper with your cousins to-night."

In the moonlight, Martin Crawford's face was a pale square beneath the brim of his black fedora. He didn't speak.

"Anne's remembered where she saw you before," Dwight told him.

Silence.

"Somalia," Dwight said.

Crawford took a deep breath and let it out so heavily I heard it from where I sat motionless.

"I was never in Somalia," he said at last.

"She says you were. Almost twenty years ago. Mogadishu. A UN peacekeeping mission."

"Really? We went out to dinner together? Had drinks?"

"You can play all the games you want, Crawford, but Anne knows what she saw."

"You're right. Forgive me. Stupid of me not to have shaved before meeting her again, but it was twenty years ago. She only saw my face briefly and not in full light."

"I imagine every detail of that night is seared in her memory," Dwight said mildly.

He didn't answer. Cold was seeping into my bones and I drew my scarf up higher around my face. Crawford stood up as if to go back inside.

"It was kind of you to drive out and tell me this, Bryant, but I'm afraid your wife is getting chilled and I'm rather tired, so if you'll excuse me . . ."

"A man was killed in a motel near here,"

Dwight said. "He was a pilot."

Crawford stopped with his hand on the doorknob.

"His neck was broken. Just the way you broke the neck of Anne's guard."

"Are you here to arrest me?"

"Should I be?"

He turned back to Dwight. "Now who's playing games?"

"Not me. The FBI's claimed jurisdiction."

In the near darkness, I saw Crawford nod as if in professional sympathy. "Turf wars? They're the same the whole bloody world over, aren't they? So why are you here instead of them if it's an FBI case?"

"It's the boy. Jeremy Harper. He saw one of your photo files with an airplane on it. Anne thinks he may have copied it off your computer while you two were outside. It may have been what almost got him killed the same night someone killed that pilot. I was hoping you'd let me take a look. Help me figure out what it was."

"Unless you have a search warrant, absolutely not," Crawford said.

"Actually, I'm not real sure I need a search warrant," Dwight drawled. "Our Constitution protects its citizens from unreasonable searches, but you're not a citizen, are you?" He looked over his shoulder at me. "The feds might could come bustin' in, but how you reckon you'd rule on that, Deb'rah?"

"Having never considered how our Bill of Rights might apply to a foreign national, I'd probably buck it up to a superior court judge," I said.

Both men laughed. I wasn't sure what was happening here, but I sensed an easing of tension between the two of them.

"I'll see you tomorrow then," Dwight said, drawing his leg back in the truck.

"I'll count on it," Crawford said. "Good night, Bryant. Judge."

We were almost home before I finished working it out.

"You warned him!" I said. "You as good as told him that the FBI might be around to question him and impound his computer. Why?"

"He saved Anne's life when he didn't have to," Dwight said quietly. "Probably at a serious personal risk. That has to count for something, don't you think?"

The best thing about Dwight's truck is the bench seat. So much more friendly than bucket seats. He reached over and drew me close to him. I leaned my head on his shoulder with my hand on his thigh and said, "I guess so."

Dwight chuckled and gave me a quick kiss on the forehead. "Now aren't you glad you didn't need to shoot him?"

CHAPTER 26

The turkey vulture often directs its urine right onto its legs. This urine contains strong acids from the vulture's digestive system, which may kill any bacteria that remain on the bird's legs from stepping in its meal.

— The Turkey Vulture Society

We got home to find an extra vehicle parked near the back porch, a white utility truck with the new company logo on the door. When Annie Sue got her electrician's license last year, Herman had wanted their new logo to read "Knott and Daughter" as a slam at Reese, who's never been motivated enough to take the exam to get his own electrician's license even though he's six years older. Annie Sue was not willing to embarrass her brother like that. Instead they had settled on a simple "Knott Family Electricians" underlined by lightning bolts tied together in loose knots.

In the living room, Lee, Jess, and Ruth were mesmerized by the TV, where that horror movie was building to a climax, but Emma had fallen asleep on the rug.

They waved and said hey as Dwight went on back to our bedroom.

"Where's Annie Sue?" I asked.

Before they could pull their eyes away to answer, Dwight reappeared. "There's a pretty young woman sitting on our bathroom floor," he said and headed down the hall to the guest facilities.

He was right. Although Annie Sue may not be the prettiest of my nieces — Haywood and Isabel's Jane Ann is generally considered the beauty of the family — none of the kids got hit with the ugly stick, and Annie Sue has been known to start a few male motors racing. Her hair, light brown or dark blonde depending on the season, was in a ponytail that she had pulled through the back of her billed hat that still had Herman's old logo stitched across the front.

She sat cross-legged on the floor, surrounded by bits and pieces of a small motor. A piece of cardboard was taped over the hole in the wall above the tub where the exhaust fan had been when we left the house.

"Oh, hey, Aunt Deborah," she chirped. "I told Uncle Dwight I could take this somewhere else, but he said for me to go ahead and finish here."

"No problem," I said. "But you didn't have to do this tonight."

"Granddaddy wanted me to reset his motion lights on the barn so Maidie could get home before they clicked off, and as long as I was out this way, I thought I'd take a look at your fan. I'm afraid it's shot, though." She began to gather up the pieces and put them in a plastic bag. "It shouldn't have quit working this quickly, so I'll bring you out a new one tomorrow and make the supplier pay for it."

I spotted her needle-nose pliers and brought her my bracelet and the new charm Dwight had given me.

She found an empty link and carefully attached the little engraved head. "It's so cool that you're going to adopt Cal. I wish I'd gotten here before he went to bed. I told him I'd bring him some red flex next time I was out so he could make some wristbands."

She handed me back the bracelet and cut her eyes at me in sudden mischief. "Reese asked me to take a look at that pig sign y'all put in the barn. Pretty cool, but it's gonna take some time to get it working."

"Get what working?" Dwight asked, sticking his head around the door.

"Your birthday present," I said quickly.

He gave me a suspicious look. "My birthday's not till May."

"All the more reason for me to get started on it right away," I said, and gave Annie Sue a wink. "I'm not sure I have enough wool and you know how slow I knit."

My niece giggled and scooped up a couple of screws that had fallen to the floor when she stood to go. "I can get you a good deal on some dog hair and LEDs if you go that route."

Dwight shook his head at our teasing. "Y'all're not going to get me to bite."

From the living room came sounds of the kids getting ready to leave. Lee pulled his sleepy sister to her feet and Dwight slipped her a twenty that she tried to refuse. "We should be paying you for the pizzas," she said with a yawn, but he just closed her hand around the bill.

There were hugs all around, a chorus of engines in the yard, then Dwight and I were left in the sudden quiet of the house.

And whaddya know? It was still Valentine's Day.

Annie Sue arrived the next morning after Dwight and Cal had left for work and school. She popped the new exhaust fan into the old cutout and had it running in less than fifteen minutes. I didn't have to be in court till 9:30, so I poured us another cup of coffee and was soon listening to why she had broken up with her latest boyfriend.

"I got tired of his dad's sniping. He thinks it's unfeminine for a woman to work a blue-collar trade. He just couldn't deal with the fact that I have my own truck and that I'm out physically pulling wire through basements and attics. He thinks Andy would be happier with a more girly girl, as he puts it. And better educated. Like a teacher or a computer programmer. Never mind that I'm already making almost twice as much as most beginning teachers."

I was appalled on her behalf. "He told you this himself?"

"No, but he told Andy."

"And Andy agreed?"

"Well, you saw where I was on Valentine's Day. Did you get stuff like this when you first became a judge? All that crap about 'what's a pretty little thing like you doing a man's job?' "

"Not really. Most of the barriers in my profession had been broken by the time I got to law school. Your granddaddy was the biggest roadblock. He didn't think my delicate ears could stand hearing all the ugly things people say and do to each other."

She laughed, knowing how he still didn't like anyone to use language around the women in his family. As if we hadn't heard it all by the time we were ten.

"And we really have come a long way," I told her. "I saw a woman working one of those monster bulldozers the other day. Power to the sisterhood!"

"One thing about my job. I don't have to worry about it going offshore. People are always going to need electricians and plumbers and carpenters. All the same, I'll be glad when people can take it for granted that we're as competent in the trades as any man."

I patted her hand. "All they have to do is look at Reese, honey."

My first case of the day could have been a textbook for Annie Sue's complaints. Ronnie Currin, 41, was charged with four counts of assault against his former boss and her other three employees, the "assault" being the adulteration of a food substance with intent to do bodily harm.

When the charges against him were read, I said, "How do you plead, Mr. Currin?"

"Not guilty," he answered firmly.

For twelve years, Mr. Currin had evidently been a satisfied employee at Braswell Hardware and Seed Store here in Dobbs. Then Leland Braswell died and his wife Linda took over. Mrs. Braswell had worked side by side with her husband and knew as much about seeds and hardware as he did, but when she decided to freshen up the store's faded appearance, expand the gardening section, and discontinue what she considered was an inferior line of hand tools, Mr. Currin took exception. He grumbled about the extra workload that the plants and hanging baskets caused, and what did a woman know about running a hardware store anyhow?

When Mrs. Braswell made it clear that he could be replaced and the other three employees told him to suck it up, he stopped joining them in the break room for coffee and doughnuts.

"He said coffee had started giving him heartburn, so he switched to ginger ale," one of them testified.

Soon afterwards, the employees began to notice that the coffee tasted odd.

They changed brands.

The off-flavor continued.

Mrs. Braswell brought in a new coffee-maker. It worked fine for a few days and then the unpleasant taste began again.

Eventually, someone noticed a yellowish liquid around the top of the pot immediately after Mr. Currin had been in the break room alone. Mrs. Braswell had it tested.

Urine.

At that point, the ADA Julie Walsh looked around the courtroom and said, "Any real big coffee drinkers here today?"

When I raised my hand, along with four-fifths of the audience, Mr. Currin abruptly decided to plead guilty and throw himself on the mercy of the court.

I have to admit I wasn't feeling all that merciful. I sentenced him to five years' supervised probation and required him to get a mental health exam, pay a $2,000 fine, and reimburse Mrs. Braswell for two coffee-makers.

CHAPTER 27

Turkey vultures, along with all other North and South American vultures, do not build nests. Instead, they lay their eggs on bare ground in concealed places, like caves or hollowed logs.

— The Turkey Vulture Society

Colleton County Sheriff's Department —
Tuesday morning

With Wes Todd firmly alibied for the time of her death and no other viable candidate in sight until Paul Kendrick returned from Mexico at the end of the month — "Assuming he does come back and we don't have to issue a warrant for his arrest," Major Bryant said gloomily — the investigation into Rebecca Jowett's murder was stalled for the time being, "so let's get out there and clean up some of this other stuff," he told his deputies at the morning briefing.

As he reviewed the pending investigations

and listened to their updates, they were joined by a tall slender woman in tailored black slacks and a white parka with a turquoise scarf looped around her neck. Her short dark hair was layered in an expensive cut with wisps of bangs that showcased her clear gray eyes. Not a haircut from the Cut 'n' Curl, thought Mayleen Richards.

"Major Bryant? I was told to come on back, but if I'm interrupting, I can wait elsewhere."

Not a Southern accent either.

"Come in, Lieutenant," he said formally as he stood up to welcome her.

Turning back to his detectives, he said, "Y'all, this is Lieutenant Harald of the New York City PD. She gave me a view of her department when I was up there last month, so I asked her in to see how we do things down here."

He described to her the cases they were working on: the arson they had just wrapped up, the murder of a Realtor, a bank robbery, an armed robbery at a local gas station, some serious vandalism at a local elementary school, and a drug-related shooting. As he finished the briefing, he asked Richards and McLamb to join him in his office.

"Coffee, Lieutenant? We just made a fresh pot."

She nodded, well aware of the psychological benefits of sharing coffee and how it would help the other two accept her more quickly.

When they were settled with the door closed, Dwight said, "There's a possibility, a rather strong possibility in fact, that the attack on Jeremy Harper could be connected to his Patriots Against Torture activities and that death out at the Clarenden, so we're going to have to tread lightly here and not do anything to tick the feds off if we can help it."

The two deputies shared a glance of surprise that he would speak of this in front of an outsider.

"Lieutenant Harald is up to speed on this," Dwight said. "I'm sure you both know of her grandmother, Mrs. Jane Lattimore over in Cotton Grove?"

They nodded.

"The lieutenant's mother was mentoring the Harper kid's community service. In fact, she may have been one of the last ones to speak to him before he was attacked."

McLamb lifted an eyebrow at that. "I don't suppose he happened to mention where he was going?"

"Sorry," Sigrid Harald said. She glanced at Dwight. "Did you tell them about his jump drives?"

"We aren't sure about this," Dwight told them, "but there's a possibility that the kid copied a computer file that might be connected to that pilot's death. Whose computer it was isn't relevant at the moment, but keep an eye out for his jump drives. Mrs. Harald said he had several."

The Harper house lay in a lower-middle-class neighborhood several blocks west of the county courthouse. Brick ranches sat elbow-to-elbow with white clapboard bungalows on small lots that featured tidy hedges and shared dirt driveways that led to separate single-car garages in the back.

Mayleen Richards and Ray McLamb parked in front of one of the brick ranches with a narrow front porch and were met at the door by Jeremy Harper's grandfather, whom they had called a few minutes earlier.

While McLamb went around the house to the back where the blue Toyota was parked, Richards went inside.

Early sixties, with frizzy white hair and rimless bifocals that kept slipping down his nose, Gene Turnage was a tubby little man with bright inquisitive eyes and an open smile that probably flashed more readily when he wasn't worried because his only remaining grandson lay comatose in a Raleigh hospital. He wore khaki pants, a white shirt and tie, and a blue WalMart vest that strained the buttons across his ample belly.

The front door led immediately into a living room crowded with two couches, three lounge chairs, and some mismatched occasional tables. Judging by the different styles and colors, Richards guessed that Jeremy's mother had brought along some of her own furniture when they lost the house in Cotton Grove. There was a built-in bookcase near the door, jammed with an assortment of family photographs. A younger Mr. and Mrs. Turnage beamed at each other in what was probably a formal anniversary picture. In other snapshots they were joined by their daughter and two little curly-top boys.

The top shelf held a photograph of a young soldier in his dress uniform, a folded American flag in a plastic case, and a framed Purple Heart.

A short hall to the right of the front door led to three bedrooms.

"I hope this won't take very long," Mr. Turnage said.

He cast an anxious glance at his watch as he showed her into Jeremy's room. "It took me a while to get this job after I got laid off at the bread company and I don't want 'em to think I can't show up when I'm supposed to."

"What time does your shift start?" Richards asked.

He pushed his glasses back up. "Not till ten."

"Oh, we should be out of here way before then," she assured him.

The bedroom was adequate if cramped and was furnished with a single bed against the outside wall, a nightstand, a chest of drawers, an armless steno chair on casters, and a desk that was nothing more than a narrow flush door supported at each end by wooden shelves. The nightstand held a cheap CD player, and the top drawer was filled with rock groups and country music in equal numbers.

A homemade bulletin board over the desk was layered with memos and photographs of school events. Atop the desk, an older boxy computer shared space with a neat stack of photography magazines, schoolbooks, a pencil jar, and a lidless cigar box full of odds and ends. A printer sat on the floor beside the CPU.

Someone must have tidied up in here, Mayleen thought, remembering the shambles her brothers used to make of their rooms. For the flicker of a moment images of Tom's indignant face flashed through her head. *"Just stay out of my room, Mayleen!"* was overlaid by Steve's angry *"You try and bring a Mexican into this family and you ain't no sister of mine!"*

Resolutely, she continued her visual examination of the room as Mr. Turnage said, "There's his computer. Just don't ask me how to turn it on or anything."

He shook his head with a wry smile and his glasses slid back down his nose. "I'm starting to sound like my dad. When I was a boy, I was the one who knew how to adjust the rabbit ears and fiddle with the horizontal and vertical holds till we got a clear picture. Now Jeremy and his mother have to show me how to record a program or play a DVD. As for computers, he might as well be speaking Chinese when he starts trying to tell me how to look something up. The only reason we got cable was so he could go on the Internet. It's expensive and we don't watch that much television, but I guess the kids nowadays need to stay up with things."

He watched as Mayleen sat down in front of the PC.

"I don't suppose y'all found his camera?"

"I'm not sure we knew it was missing," Mayleen said, pressing the power button.

"Maybe no one thought to say, but yeah, when we went to get his car, his camera bag was gone and he always has it with him."

Mayleen poked through the cigar box. "What about his jump drives?"

"His what?"

"Portable memory sticks."

When Turnage continued to look at her blankly, she reached into her pocket and pulled out her car keys. Two jump drives were on the chain.

"That what you call them things? Yeah, I think he did have some." With his index finger, he pushed his glasses back into place and looked around the room with a helpless air. "I don't know where he keeps them, though."

He pulled open a dresser drawer and felt around the edges.

"Why don't you let me do that?" Mayleen said. "His computer seems a little slow to load."

"Yeah, he's always complaining about that." He turned away from the dresser. "How 'bout I fix us all a glass of tea?"

"That would be nice," Mayleen said encouragingly.

As soon as the older man left the room, she quickly and efficiently checked all the dresser drawers as well as the drawers in the nightstand. She slid her fingers into the pockets of the jackets in his closet, patted down all the slacks and jeans, then looked under the bed and lifted the mattress.

Nothing.

The computer finally came to life and the screen saver was a picture of Jeremy's brother, dressed in Desert Storm–type cammies as he leaned against a sand-colored Humvee. Although she had only seen Jeremy when he lay wounded and bloody the morning he was found, she noted the resemblance between the two brothers, the same thin necks, the same frizzy blond hair even though the dead brother's hair was clipped short. Every time Jeremy booted up his computer, this was what he would see, she thought sadly.

With a sigh for all the young men and women who had died or been wounded in this misguided war, she turned back to the task at hand. Happily, the computer did not seem to be password-protected. She went first to the history of websites the teenager had visited. In the week leading up to his attack, they consisted mostly of Facebook pages, Google searches for what might be school subjects, newspaper stories, and some games. He had also looked up the Disabled American Veterans websites, Anne Harald's Wikipedia entry, and had tried to find a Martin Crawford.

No luck there.

But Crawford? Oh yes, she thought. The guy who had found him. Now how did Jeremy know Crawford?

One of his last searches was of the FAA's registry, which made sense in light of Major Bryant's cryptic statement that he might have copied something linked to the FBI's case. His last search had been the Colleton County yellow pages, but he must not have clicked on anything specific. On the other hand, the phone directory was atop that stack of magazines at the end of the desk.

Mr. Turnage returned with a tall glass of iced tea and Mayleen thanked him as she took a deep swallow. Nice and sweet, just as she liked it.

"I took a glass out to your friend. He doesn't seem to be finding anything."

"Does Jeremy have a cell phone?" she asked.

Turnage adjusted his bifocals and shook his head. "It quit working last week and he was saving up to get a new one. Something else this generation's got that ours didn't have. When we were kids, we thought the twenty-first century would find us all flying our own personal airplanes. Never dawned on us that we'd cut the cord and carry our phones around in our pockets. Never dawned on us that one phone wouldn't last you thirty years either. Way Jeremy acted, you'd've thought somebody'd cut off his right arm."

Mayleen smiled and finished skimming through the boy's email — the usual teenage boy talk. A group message to tell some friends that his phone was fried. *"Bummer."* A short summary of his day in court and how "that asshole DA doesn't have a fucking clue as to how this country's being taken over by those Blackwater supporters."

Regretfully, Mayleen realized that the computer was no help. "Who straightened up this room, Mr. Turnage? I can't believe any teenage boy is this neat."

"Me," he said. "And you're right. It was a mess. My wife and daughter have to be in Raleigh at eight-thirty and it's nearly suppertime before they get home, so since I'm only working part-time, I try to do what I can to help out. I always knew how to cook, but now I've learned how to run the washer and the vacuum cleaner."

She pointed to the phone directory. "Was

that on the desk when you started straight-
ening up?"

He shook his head. "No, it was there on
the floor right where he left it."

"Open or closed?"

"Open," he answered promptly.

"I don't suppose you noticed where?"

"Sorry. You reckon it was important?"

"Hard to say," Mayleen told him.

"It was in the yellow pages section,
though."

The Colleton County yellow pages were
barely half an inch thick. Turnage picked it
up. "Best I can remember, maybe halfway
in?"

He riffled the pages. Halfway in meant the
H's — harnesses, health clubs, hearing aids,
and heaters.

"No, maybe it was a little bit more than
halfway, now that I think about it." He
flipped over several more pages to mulches,
music instruction, and nail salons. "Sorry,
ma'am. I just can't say."

McLamb came inside to search the bedroom a final time, while she went out to run
fresh eyes over the car, but if Jeremy Harper
had hidden a jump drive in either, they
could not find it.

As they drove back to work, Mayleen said,
"What about that Crawford guy, Ray?"

"Who?"

"The one who's staying out there writing about buzzards. The one who found the Harper boy and called it in."

"What about him?"

"Jeremy Googled him."

"So?"

"So how'd he know the guy's name?"

"You think he's the one Jeremy went to see?"

"Well, the kid was pretty close to being buzzard food, wasn't he?"

CHAPTER 28

Turkey vultures can often be seen near rivers, feasting on washed-up fish.
— The Turkey Vulture Society

Dwight and I had agreed to meet for lunch at the Landing, a fish house overlooking the river that flows along the southwest side of Dobbs. It's a bit pricier than the chain restaurants and is seldom crowded for lunch. Fresh seafood is trucked in from the coast every morning and we were both hungry for oysters. On the drive over, I passed Braswell Hardware and noted that the storefront had indeed been given a facelift since I last noticed it. The faded white lettering across the top was now painted in gold that glistened in the sunlight. Inside the show window, someone was dismantling a big heart made of red-handled hand tools while a colorful sandwich board on the sidewalk announced the arrival of seeds for the spring garden.

Go, Mrs. Braswell! I thought.

I was first at the restaurant, so I went ahead and ordered our drinks. Iced tea for me, water for Dwight, hold the lemon on both. The hostess had seated me at a booth that offered a panoramic view of big white-trunked sycamores along the river. Sunlight sparkled on the muddy brown water, which was still high after all the rain and nearly level with its bank.

When I heard Dwight's voice and looked up from the menu, I was surprised to see that Sigrid Harald was with him.

"Well, hey," I said. "Dwight didn't tell me you were visiting his office today."

"That's because you don't have your phone on," he said, sliding into the booth beside me.

"I don't?" I retrieved it from the pocket of my coat and saw that it was indeed switched off. "Sorry. I thought sure I put it on vibrate."

Dwight rolled his eyes.

I switched it on and immediately saw his text message that Sigrid would be joining us.

"Hope you don't mind," she said, taking the opposite seat and removing the white parka I'd seen her wear in New York. Beneath was a white turtleneck sweater, and she left her turquoise scarf loosely tied around her neck. "Martin called Mother this morning and wanted to see her. Alone. So I thought I'd take Dwight up on his offer to show me his department."

"You should have come up to my courtroom," I said and told them about the coffeepot case and how that disgruntled employee resented working for a woman. "I guess you must have faced some of that yourself when you took over your homicide squad?"

Sigrid nodded, but did not elaborate as our waitress came to take our orders — steamed oysters on the half shell for Dwight, lightly fried oysters for me, grilled sea bass for Sigrid, accompanied by salads and cornbread squares heavily laced with onions.

"What's the proportion of sworn female officers in your department?" she asked Dwight.

"Less than twenty-five percent," he admitted, "but Deborah will tell you that I talk it up every time I speak at a high school career day or to the criminal justice classes out at our community college."

"I'm afraid it's still seen as a guy thing," I said. "And the pay's not enough to tempt many adventurous young women. Take my niece. She just broke up with her latest boyfriend because he didn't approve of her job."

"What does she do?"

"She's an electrician," Dwight said. Annie Sue's expertise delights him, and he told a couple of family stories, including the time she was grounded and spent her enforced house arrest rewiring the wall switches so that none of them turned on the expected lights. "She was thirteen at the time and now she has her own truck and her own set of tools."

He hesitated and a slight frown crossed his face.

"What?" I asked.

"Nothing. For a moment there . . . ever get the feeling you're about to remember something important and then it's gone?"

Sigrid nodded. "More often than I'd prefer. I think it comes from trying to fit too many pieces together from too many possibilities."

"Annie Sue? Electricians?" I prompted. "Tricks?"

He shook his head. "It's gone."

Our food came and talk turned back to Martin Crawford and Anne Harald's narrow escape in Somalia.

"I knew she'd had a close call back then,"

Sigrid said, "but nothing like what she told us last night. I was studying for my sergeant's exam around that time so I guess I wasn't paying enough attention. Besides, she always downplayed any danger and said I put myself in harm's way more often than she did."

I tried to take a square of cornbread from the basket. It was so tender that it crumbled in my fingers and I had to use a fork to transfer it to my plate, but it was worth the effort, buttery and savory at the same time.

Sigrid followed my example and seemed surprised by how delicious cornbread could be. "Mother keeps taking me to places that serve deep-fried hushpuppies with the texture of dried-up oatmeal."

"Not enough self-rising flour," I said.

She gave me a blank look. "I'm not much of a cook. Besides, my housemate —"

She was interrupted by the ringing of Dwight's phone. He checked the screen and said, "Sorry. I need to take this. It's Richards."

As he walked away, I said, "Did you meet Deputy Richards?"

She nodded.

"Now there's a case of another woman who bucked her family tradition." I described how Mayleen had left a good

computer-related job in the Research Triangle to join the sheriff's department despite
her father's strongly voiced opposition.

"Any luck?" Sigrid asked when Dwight
rejoined us.

"Nothing on his computer and no sign of
any jump drives in the house or his car," he
said and explained to me that he'd sent
Richards and McLamb out to Jeremy Harper's house that morning. "His camera case
is missing, though, and so is his camera.
But his grandfather said he'd left the phone
directory open to the yellow pages. Richards thinks he looked up a business just
before leaving the house."

"No scrap of paper with cryptic nota-
tions?" I asked, only half facetiously.

"No, but he did Google Anne and got her
Wikipedia entry and some of the web cita-
tions. She said he tried to Google Martin
Crawford as well and how did Jeremy know
his name."

I was curious. "You didn't tell them about
Martin? How did you explain the copied
computer file?"

"I just said it might be something connected to the FBI's case and I was keeping
it on a need-to-know basis for the time being."

"What *about* the FBI?" Sigrid asked. "Will

you tell them?"

"Anything I have is only speculation based on what Anne told us. Hearsay. Would you?"

"Not my case," she replied.

"Mine either," he said and gestured to the waitress for more water.

I was troubled by the mixed signals I was getting from them. We're all three officers of the court, sworn to uphold the law. In the normal run of things, wouldn't they bring Crawford in for questioning? Ask for alibis? Probe for a connection to the victim?

Dwight had always seemed like an open book without footnotes. Now it was as if some of his pages were written in Urdu and I realized that I couldn't read him as well as I always thought I could, that there seemed to be things in his past that made him unwilling to cooperate with the feds or to cast suspicion on Crawford, things that might have more to do with his own personal history than with how Anne was rescued twenty years ago.

(*"And what about the things Dwight doesn't know about you?"* whispered my internal preacher.)

(His pragmatic roommate nodded. *"Before you sit in judgment, you gonna tell him exactly how you were first appointed to the bench?"*)

Conflicted, I steered the conversation into

safer waters. "What about Becca Jowett's murder? Any progress there?"

"That Realtor I told you about," he said to Sigrid. To me, he said, "Another brick wall, I'm afraid. Her husband has a water-tight alibi and so does our first suspect, the one with a hair-trigger temper who cheats on his wife yet wants to keep his marriage. The other guy she was getting it on with has taken his wife to Mexico for the rest of the month. His alibi's not as tight, but we'll have to wait till they get back before we can tackle their stories again."

Wife? Alibis?

"Annie Sue's truck!" I exclaimed.

"What about it?" Dwight asked.

"Does Wes Todd's wife have a truck, too? Is that what you almost remembered before?"

Dawning comprehension spread across his face. "Well, damn!" he said, and kissed me there and then to Sigrid's amusement.

"This is why I keep her," he said. "How the hell could I have overlooked that? She couldn't stop herself from rubbing Todd's nose in that love bite on Becca Jowett's neck and she was the one who insisted on looking over the house at the last minute before the closing. I bet if he hadn't said something about that couch, she'd've found a reason to move that afghan and find the blood herself."

His speculations suddenly drew up short. "But she said she was with her kids and their grandparents during the relevant times."

"Did anyone actually confirm that?" Sigrid asked.

"I don't think so," he said slowly. "But you know something? I got the impression that she's the one who went back out to Creekside next morning to dispose of the trapped rats and set new traps. If she did, that would certainly put her in the vicinity of the dump site early Sunday morning."

He smiled at me. "It's your theory about the husband, applied to the wife. Kill Becca Jowett, hide her body in the back of the truck, dispose of it at her convenience."

"But why would she kill the woman in the first place?" Sigrid objected. "Didn't you say the affair was brief and already over? Isn't divorce easier?"

"You've evidently never been through one," I said dryly. "Especially a contentious divorce that involves children and a business partnership. Not to mention the humiliation of having your friends know. If they were supposed to close on the house this week, then they would be past the point

356

of being able to walk away without losing money. How would you feel about buying a house from someone your husband had sex with, knowing that she was going to collect a healthy commission on it, and wondering if he was so enthusiastic about the house because of her?"

"Why don't I ask her?" Dwight said, punching Mayleen Richards's number on his contact list.

When she answered, he instructed her to invite the Todds to come in and talk to them.

Now.

"Want to sit in on it?" he asked Sigrid.

"Sure," she said.

I shook my head when the waitress offered us the dessert menu. A check of my watch showed I was due back in court in ten minutes. Regretfully, I said, "Y'all have fun," and headed back to the courthouse.

CHAPTER 29

Genders appear identical and it is impossible to visually distinguish males from females.

— The Turkey Vulture Society

Colleton County Sheriff's Department — Tuesday afternoon

The Todds were angry and apprehensive when they arrived at the sheriff's department.

"She came in her own truck, too," Mayleen Richards told Dwight when she let him know that the Todds had been put in separate interview rooms.

"Check to see if the search warrant we used before can be stretched to cover all company vehicles and put Denning on it," Dwight said. "We'll start with the husband first."

"What the hell's going on?" Wesley Todd asked belligerently when Dwight and Sigrid entered the room. He included Sigrid in his glare, but seemed to assume she was another deputy. "You said you wouldn't tell my wife."

"And you said you were telling me the truth about Saturday night," Dwight said.

"I did! Ask the Applewhites. They called me around six-thirty and I was out there by seven. Left around eight-thirty and got home a little after nine. Ask Ginger."

"She said she took y'all's children over to her parents' house and stayed to visit awhile. Was she really home when you got back or is she just saying that to give you an alibi?"

"She was there! Ask her. Hell, ask her parents."

"We will," Dwight promised. "And it was a legitimate callout? You did find rats in your trap when you went back next morning?"

"Absolutely." He glanced up and met Sigrid's clear, steady-eyed gaze. It made him hesitate. "Well, actually, Ginger did. She's an early riser and she lets me sleep in on Sundays if the kids are with her parents or mine. Long as she was up, she went out to check."

Again, he seemed to need to explain why his wife had done what most people would consider a man's job. "Rats don't bother

her, see? Just don't ask her to do snakes. She said there were rats in four of the traps, so she set new ones and plugged a hole in the crawl space that I had missed. Monday morning I found one more, so I left the traps in place for the rest of the week. But that was the end of them. Applewhite's happy and so is his daughter, so what else you need to know?"

"She drive your truck?"

"Hell, no! Mine's a gearshift with four-wheel drive. She won't drive anything but an automatic. Why? Y'all find something on my truck when you searched it Thursday?"

Dwight stood. "Sit tight for a few minutes while we talk to your wife and we'll get back to you."

"You're not going to tell her, are you?"

"Are you a hundred percent sure she doesn't already know?"

"I know she doesn't." He shot Sigrid an apologetic look. "I don't mean to talk dirty in front of a lady, ma'am, but last time, she said if it ever happened again, she'd squeeze my balls till I wouldn't have a penny left by the time she finished with me, but hell, when a woman hot as Becca Jowett comes on to you, what're you supposed to do? But Ginger doesn't have a clue about this. It's over and Becca's dead, so why cause trouble for me, okay?"

Dwight didn't answer and Sigrid, who still had not spoken, followed him from the room.

Denning and Richards met them in the hallway and Denning did not have a happy look on his face. "Either she's the neatest workman you ever met, Major, or the truck's been detailed in the last week. Looks like the cab was vacuumed, the bed's been hosed down, and I can't spot a thing that looks connected with the victim."

"What about the tires?" Dwight said. "Does the tread match the one you found when the boy was dropped?"

"Same tread, and I can see where a roofing nail might have been, but it must've worked its way out. One thing, though," Denning said. "No plastic sheeting in her truck. She may not ever have had any, but both trucks seem to carry the same equipment, so . . ."

"Where's Wes?" Ginger Todd asked when they opened the door and joined her at the interview table. She had pulled off her ball cap, and under the fluorescent lights her orange hair looked even brighter, while her pale skin was almost without color at all.

"Why can't he be here?"

"It'll be fine," Dwight said soothingly. "We needed to ask him some questions, and if you give the same answers, this will all be cleared up."

"What questions??"

"About Saturday night and where you both were."

"We told you. Wes had to go see about some rats and the children and I visited with my parents."

"Did you both leave the house at the same time?"

She shook her head and her long ponytail swung against the shoulders of her brown work clothes. "No, Wes left first. Around six-thirty. I finished giving the children their supper and then drove them over to my mom's. She loves to have them spend the night and it gives us a chance to sleep in on Sunday morning."

"Except that you didn't sleep in," Dwight said.

"Is that camera on?" Ginger Todd asked abruptly.

Dwight nodded. "That's okay, isn't it?"

She frowned. "I guess."

"Wes says you got up early Sunday morning and went and picked up the rat traps he set the night before. Is that true?"

"Of course it's true. You trying to say he didn't actually set any traps?"

"No, ma'am. Just trying to get a full picture here."

"Well, he did. Ask Mr. Applewhite. He thought his daughter was exaggerating about the noise the rats were making. He thought they were going to be just little field mice. He couldn't believe it when he saw the traps next morning. He met me in the yard and couldn't wait for me to get rid of them."

"What do you do with the rats you catch?" Sigrid asked.

"Depends. We keep a barrel of water out back. Sometimes we drown them. Sometimes, if we're out in the country, we just let them go. Lots of foxes and hawks and stray cats around."

"Which did you do Sunday morning?"

Sigrid's tone held only friendly curiosity, but Ginger Todd visibly froze.

"I — um . . . where Old Forty-Eight crosses Possum Creek? I dumped them into the creek. There's no houses near there, so I figured something would eat them."

"Really?" said Dwight. "You sure you didn't dump them in the woods beside Grayson Village?"

"No! I'd never turn them loose near

anybody's house."

"But you do know about those woods?"

Ginger Todd stared at them without answering.

"Where's your plastic sheeting, Mrs. Todd?"

"What plastic sheeting?"

"The sheeting you and your husband both carry in your trucks."

"He tell you that?"

When they didn't answer, she said, "I don't know. It's still there, isn't it?"

"When did you have your truck detailed?"

She seemed to shrink back into her heavy brown work jacket. "I don't know. Monday? Tuesday? It was getting pretty dirty, so one of our workers took it over to the Handi-Wash to get it cleaned up."

"What's his name?"

"Tito. Tito Morales." She brightened. "You know something? If my roll of sheeting's gone, I bet someone there took it. We're always losing stuff off the trucks."

"When did you last see Becca Jowett, Mrs. Todd?"

The abrupt change of subject made her hesitate. "Saturday morning," she said after a short pause. "When she showed Wes and me the house for the last time."

"You sure you didn't see her Saturday

night when you were driving home alone? You didn't swing past that house and see her out jogging?"

"No!"

"You saw that mark on her neck Saturday morning and you knew that your husband was attracted to her."

"Todd wouldn't —"

"Wouldn't he?"

"And even if he did, why would he kill her?"

"He wouldn't but you might. You'd had all day to stew about it, and when you saw her there by the house, alone? What did you do? Tell her you wanted to take another look? Check on one of the features? Ask her how many times she'd had sex with your husband on that couch?"

"No!" Ginger Todd stood up. "Turn off that camera. I'm not going to stay here and be talked to like this. Am I under arrest?"

When Dwight didn't answer, she said, "I know my rights and I'm leaving."

She stalked from the room and Mayleen gave her boss a wry smile. "Her husband did say she watches a lot of crime programs."

"*CSI* has a lot to answer for," Sigrid said.

Dwight sighed. "Go tell Todd he's free to go, too."

"Do I tell him his wife knows?" Richards asked.

"Let's let it be a surprise," Dwight said sourly.

CHAPTER 30

It is illegal to harm turkey vultures because the species is federally protected under the International Migratory Bird Treaty Act of 1918.

— The Turkey Vulture Society

Colleton County Sheriff's Department — Tuesday afternoon (continued)

"Sorry, Dwight," Sigrid said when they were back in his office. "What will you do now that there's no physical evidence to link her to the murder?"

"The usual slog. We'll talk to her parents, see exactly how long she was there Saturday evening. Canvass the neighborhood again. Talk to the guy who washed her truck. Hope we get lucky and that someone will've noticed her truck around seven or seven-thirty. The owner of the real estate agency told me that one of the selling points of that house was that it was nearer Ginger Todd's parents. That's the same neighborhood Becca Jowett used to run in, so it's only logical that Ginger saw her and one thing led to another, but right now there's not enough to get a warrant to search their house for bloody clothes."

"You couldn't get Deborah to sign one for you?"

He gave a half smile. "Forbidden under our separation of powers agreement."

"I was wondering how that works," Sigrid admitted.

"Besides, if she had the truck cleaned, I doubt if she kept any bloody clothes. Everybody knows about DNA these days." Dwight picked up the mug on his desk and contemplated the cold coffee inside. "What's interesting to me is that Wesley Todd swaggers around like an alpha male and she acts like the submissive little wife with him and yet she seems to hold the balance of power."

"Confirming Deborah's take on divorce?"

"Either that or she's hell on wheels when she gets fired up."

Sigrid took her phone from the pocket of her parka. "And you're still no closer to finding the Harper boy's attacker?"

"No. I told Crawford I'd be back out today. You reckon he's still with your mother?"

"I was about to call her and ask that myself. Get out of your hair." She touched the buttons, waited for Anne to answer, then asked if Martin was still there. *"What?"*

She looked at Dwight in dismay. "When? Why didn't you call us?"

"What?" Dwight asked.

"Mother's on her way home from the Raleigh-Durham Airport. She dropped Martin off there about a half hour ago. His plane leaves this afternoon. Mother? I'm going to put you on speakerphone."

Dwight heard her protest, but overrode it. "What airline, Anne? What time?"

As soon as she told him, he grabbed his hat and jacket and headed for the door. It was now 4:42, Crawford's plane was scheduled to leave at 6:00, and the airport was west of Raleigh.

"I'll come, too," Sigrid said, and before he could decide whether or not this was a good idea, they were out in the parking lot and he was sliding a key into the ignition switch of a prowl car.

With blue lights flashing and sirens wailing, he dug out of the parking lot and headed for I-40.

As a rule, Dwight liked to amble along no

more than a mile or two above the speed limit, but when expediting, he turned into Richard Petty, expertly weaving in and out of the westbound rush hour traffic, zipping past the cars and trucks that slowed and moved over.

Sigrid, who appreciated competence wherever it was found, realized that there was more to this big, slow-talking lawman than his laid-back surface implied.

Like Martin, she thought. Kate had once mentioned a military intelligence background, but it hadn't fully registered till now.

No wonder he so quickly tagged Martin as MI6. Like calling to like? He cut between two cars with only inches to spare, but she didn't flinch, so confident was she now that he knew exactly what he was doing. Despite the traffic, they pulled up in front of the international terminal with almost a half hour to spare.

They flashed their badges at security and checked the board for the flight to Gatwick, then raced down the concourse, dodging luggage and passengers, to the proper gate.

And there sat Martin Crawford, neatly groomed and looking like an ordinary tourist in his tailored black suit with his carry-on roller bag by his feet. Sigrid noted that he wore the old-fashioned black onyx signet ring that she and Anne had brought home from Mrs. Lattimore's bank, a heavy gold ring that had belonged to Martin's grandfather. He seemed engrossed by the screen of his laptop, yet appeared unsurprised to look up and see them approach.

"Ah, Bryant. Sigrid. Come to arrest me?"

A woman seated in the next row turned and stared at them.

Dwight looked around as the loudspeaker called flight numbers and destinations and arriving passengers streamed toward the exit. Opposite this waiting area was an unlit, vacant gate where no one was seated. "Let's move to where we can talk," he said.

"If you wish." Crawford closed his laptop, slid it into a side pocket of his carry-on, and followed them over.

"Why the hurry to leave the country?" Dwight asked him.

"Hurry? No hurry." Crawford sat down and looked up at Dwight calmly. "I booked this flight Friday morning."

Dwight and Sigrid took seats across from him and Dwight said, "After killing Frank Alexander the night before? You didn't waste any time."

"Frank Alexander? Was that his name?"

"Or did you know him as Alexander

371

Franklin?"

"I repeat: are you here to arrest me?"

Dwight glanced at Sigrid. Her neutral look told him nothing.

"Shall I assume then that you haven't told the FBI about me?"

Dwight gave an impatient wave of his hand. "All I want to know is what was in that file the Harper boy copied."

Crawford made a show of looking at his watch. "They'll be calling my flight soon. Will I be on it?"

"Yes," Sigrid said, even though she and Dwight had not discussed this.

Her cousin lifted an eyebrow. "Thank you."

He turned back to Dwight. "I believe there's enough time to tell you a story. Let's say there were once two little boys who met in Egypt. One was from Islamabad, the other from London. Both were lonely and both liked to watch birds. They bonded over a wounded Egyptian vulture that they nursed back to health. They met again at Cambridge and took rooms together. After leaving university, they were recruited by an agency that thought their language skills would be useful. They were still young and idealistic and they believed they could help make the world a better, safer place even if, as time went on, they were repelled by some of the things that agency occasionally condoned."

Across the way, a flight clerk had arrived at the departure desk and the passengers there were gathering up their belongings, stashing them in their carry-on bags, and starting to move restlessly.

"Fast forward to last spring," Crawford said. "One of them was anxious to get home to his wife and teenage son, so he hitched a ride on an unscheduled flight even though he'd heard rumors about the copilot's sadistic practices on powerless . . . shall we call them passengers?"

"Passengers or prisoners?" Dwight asked.

Crawford ignored his question.

"Both the passenger and the hitchhiker died on that flight, but it was hushed up and the copilot reassigned. When the hitchhiker's friend tried to learn what had happened, he wound up in front of a bus and was left for dead."

"Was that hitchhiker the other 'Arab' in Somalia?" Sigrid said.

Her cousin nodded and stood up as the departure clerk announced that the six o'clock flight to London was now boarding.

"So that's why you killed Alexander Franklin," said Dwight as he and Sigrid stood, too.

Martin Crawford gave an ironic smile. "When a man's partner is killed, he's supposed to do something about it. Isn't that what they say?"

Sigrid was not a demonstrative person, but she put her hand on Crawford's arm. "Thank you for what you did back then, Martin. For saving my mother's life."

He covered her hand with his. "My dear, how could we not?"

As he headed toward the queue now passing through the boarding gate, he turned and said, "Bryant? Do me a favor? Ask your wife's nephew to sling an occasional squirrel or rabbit onto my vulture table for me?"

Dwight gave him an affirmative salute.

"Oh, and my aunt has something for you."

The drive back to Dobbs took the full fifty-five minutes. Except for leaving Deborah a message that he would be late getting home and could she pick up Cal, neither Dwight nor Sigrid had much to say and they rode mostly in silence.

"Will Deborah understand why you didn't call the feds or try to stop him?" she asked as they neared the courthouse where her car was parked.

"I don't know," he answered candidly.

"But it wasn't too long ago in this county when a valid defense for some murders was that the victim needed killing."

He checked by his office, then followed Sigrid back to Cotton Grove in his own truck.

The iron gates had been left open and Anne met them at the door.

"Mother's asleep," she said, "but Martin gave her this as he was leaving and said it was for you."

"This" was a plastic flash drive.

"Let me get my laptop," Sigrid said.

Minutes later, they were looking at a slide show of turkey buzzards in flight above the concrete slab that Martin had called his vulture table. And there was Martin himself pointing directly at them.

"He's holding a remote control," Anne said softly. "He put a miniature camera on the bird's leg. That's how he got all those unique shots. He told me he had it rigged to take three pictures at a time."

Every four seconds as the slide show continued, the perspective widened out. Leaning over Sigrid's shoulder, Dwight and Anne saw the old house Martin had camped in, the whole pasture and his vulture table, Grayson Village, the surrounding roads, with cars and school buses, and even Reese's trailer and the house of a brother-in-law. Eventually, they saw the small airstrip where Alexander Franklin had landed. Only one plane, a Gulfstream, had visible numbers. Dwight knew that Franklin had been piloting a Learjet. So what was the significance of this plane? Jeremy had searched the FAA site. Did the Gulfstream belong to someone who shouldn't have been there? Was that who Jeremy was looking up in the phone directory?

He didn't realize he'd spoken aloud till Anne shrugged and said, "I don't get it either, but Martin definitely said this must have been the file the Harper boy stole. It was the only one that had a plane for the identifying picture on the file."

"Go back to the beginning, please," Dwight said. "That last frame was time-stamped 10:48 a.m., February seventh." He checked the calendar on his phone. "That was Monday a week ago. What was the first one?"

A few clicks of the mouse brought them back to the beginning.

"February third, 8:06 a.m.," Sigrid said.

"A Wednesday."

"Sit here," Sigrid said, handing Dwight the mouse as she relinquished her seat in front of the computer screen.

She showed him how to put it on maximum magnification and he started back through the slides manually, one by one, and then he spotted it off to the lower left side of the frame: a beige utility truck parked by the dump between Grayson Village and the Ferrabee pasture. In the first of that three-frame cluster, a foreshortened figure stood on the edge of the embankment and seemed to be tugging at some sort of diaphanous material that half covered a cylindrical shape. The material shone like silver in the early morning sun.

The early morning sun of Sunday, February 6.

The second and third shots showed a body lying atop what Dwight knew to be a rotten mattress. The hat was missing from the head of the person looking down at the exposed body, but the hands held a sheet of plastic that billowed in the wind.

Ginger Todd's bright orange hair shone as brightly as the plastic sheeting that had encased the body of Rebecca Jowett.

CHAPTER 31

These unique birds have a variety of interesting habits.
— The Turkey Vulture Society

Colleton County Sheriff's Department —
Tuesday night

When they unlocked the handcuffs in the interview room, Ginger Todd rubbed her wrists fretfully and said, "Do I need a lawyer?"

"That's certainly your right," Dwight told her.

Heretofore, they had seen her only in those brown canvas work clothes that made her look like a tagalong tomboy. Tonight, she wore a black leather jacket over a green jersey and skinny jeans. Tendrils of bright copper-colored hair framed her pretty face. The rest was pulled back and tied low at the nape with a thin silk scarf patterned in tones of gold and green. She looked like the competent woman they now knew she was, and once the handcuffs were off, there was no fear in her large brown eyes.

Raeford McLamb sat beside Dwight with a closed laptop on the table before them while Mayleen Richards activated the video camera.

Dwight stated the date and time and the names of all who were in the room. Even though the arresting officers had Mirandized her when she was brought in, he went through it again and asked if she understood her rights.

"Yeah, yeah," she said, more concerned with the camera. "I didn't give you permission to film me."

"We don't need your permission now," Dwight said. "For the record, you have been arrested for the murder of Rebecca Jowett and for assault with intent to kill Jeremy Harper. Assault with intent because he didn't die. In fact, he opened his eyes this evening and spoke his mother's name for the first time. We expect that he'll be able to identify his assailant any day now. Would you like to comment, ma'am?"

When she didn't speak, he said, "Deputy McLamb, please show Mrs. Todd those pictures."

McLamb turned the screen around. The

three pertinent pictures had been isolated and enlarged yet again. They ran on a continuous loop that repeated every five seconds. Mrs. Todd turned white and went rigid.

In a suddenly shaky voice, she said again, "Don't I get a phone call?"

Dwight slid a phone across to her. "Be my guest."

Ginger Todd stared at the phone as if it were a copperhead. "Wait a minute! Aren't you going to offer me a deal?"

"A deal?"

"On television, when the police say they can prove something like this, they'll offer the person a deal if she'll confess to a lesser charge before she gets a lawyer. If I confess to unpremeditated manslaughter — ?"

As if genuinely puzzled, Dwight said, "Why on earth would I offer you a deal like that?"

"So there won't have to be a trial. Save the state some money."

"Mrs. Todd," he said patiently, "you killed a woman and you came very close to killing a teenage boy."

"But if it wasn't premeditated? Like if someone tries to blackmail you, who thinks that because you're a woman you'll just roll over and shell out five thousand dollars —"

Dwight held up his hand. "Please! Call your attorney."

"I don't want one. I want to cut a deal."

Dwight took a deep breath and said, "If you've watched a lot of crime programs, you know you have a right to an attorney. I'm asking you one more time. Are you giving up that right?"

She nodded and signed the form Mayleen Richards gave her, then looked at Dwight expectantly.

"Involuntary manslaughter?" she asked.

"Let's just talk hypothetically first," he said. "See if that's a possibility."

"If there was no intent to kill, no premeditated intent, I mean? Isn't that the definition of manslaughter? And doesn't 'involuntary' mean you didn't know what you were doing could actually kill somebody? Like it was almost an accident?"

Sigrid was right, Dwight thought wearily. Those police procedurals had a lot to answer for.

"So when you saw Rebecca Jowett running through what was supposed to be your new neighborhood, you had nothing more in mind than maybe warning her to stay away from your husband?"

"*If* I saw her. We're still talking *if*, right?" she said brightly. Regaining confidence now, she reached back and pulled the scarf from her ponytail to let her luxuriant fiery red hair fall onto her shoulders and cascade down her back. "If I saw her, yeah, I might've been thinking how she came on to Wes and how he probably gave her that hickey and, yeah, I might've got her to come inside the house with me. But if I did, it would've been to tell her why we weren't going to buy the house, not to kill her. But then she started — I mean, *if* she started throwing off on Wes, if she called him a crude redneck and said that we couldn't walk away from the house without losing our earnest money and I could just suck it up? If she said all that, it could've made me lose my temper enough to just smack her with —"

She paused and twisted her scarf into a thin cord.

"Smack her with what?" Dwight asked quietly.

"I don't know. Whatever I might've had in my hand. It's not like I would have brought one of my hammers in with me. That would be premeditated."

"But once she fell back onto the couch and was bleeding, what would you have done? Your husband was due home. Why wouldn't you just leave her there?"

"I might've been worried about DNA. I might've forgotten that it wouldn't matter if y'all found my fingerprints or my hair or something because I'd been in the house before. I might've thought I needed to just make her disappear for so long y'all would never figure out what happened."

She threaded the thin silk scarf through her callused fingers, then pulled it free.

"So you wrapped her up in your plastic sheeting and stashed her in your truck, then let your husband sleep in next morning while you disposed of both the rats and the body," Dwight said.

"Yeah, that's what I *might* have done. *If* I'd killed the little bitch." Her scarf was now wound tightly around one thumb and she gave it a sharp yank.

Dwight gestured toward the laptop that McLamb had paused on the picture of her pushing the body over the edge of the ravine. "So if Jeremy Harper showed up with those pictures, you might've decided he needed to go, too?"

She leaned forward and peered at the screen. "Who took those pictures anyhow? Somebody in an airplane?"

When Dwight didn't answer, she sat back in her chair and began playing with that band of colorful silk again.

"So do we have a deal?"

"If those programs you watch are accurate, Mrs. Todd, then you must know it's the district attorney who decides what you'll be tried for, not the sheriff's department."

"But you can put in a recommendation, can't you?"

Tired of bandying words, Dwight nodded to McLamb. "Take her over to the jail and book her."

Ginger Todd gaped at them. "But it wasn't premeditated. It *wasn't!*"

"I'll be sure and tell the DA you said that," he promised.

CHAPTER 32

They are very graceful, many even say beautiful.
— The Turkey Vulture Society

Tuesday night (continued)

The moon, four nights from full, was high in the western sky as Dwight drove home along endlessly branching back roads that were nearly deserted at that hour — deserted, that is, of humans and their vehicles. Every few miles his headlights were reflected in the eyes of a rambling possum or a feral cat crouched in the weeds of a ditchbank. As he drove through the creek bottom near the farm, he slowed to let a fox safely pass in front of him. Had he been going faster, he thought, Crawford's abandoned buzzards would have had fresh meat for breakfast.

He had driven even slower than usual, using the time to turn the day's events over in his mind and uneasy about what the rest of this day might hold. Despite his earlier flip answer to Sigrid, he knew that Deborah was troubled that Martin Crawford hadn't been arrested nor even officially questioned.

True, it was the FBI's case. True, there was no physical evidence to link him to the motel murder; and yes, it was true that he had rescued Anne and her colleague.

But to condone a cold-blooded murder because the CIA only demoted and reassigned the man who had killed Crawford's partner and closest friend? Who had almost killed Crawford himself?

He could live with what he'd done, but could Deborah? Or would this taint what they had together? She was a judge, and while she had skirted close to the letter of the law, she had never actually broken it . . . except . . . well, yes, there *was* that time she stabbed Allen Stancil.

And he couldn't help grinning as he remembered how she couldn't be trusted around an unguarded neon sign. As a teenager, she had stolen a blue guitar, and he'd never heard a clear explanation of how she acquired that OPEN TILL MIDNIGHT SIGN.

All the same, taking a life was a hell of a lot different from taking a neon sign. Those were things she'd done before she became a judge and took an oath to uphold the law, an oath he knew she took seriously.

Except for a light in the kitchen, the house looked dark. Nearly midnight. She was probably already in bed, he thought. Asleep. He had half expected her to call sometime during the evening, but she hadn't, which made him even more apprehensive. Taking a deep breath, he closed the door of the truck and stepped onto the back porch.

As he reached for the doorknob, Deborah opened the door. She was still dressed, and without speaking, she went into his arms for an embrace that melded into a long, slow, hungry kiss that he wished would never end.

Nevertheless, he sensed an underlying uncertainty in her kiss that made him step back and look down into her eyes. "We need to talk."

"Yes," she said.

Lifting a jacket from a peg beside the door, she joined him in the yard; and as they walked toward the pond, she linked her arm through his, which gave him hope. He found himself remembering another moonlit night down there on the pier, a mild spring night when she was home from hearing a divorce case over in Moore County and getting over a breakup with her latest boyfriend. It had taken all his willpower to keep his hands clasped around his drink, to keep from confessing that he'd loved her for years and wanted to be with her forever.

Sometime during his drive home, the wind had shifted. Instead of bone-chilling gusts out of the northeast, he felt a flow of warmer air from the west. Overhead, veils of thin clouds scudded across the moon, yet there was more than enough light to let them walk the familiar path without stumbling.

He told her first about Ginger Todd, of the incriminating pictures Martin Crawford had taken of her with a camera fastened to one of his circling buzzards, and of how Jeremy Harper had copied those pictures and tried to blackmail Mrs. Todd.

They walked out on the pier and moonlight glistened on the still dark water. She listened without comment when he repeated the conversation he and Sigrid had with Crawford at the airport. He also told her what his former colleague had said about the murdered pilot. "I'm not trying to justify it, Deb'rah, just saying that I know where he's coming from."

"Because you know where he's been?" There was no judgment in her question.

Indeed, it was not really even a question.

The silence stretched between them.

"Maybe I should have arrested him or turned him over to the feds, but . . ."

"But it got complicated, didn't it? Bits and pieces of your own life got caught up in the equation."

She started to move away, but he put his hand on her shoulder and turned her back to face him.

"Do you really want me to tell you what happened in Germany?"

She returned his steady gaze for a long moment without flinching, then the consciously neutral lines of her face softened in the moonlight.

"Someday," she said as she reached up and gently touched his face. "When you're ready. If you want to."

She walked down to the post that Annie Sue and Reese had wired with a switch at Christmas. Red, blue, and yellow lights gleamed through the water off the far end of the pier. The surface above bubbled and foamed, then that silly fountain the kids had installed suddenly shot up into the air, changing colors as the lights revolved.

He followed and put his arms around her, and when she leaned back against his chest, he knew she was okay with his decision.

"Cal was out in the garden this afternoon," she said, fitting her body more closely to his. "He says our peas are coming up."

A light breeze ruffled her hair as the wind shifted further to the west.

It held the promise of rain, the promise of spring.

APRIL 2011

STATE OF NORTH CAROLINA

COLLETON COUNTY

IN THE GENERAL COURT OF JUSTICE
DISTRICT COURT DIVISION
BEFORE THE CLERK

SP _____

PETITION FOR ADOPTION
OF A MINOR CHILD
(STEPPARENT)

Deborah Knott Bryant
Full name of petitioning ~~Father~~ [Mother]

Calvin Avery Bryant
(Full name by which adoptee is to be known if adoption granted)

To the Honorable _Ellis Glover_, Clerk of the Superior Court of _Colleton_ County:

I, the undersigned, _Deborah Knott Bryant_, _F_, do hereby petition the Court to adopt

(Name by which the adoptee is to be known)   (Sex)

1. That the petitioner herein seeking adoption has lived in or been domiciled in North Carolina for at least six consecutive months immediately preceding the filing of this Petition; **and** the adoptee has lived in North Carolina for at least six consecutive months immediately preceding the filing of this Petition.

2. That the petitioner's spouse is the parent of the adoptee and has had legal and physical custody of the child.

ld

child; and upon adoption, the said adoptee shall inherit real and personal property by, through, and from the said petitioner in accordance with the statutes of descent and distribution.

This _14th_ day of ___February___, 20_11_

Deborah K. Bryant
_____
                                                Petitioner

Deborah Knott Bryant being duly sworn, deposes and says that _she_ has read the
Full name of petitioning [Father] [Mother]

foregoing Petition and that the facts set forth therein are true to _her_ own knowledge, except as to matters therein set forth upon information and belief, and as to such matters _she_ believes them to be true.

Deborah K. Bryant
_____
                                                Petitioner

Subscribed and sworn to before me this _14th_ day of _February_, _2011_
Ellis Glover
_____
Clerk Superior Court

Granted
4/4/2011
EG

ACKNOWLEDGMENTS

My continuing thanks to Rebecca Blackmore, Shelly Holt, John Smith, and Shelley Desvousges, who went to law school and became district court judges so that I didn't have to. Without their expert knowledge and their willingness to share that knowledge, Deborah Knott could not have been elected dogcatcher.

Brenda Foldesi, Sharon Woods Hopkins, and Lisa Logan walked me through the process of buying a house in Colleton County.

Brainstorming sessions with Bren Bonner Witchger, Mary Kay Andrews, Alex Sokoloff, Diane Chamberlain, Katy Munger, and Sarah Shaber — the other six of our *Weymouth 7* — were indispensable when I wrote myself into a corner with this book and couldn't get out. And Weymouth itself continues to welcome us twice a year.

Vicky Bijur, who will be my agent and

friend till one of us dies, has been my trusted advisor and support since we were both newbies.

ABOUT THE AUTHOR

Margaret Maron grew up on a farm near Raleigh, North Carolina, but for many years lived in Brooklyn, New York. When she returned to her North Carolina roots with her artist-husband, Joe, she began a series based on her own background. The first book, *Bootlegger's Daughter,* became a *Washington Post* bestseller that swept the top mystery awards for its year and is among the 100 Favorite Mysteries of the Century as selected by the Independent Mystery Booksellers Association. Later Deborah Knott novels *Up Jumps the Devil* and *Storm Track* each won the Agatha Award for Best Novel. In 2008, Maron received the North Carolina Award for Literature, the state's highest civilian honor. To find out more about the author, you can visit www.MargaretMaron.com.